Essence:
ASSAULT ON THE MIND

Book 1 of the Essence Series

To my beautiful and brilliant wife, Donna, and our four children, Joseph, Rebecca, Gabriel, and Teresa

Table of Contents

PREFACE

"Hell is other people," Sartre's character proclaims at the end of the play, "Huis Clos" (No Exit). *It's true!* Or so we might think when cut off on the highway or when dealing with a particularly rude individual. While there are elements of truth in all philosophies, including Existentialism, where is *all* truth? Is there such a thing–absolute consistency, the source of perfectly logical, reasonable answers to all questions? And if so, can we find it?

According to Socrates, we have to try. "The unexamined life is not worth living," he stated in his defense after being condemned to death for teaching his philosophy. Why are we here? Do we have souls? Why must we suffer? These are the questions that beg examination, and which haunt the characters in this novel, as they do most of us making our way through life. To address them, we must wonder, examine, and come to our own conclusions through calm, rational reflection. To do this we need faith. Not to tell us what to think, but to allow us to think. As one of the characters in *Essence* states, "Faith is the willingness to follow truth wherever it leads you," even to the fantastic and supernatural. It takes faith to understand Einstein's concept of spacetime or the extra dimensions predicted by string theory physics. Moreover it is through faith that we can break free of thought control.

Polarizing news reports, propaganda, and subliminal advertising are today's surreptitious forms of thought control. In *Essence*, such thought control is exerted openly and boldly by Dr. Karl Hoffman, who controls minds through string theory's hidden dimensions. It's there that our minds are said to interact with each other, and where we choose the direction of our will. It is the birthplace of good and evil.

The German philosopher, Nietzsche, claimed to transcend the concepts of good and evil, identifying the driving force in nature as the *will to power*, the will that once fully realized, would lead to the ultimate human condition. Christianity proposes a different path to ultimate human existence: an alignment of one's will with the will of God. Since God is love, as Saint John writes, this would be the *will to love*. And so, *Essence* presents the classic battle between good and evil as the *will to love* versus *the will to power* fought in the dimension of the mind.

At times, the line between science and metaphysics is blurred in this novel, all the better to have a perspective from which to examine the relationship between the two. Does morality reflect the will of God, or is it a by-product of evolution? Is there absolute right and wrong, or does that distinction depend solely upon those who have the power to decide? Is Christianity the fullness of truth, or is it just one of many equivalent religions? Is atheism a scientific conclusion or a religion unto itself? Sincere, intelligent individuals can and do arrive at different answers to these questions, but to even begin to address them adequately, we all need the freedom to think for ourselves. We all need faith.

There is more before us than meets the eye. While it is true that hell can be seen in other people, so too can heaven. If we resist the thought control and take a leap of faith to consider the unseen, putting no artificial restraints on our queries, there's no limit to what we may find. Life is short, and time is precious. The time to examine is now.

As Saint John of the Cross writes, "Oh my soul created for these grandeurs and called to them. What have you been doing? How have you been spending your time?"

Essence:

ASSAULT ON THE MIND

A Novel

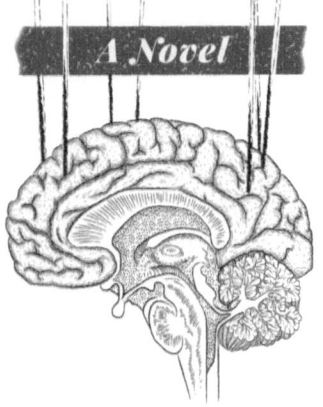

Mario Loomis

Part I

KARL HOFFMAN

0

1

66*I* won't allow it!"

The voice boomed through the Upper East Side apartment walls, down to the Manhattan streets below. It was the voice of a man pacing back and forth before the apartment's window.

"I won't allow it!" he repeated.

The man was Dr. Karl Hoffman, a tall, muscular man in his mid-fifties with short gray hair and a closely trimmed Van Dyke beard. He swung his hands through the air as he spoke, pointing at another man, Dr. Paul Silverman, seated just opposite the window. Dr. Silverman, who immigrated from Eastern Europe twenty years earlier, was in his sixties, with a receding hairline and long white hair that flowed over his ears. The two were colleagues at a local university, Hoffman, a professor of neuroscience, and Silverman, a physics professor specializing in string theory, a theory that posits multiple unseen dimensions.

Hoffman stopped pacing and pointed a finger at Silverman, continuing his rant. "Do not publish that paper now!"

"Karl, I'm simply sharing my work."

"Your *work*–your great revelation!" He stopped pacing and held his arms outstretched. "Our minds are in another dimension. Who cares?"

"If no one cares, why do you?"

"Because they *will* care, very soon, and your detailed explanations could prove troublesome. Once I..." Hoffman stopped short and grinned at Silverman. It was a grin that combined a slight curl at the edge of the mouth with enough of a frown to offset any pleasantness, conveying instead, utter disdain. "That's it, isn't it? You want to save the day. Dr. Silverman–the savior, the white knight who comes to the rescue–the *ethical* one." He spoke the word with an evident loathing.

"We must all pay attention to ethics."

"You can keep your ethics," Hoffman scoffed, "your sacred cow. You know it's nothing but a euphemism for the weak controlling the strong."

"You would rather the strong control the weak?"

Hoffman stared at Silverman, expressionless. "What could be more natural?" He fixed his eyes on Silverman's, his gaze unwavering, his neck taught. His cheek muscles quivered as his teeth ground together quietly. The furrow between his brows tightened and several beads of perspiration appeared on his forehead. The two men were motionless. Hoffman stood like a wax figure, his hands just above the lower edges of his jacket, his shoulders and trunk perfectly erect, and his head tilted ever so slightly down at Silverman. Silverman sat with his hands resting on his lap, his shoulders slumped forward, and his neck extended to look up at his colleague. It was as though time itself were frozen in that moment, or the scene were being played back on a screen and some technical malfunction had stopped it cold. The only traces of motion breaking the unnatural stillness were the beads of perspiration forming on Hoffman's forehead and the subtle quivering of his cheeks.

As suddenly as it began, Hoffman's frozen affect softened and his face dissolved into a serene, placid look.

"Very well," he capitulated. "I'm heading over to Brooklyn now."

The corners of Hoffman's jacket flapped against his sides as he marched toward the door. Meanwhile, Dr. Silverman quietly got up from his chair and moved to the kitchen, filling a glass with water. Drinking it down, he filled another and said, "Have a good day, Karl."

"Yes, you too, Paul," Hoffman said with a furtive smile as he watched Dr. Silverman filling his glass. A moment later, Hoffman was out the door.

Dr. Silverman's nephew, Jonathan, who was visiting from Virginia, emerged from another room. "Where does he get off?" he asked.

"He's passionate about his work," Dr. Silverman explained.

"He's an arrogant SOB. How can you stand him?"

"Oh, I've known Karl for many years. He's... well, he's very accomplished. Maybe too accomplished," he added under his breath.

"What's that, Uncle Paul?"

"Oh, well, you see, he's made an app to connect your brain to your phone. No wires; you think of a letter and it appears on the screen."

"For real?"

"Yes, for real," Dr. Silverman laughed.

"How? No wires? How can your thoughts just *go* from your brain into your phone?"

"Thoughts are electricity, Jonathan. You know EEGs, when we measure that electricity, yes? Well, that electricity changes the electromagnetic field around your head, around your body, even around your hand holding your phone."

"That's amazing."

"Yes, but..."

"But what? You're worried about something, aren't you? What was that about ethics?"

"Connections go both ways," Dr. Silverman explained.

"If your brain can connect to the phone, the phone can also connect to your brain."

"What do you mean, like subliminal advertising? So when I'm surfing for something my phone will tell me, 'Buy that?'" Jonathan chuckled. "Better turn off that one-touch buying."

Dr. Silverman nodded. "It's more than that. You tell people what to buy, okay, but then you tell them what to think, how to vote–where does it end? That much power corrupts even the strongest of men."

"You think there's that much power in a phone app?"

"It's not in the phone!" Dr. Silverman exclaimed with such fervor that Jonathan was visibly startled. "I'm sorry Jonathan. I'm sorry." He put a hand on his nephew's shoulder and led him to the sofa where they both sat down. "You see," he continued, "without free thought, there is no freedom. Justice, injustice, right, wrong, good, and evil: what do these words mean? You must be free to think for yourself. It cannot be dictated to you. You know, I've told you this." His nephew nodded. "I've seen the evil that comes when people stop thinking." He looked past his nephew, and frowning, closed his eyes. Dr. Silverman had spent most of his life in communist Bulgaria, and had lost friends, colleagues, and family members to political imprisonment and execution.

"So, why doesn't he want you to publish your paper? What's in it?" Jonathan asked.

"The antidote, if it's not too late." Dr. Silverman gazed across the room toward the door Hoffman had just gone out of. His eyes widened, as though trying to see past it, then regained their usual gentle, smiling appearance. He took a deep breath and, sharing a broad smile, added, "Maybe I just worry too much. Karl's a good man. The things I've seen— that was another time."

"Yeah, well, don't let him bully you, Uncle Paul. Listen, are you okay? Do you need anything? I was going to meet up with the guys for the day, but I can call it off."

"No, no, you have a good time and I'll see you when you get back."

"Okay Uncle Paul, I'll see you later then," Jonathan replied as he put on his coat and headed out. Dr. Silverman looked out the window at the East River. Letting out a soft sigh, he returned to the kitchen to refill his glass.

*T*he morning sun was still low in the sky when Hoffman arrived at his destination in Brooklyn, a warehouse loft near a highway overpass. He appeared tall, even in the large open space of the loft, taller still as he towered over two other men who stood at his side. One was Henry Miller, a congressman, conspicuously well dressed in a silk suit with a brightly colored tie and polished shoes. The whiteness of his teeth glimmered sporadically through his barely parted lips, and his hair, exceptionally dark and full, contrasted with his forehead and cheek lines that divulged his true age. The other man was Kyle Williams, a Wall Street stock broker, about the same height as Miller, but much rounder, his protruding abdomen an insurmountable barrier to his suit's closure, a suit custom tailored a year earlier. He was nearly bald, and though half Miller's age, appeared to be more his contemporary than his younger companion. He shifted his weight nervously from left to right foot, looking quickly at Miller then Hoffman.

"Why did you want to meet here?" Williams asked Hoffman, who was drumming his fingertips on the glass window pane.

"Did you know glass is a liquid?" Hoffman asked, continuing to tap the glass.

The two men frowned at each other.

"No," Williams answered finally. "Didn't know that."

"It's a slowly moving liquid, not a solid. You see it in old buildings like this. Look at the waves in this glass. For the past sixty years, this glass has been streaming downhill with gravity, moving so slowly that no one could see it move. But, after decades have passed, one can see the evidence that it *has* moved in this rippling distortion. Now, of course," he stopped drumming his fingers and glanced toward the two men, "it's too late."

"Too late for what?" Williams asked.

"Perception," Hoffman responded.

The congressman, Miller, sighed audibly, rolling his eyes at Williams.

"Perception is power," Hoffman seethed. "You want power, don't you?" he asked, pivoting toward the congressman who looked away when he caught Hoffman's glance. "Then you need to be more perceptive."

"Okay," Williams acknowledged, sending an impatient glance toward Miller who continued to roll his eyes but sighed more quietly. "Everything's going very well," Williams continued. "We've got over a million users now. I can run the numbers for you, even show you where they are geographically, but I need my computer. Why are we in this old warehouse?"

"We need some muscle," Hoffman answered.

"Look," Miller barked, "I could get muscle for a hell of a lot less than I'm paying you. You guaranteed me votes, not coercion."

"Who said it was for you?" Hoffman asked dryly.

Silence hung between the men like a shroud, broken finally by the sound of an opening door scraping along the floor. On the opposite side of the room, five men moved like a spearhead trough the doorway. The man in front, trailed by two on each side of him, stopped, and the others lined up alongside him.

"Which one of you's Hoffman?" the man in front asked.

"That would be me," Hoffman replied, remaining by the window and staring intently at the man. "You're Spinosa?"

"I heard you might be interested in our services," the man answered without acknowledging Hoffman's question.

"Protection. We need protection. You can provide that, can't you?" Hoffman inquired.

"Yeah, for a price."

"I can offer you something more than money," Hoffman retorted.

"Don't waste my time."

"How would you like to be invincible?" When Hoffman asked this, the man turned his head to his associates and laughed.

"Invincible? I'm the most invincible guy in this room. You want to see invincible?" He drew a gun from his waist and raised it to point at Hoffman when suddenly, he collapsed onto the floor, the gun resting on his right palm, his fingers twitching as they struggled to regain their grip. His face was tightened, his eyes fixed on his gun hand, with his arms and legs motionless as if bound to the floor. His men rushed to his side and tried to lift him back to his feet. Although there were four of them, they were unable to lift even his head. Trying different holds and leverage points to no avail, they drew their weapons and stood facing Hoffman.

"Place your weapons on the floor or your boss dies," Hoffman ordered calmly.

The men looked at each other and Spinosa's immobile body, then slowly complied. Immediately after the men placed their guns on the floor, Spinosa began to move again and got back onto his feet, leaving his gun on the floor. Franco, the last of Spinosa's men to place his weapon on the floor, surreptitiously reached for an ankle holster as he kept his eyes fixed on Hoffman. Hoffman snapped around to face Franco and stared at him for several moments. Franco returned Hoffman's gaze with an unabashed look which quickly became timid and meek. He looked away from Hoffman, focusing his attention instead on the floor around him. His eyes shifted sporadically, seeming to scan an arc of empty space before him. His hands, so cool and steady a moment before, now trembled before him, on his left side, then his right.

"Boss," he whispered.

"It would be wise not to challenge me," Hoffman explained as he turned from Franco, who continued to stare nervously at the surrounding floor. Gesturing toward the space around Franco, Hoffman added, "They don't like you. You'd better run."

Franco backed away from the floor space he had been tremulously holding out his hands against. He turned his legs and stumbled into a run while still looking over his shoulder.

"Franco, relax," one of Spinosa's men whispered.

Franco did not relax. In fact he ran the length of the room, thrashing his arms to one side, then the other. His gaze was so intent on the floor alongside him that he ran straight into a light wooden railing surrounding an elevator shaft. The railing splintered and Franco fell with a shriek into the darkness of the thirty-foot shaft.

The shrieking ended with a loud thud, then a muffled silence which hung over the men in the room.

"I hope we won't need any more demonstrations," Hoffman announced as he moved for the first time from the window. Spinosa had collected himself and was standing now, with his remaining three men close by.

"What are you doing?" Williams whispered to Hoffman anxiously.

"You ask too many questions, Williams. Are you with me? Because if you're not with me, you're against me. Which is it? Decide quickly."

"I'm with you, absolutely, all the way," Williams stammered.

"Then, no more questions." Hoffman raised his voice, speaking now to Spinosa and his men. "As I was saying, I can make you more powerful than you can imagine."

"What for?" Spinosa asked. "What do you want from me?"

"I need your guns and your men. Are you interested, or

should I be speaking to another organization?"

"I'm interested," Spinosa snapped. "I'm interested in how you did that to me."

"One thing at a time."

"What's our percentage?"

"What do you want? Control? Turf? Just do what I need you to do first. How many men do you have?"

"Thirty, but I can get sixty easy."

"Let's talk." Hoffman gestured for Spinosa to come over by him. The two men moved over to the side wall and spoke quietly, leaving Miller and Williams standing alone opposite Spinosa's men. The five men were casting intermittent glances at the elevator shaft.

"Should we see if he's alive?" Miller asked. Spinosa's men took the lead and scuttled to the top of the shaft. Franco was motionless on the platform below.

"Boss," one of Spinosa's men interrupted, "You want us to check if Franco's alive?"

Spinosa turned toward his men and opened his mouth to speak.

"He's not," Hoffman rebutted, "but if you'd like to see for yourself, go ahead. Bring up the elevator."

The five men stood around the elevator shaft as the unpleasant sight drew nearer and nearer, the sound of the elevator motor and cables blotting out Hoffman and Spinosa's ongoing conversation. While Spinosa's men were no strangers to blood or dead bodies, the sight was a novel experience for the congressman and stock broker, who shifted their positions frequently, stepping back in increments as the elevator platform brought its load up further and further into plain sight.

It was an ugly sight. Franco's body was twisted upon itself, contorted by the violence of his fall. Neither Miller nor Williams had ever witnessed a man's death before. They stood like gapers alongside a highway accident, consumed with curiosity, revolted by what they saw, yet unable to turn away.

Within a few minutes, Spinosa returned to his men and gave them some quiet instructions. The three men then carried off their comrade, walking behind Spinosa, while Miller and Williams returned to Hoffman, keeping their eyes fixed on the floor with only a few momentary glances toward Hoffman.

*T*hat evening in Manhattan, Silverman's nephew, Jonathan, returned to his uncle's apartment, finding him sitting in his chair by the window, a glass in his hand and a pitcher on the table beside him. "How are you doing, Uncle Paul?" he asked him. "Heard anything more from, what was his name?"

"Karl? No. Karl Hoffman. That's his name. You should remember it. I'm sure he'll be famous someday."

"I don't trust him."

"Oh, he may be a hot head, but what is he going to do? Stop me from publishing my own research? This is my work. He has no say in it, right?" Dr. Silverman asked, as he filled his glass with water from the pitcher.

"Absolutely," Jonathan affirmed looking at his uncle with some concern. "Are you sure you're all right? You seem awfully thirsty."

"Yes, I'm fine, just a lot on my mind," Silverman said, rising to go to the bathroom.

"You going to bed soon?" Jonathan asked as he went into the guest room to get ready for bed.

"Yes, yes, but you go ahead. I'll just be up a little longer," his uncle responded. When he came out of the bathroom, he started down the hall toward his bedroom then halted, going to his chair by the window instead. Standing over his chair, he drank another glass of water, then brought the pitcher to the kitchen sink where he filled it to the rim. He sat back down in his chair, refilled his glass and held it close to his lips with both hands, as a man drawn out of freezing waters might hold a hot cup of coffee. He drank the water in a steady, purposeful manner, staring out at the lights across the East River.

The following morning, the sun was again shining through the window as it rose over Brooklyn, sparkling in the water at the bottom of Dr. Silverman's glass which rested on a small table beside his armchair. Jonathan came out from his room to find his uncle still in the armchair, his head slumped forward.

"You fell asleep in the chair?" Jonathan asked him. "Come lie down for a bit or you'll have a stiff neck." Jonathan put his hand on his uncle's shoulder to pull him upward when, touching the skin of his neck, he recoiled at an unexpected coldness. He knelt down in front of the chair and gently pushed his uncle's shoulders back, falling away in horror as his uncle's knees rose in unison with his torso, his body stiff with rigor mortis.

His uncle was dead!

Paramedics confirmed Dr. Silverman's death at the scene, and when the police arrived, Jonathan insisted that Karl Hoffman had done something to his uncle the previous day. Frantically, he described the scene he had witnessed, the anger with which Hoffman had spoken to his uncle, and how he had threatened to stop him from publishing his work. The police asked the usual questions, looking for means and opportunity. Had Dr. Hoffman given Dr. Silverman anything to eat or drink? Did he have access to his food, his water, any other means of poisoning him? Jonathan answered all the questions by shaking his head. He had just come in, started yelling at his uncle, paced back and forth, and then left.

"He did something, I tell you," Jonathan reiterated. "He did something. He got into his head somehow." This last suggestion brought an end to the officers' questioning. They traded looks with each other, notepads were closed, and Jonathan was reassured that they would do everything possible to investigate the case thoroughly. In the interest of completeness, two uniformed officers were dispatched in Brooklyn to question Hoffman at his home.

The assignment fell to two rookies, William O'Malley and Rick Hardin. The two arrived at Hoffman's residence, and, finding the front door ajar, they entered the house, sidestepping boxes of books on the floor. Hardin took the upstairs and had finished clearing all the rooms when he heard a sound below. Running downstairs, he discovered O'Malley collapsed in a hallway. Checking his partner's pulse, Hardin drew his weapon and moved to the end of the hallway where he saw Hoffman making his way toward the back door.

"Turn around with your hands up." Hardin leveled his weapon at Hoffman and stood immobile for several seconds, as his partner O'Malley rose from the floor.

"What are you doing?" O'Malley asked, coming alongside Hardin. "Cuff him!"

"Where is he?" Hardin yelled out, glancing back and forth. The two looked at the small entryway, the closed back door and the walls on either side.

"Did he go out the back door?" O'Malley asked.

"The door never opened," Hardin insisted. "I was looking straight at him, then he was gone."

"He disappeared?"

"I was looking straight at him, then I was looking at the back door. It never opened I tell you," Hardin repeated. Then, turning toward O'Malley, he asked, "Are you okay?"

"Yeah, I'm fine." The two went to the back door, opened it and looked out into the small back yard. Additional police officers arrived, and together they carried out a thorough search, upstairs, downstairs, and around the entire grounds of the house, but Hoffman was already gone, making his way with calm, resolute strides through the back alleyways of Brooklyn.

JOHN ROCCO

02

*T*wo days later, a pervasive gray fog enshrouded Brooklyn, obscuring the light of dawn as well as cars and traffic signals. Along the East River separating Brooklyn from Manhattan, the top floor of a factory building rose like a great whale surfacing from the sea of gray. The factory stood as a monument to the generation of hardworking immigrants who had made up the local community. Its sturdy brick construction had outlived its obsolete purpose, the mass production of television vacuum tubes, so it now housed mostly empty office spaces.

Inside the top floor, John Rocco was waiting. Rocco was an agent with the FBI, leading a task force brought in to investigate the Hoffman case. Rocco stood at the window, his dark eyes taking in the New York skyline above the fog. The creases running across his forehead would have seemed harsh were it not for the downward slope of his lateral brows which gave him a disarming, concerned look. At thirty-two, his hair was full and thick, falling naturally across his forehead. He had chiseled features that were rugged but still youthful, and his frame was well developed and lean.

Rocco had been with the FBI for ten years and was familiar with a wide range of criminal activity, including cryptic methods of poisoning and clever illusions. He was well known throughout the bureau for his hard work, especially on the tough cases. Two years earlier, he had been recognized for solving a highly publicized murder of an eight-year-old boy, doing most of the work on his own time over several years. He had won the award for top agent in his district four times and was considered to be first in line for the next director's position. To him, every case, every question had an answer. Finding it was only a matter of time and "bullheadedness," as he would say. Today, he was meeting with three other agents, Dr. Silverman's nephew, and other witnesses.

As Rocco looked across the sea of fog, wispy white clouds raced by the peaks of familiar skyscrapers. He had lived in Brooklyn once, though he had not been back for many years. Not far from here, he remembered, he and his brother would sit on the roof of their apartment building and look across the river at the New York skyline. "Someday, you and I will be working there," his brother would say to him, "partners or something, in one of those big tall buildings. Won't that be cool?" Then they would sneak up on pigeons, trying to grab one, or play on the fire escape until their mother poked her head out the window to call them in for dinner. *The last time I saw this skyline...* he began thinking, then stopped himself. A tightness rose in his chest and ran up his spine, raising the hairs on the back of his neck. His shoulders slid backwards and his chest extended outwards, arching his torso into a military-like position of attention. His gaze shifted to the sky above the city as his teeth clenched tightly together. Anger pulsed through him, from his temples to his hands which twitched in tight fists at his sides. He stood in this position of defiance for several moments, after which his breaths became deeper and slower.

The reaction was a familiar one for him, a sort of equal and opposite reaction to the rising of an underlying darkness. As the tightness relaxed and the darkness receded, he turned away from the skyline, exhaling through tightly pursed lips.

His left hand unconsciously rubbed the aching pain in his hip, a regular companion of such overcast days even now, ten years after his bone marrow donation. A collage of memories played through his mind as he massaged the scar: the trip to Seattle; the brief conversations with the doctors; the anguish of seeing his brother in an isolation room; his body's immune system destroyed by the chemotherapy, waiting for

John's donated marrow cells to multiply and spread through-out his body to make him whole again, to save him. He re-called the novena prayed nightly in the hospital chapel, led by his aunt who had always been the spearhead of faith in the family, a faith John hardly knew then, and which would soon perish along with his brother, wasting away to nothing beneath the dreary Seattle skies.

Rocco moved from the window and walked around the room. Stopping at an odd picture on one of the walls, he stared at the mass of swirls and lines for several minutes. He'd seen these pictures before–apparent chaotic scribbles from which, if you stare at them long enough, a hidden picture emerges. There was always a small collection of people around these pictures who, one by one, cried out, "I see it!" He was never one of those people. Merely look-ing at the picture annoyed him. It was useless, serving no purpose but to give people another game, another excuse to waste time. It was not that Rocco never engaged in idle recreation. He could relax after work with his coworkers, have a few beers, shoot pool and laugh at jokes, although he always seemed to be the first to stop laughing. *I hate these things*, he thought as he turned from the picture and went back to the window.

Clare Bristol was the first of his team to arrive. As she entered the room, they shared a brief, subdued greeting. They had not spoken for several months, having come off of a fairly close relationship that had ended three months earlier on less than good terms. Rocco found himself staring at Clare's face. Her blue eyes seemed particularly striking that morning, bold and bright, accented by her long lashes, scanning the room with graceful movements beneath a lock of blonde hair that had escaped her ponytail. A few years younger than Rocco, still in her twenties, her face had all the signs of youth, smooth curved cheeks, full lips with a slight upturn at the corners of her mouth, and a pristine jawline that flowed gracefully into her long neck. He had forgotten how attractive she was.

"What?" she snapped, with a glare that shattered his momentary adoration. Like Rocco, Clare was well respected in the Bureau. Several years earlier, she had received an academic scholarship at Princeton, but resisting her parents' desire for her to pursue law or medicine, entered the FBI. It was, "To right wrongs and protect the public," she would say. Her father, a successful businessman, had passed away shortly after she joined the Bureau. She had been very close to him, speaking with him almost every day. After his death, she focused only on her work and tended to deflect advances from men. Her friendship with John Rocco had been the closest thing to a relationship she had had since joining the FBI.

The awkwardness of the moment was relieved by the arrival of two more agents, Vince Ambrosi and Jake Steinman, both of whom had known Rocco and Clare previously. They had just been at the morgue where the Medical Examiner was investigating the cause of Dr. Silverman's death. Jake and Vince had been working together for two years. Jake was the only child of an Orthodox Jewish family in Manhattan, his father a well-known local rabbi. He had curly red hair, a ruddy complexion, a medium build, and no noticeable accent, unlike his partner, Vince, who had an unmistakable Brooklyn accent. Vince was the oldest child from a Brooklyn Italian family, always impeccably dressed and groomed with slick black hair. He had a peculiar way of cocking his head while speaking, which gave him the look of a confused puppy tilting its head. The smiles this invoked usually represented ridicule rather than affection, but Vince nonetheless took it as positive feedback. The four agents sat at a table in the middle of the room.

"Vince, Jake, what's the story at the morgue?" Rocco asked.

"So far," Vince began, "it looks like Silverman died from something called"–he paused, pulling a note card from his top pocket–"Psychogenic Polydypsia."

"What's that?" Rocco asked.

"Well, the Medical Examiner said it's this condition where a person can't stop drinking water. They keep drinking and drinking and their blood gets so diluted that they have seizures and die. Usually, they wind up in psych hospitals where they have to lock the sinks and even the toilets to keep them from drinking too much water."

"Nice," Clare said with a frown.

"I know, right?" Vince answered with his signature head tilt.

"So why wasn't this guy in a hospital?" Clare asked.

"Well, that's just it," Jake added, leaning in to join the conversation. "Silverman's nephew was at the morgue too this morning, and once the doc starts talking about this psychogenic condition, he insists that his uncle never had any such thing. He thinks Hoffman made him do it somehow, like a hypnotic suggestion or something."

"Yes," Rocco added, "he's been saying that all along. We'll talk to him shortly, along with the two police officers that confronted Hoffman in Brooklyn. This nephew says his uncle's research paper will show us how to stop Hoffman before he does whatever it was his uncle was afraid of. What have you turned up, Clare?" Rocco turned to her with renewed confidence, having moved on from their awkward first greeting to his current commanding role as team leader. Clare, apparently, had not yet made that move.

"Well," she replied, looking at Jake and Vince and avoiding eye-contact with Rocco, "I found the paper Silverman was about to publish which was pretty slow-going, but between that and his email communications to Hoffman, I think I have the gist of it. Silverman was a physicist specializing in string theory." Clare explained how string theory physics predicted the existence of multiple dimensions beyond our three dimensions of space, and the fourth dimension of time. "So outside of space and time, there are these other dimensions. We can't see them, but we're connected to them. There's like an extension of ourselves there, if that makes any sense."

"What does that have to do with Hoffman?" Rocco asked.

Clare reluctantly turned in Rocco's general direction, still not looking him in the eyes. "Well, that's where Hoffman said he could manipulate other people's minds, reaching them through this phone application he created called 'eTelepathy.' It supposedly reads brain waves. You think of a letter and it appears on your screen. Silverman was worried that Hoffman's technology could lead to widespread mind control."

"With just an app?" Jake asked.

"Hoffman was bragging about that ability. Here"—she shuffled a stack of papers in front of her—"in one email he wrote, 'Once I have their attention through the app, then I have them, thousands at a time.'"

"Did he say how exactly?" Rocco asked.

"He referred to a protocol of drugs and electrical stimulation that helped him connect with the app users in this other dimension." Clare finally looked at Rocco after this last statement.

"I don't get this other dimension thing," Vince said, shrugging, "What is it again?"

"Silverman said it's a dimension that contains our *essence*, like our souls or something."

"Our souls? You're joking, right?" Jake asked. Jake was neither philosophically nor religiously inclined, even though his father was a rabbi. In fact, Jake had not spoken to his father in years, due to a Thanksgiving Day argument about religion. "Why would a physicist be talking about souls?" Jake asked.

"Silverman used the word, 'soul' while Hoffman always said, 'mind,'" Clare explained. "Anyway, that's how he said he'd get to people."

"What about the app?" Rocco asked. "Any clues there?"

"I did an internet search and found a group of three teenagers bragging about their telepathic powers with the app. They're outside now waiting to talk to us," Clare explained, looking at Rocco once again.

"They're here now?" Rocco asked. "You brought them here?" Clare scowled as though ready for a fight. "That's excellent," Rocco exclaimed. "Fantastic! Nice work Clare. Bring them in." Clare's look softened slightly as she went out into the hallway and led in three boys who glanced repeatedly over their shoulders as they followed her in.

"Are we in trouble?" one of them asked.

"No," Clare reassured them. "We just want to talk to you

about this eTelepathy app." The oldest of the three handed Clare his phone and pointed out the app. Clare tapped on the icon. "How does it work?"

"Well, you need to tap the new user button there... now just wait until you're registered."

"That's it?"

"Yeah, there... see, read those letters as they're appearing. Keep doing it until it says you're registered." Clare kept her eyes fixed on the phone.

"Would you mind if we keep your phone for a bit?" Clare asked. "There must be an answer in here somewhere."

"You could put it on your own phone," the oldest teen suggested.

"Yeah, it's free," another chimed in. The three boys stared at Clare, then in unison, turned toward Vince, then Jake. The uniformity of their motions startled Vince who frowned and pulled on Clare's arm to get her attention.

"You know Clare," Vince interrupted, "I don't think that's such a good idea. Maybe it's like cookies that websites put on your computer, you know, so they can recognize you later. Maybe this app does something like that. It might put a cookie in your brain."

"How?" Rocco laughed.

"You heard Clare," Vince protested, "Hoffman said all he had to do was get people's attention. Well, aren't you giving him your attention now Clare?"

"I'm looking at the phone, not him."

"There's a camera on that phone, look." Vince tapped the camera icon, flipping it to selfie mode. "See, you look at it and it looks back at you."

Seeing her face on the screen, Clare dropped the phone on the table.

"Are you saying Hoffman actually looks at each individual person who logs in? That's impossible!" Jake protested.

"It can take a long time to register," one of the teens offered. "I had to do it about ten times before I got through."

"And now it works for you?" Rocco asked.

"Every time! It's even giving me tips and things. It told me Billy was coming over, and then a few minutes later, he's knocking at the door!"

"Well, delete that app from your phones right now," Rocco commanded. "Jake, contact the distributers and pull the app from the online stores." After the teens had reluctantly complied, Rocco told them they were free to go.

"There's something else," Clare said quietly to Rocco, "Hoffman had exchanged emails with someone who called himself 'the machinist.' He said he was interested in Hoffman's services and Hoffman had agreed to meet with him in Manhattan later today, at a cafe in the village. Who knows if he'll go through with it now, but it's probably worth staking out the area."

"Absolutely. When was the meeting time?" Rocco asked.

"Three PM, six hours from now," Clare responded while glancing at her watch.

"Good work," Rocco said, pausing as he looked for a sign of appreciation from Clare, but seeing only her down-turned head, he added, "Let's bring in our other witnesses."

"Those kids were weird," Vince blurted out once the teens were out of the room. "Did you see how they all stared at us?"

"It is intimidating being interviewed by the FBI," Rocco suggested.

"But did you see how they all winked at the same time?" Vince asked.

"They winked at you?" Jake chuckled.

"At the same time!" Vince stressed. "Who does that? I'm telling you, something's weird about them."

The door at the stairwell opened and officers Hardin and O'Malley, who had confronted Hoffman at his home, and Jonathan, Silverman's nephew entered the room and were introduced by Rocco. Jonathan looked around the room at the agents, pausing at each one as if making a mental note of their faces. As he sat down, Rocco asked him, "Jonathan, you seem pretty certain that Hoffman had something to do with your uncle's death. Why is that?"

"Not something to do with it, he did it," Jonathan insisted. "Hoffman didn't know I was there. I was in the other room, but I heard everything. My uncle was afraid Hoffman would misuse this app of his. At first, I just thought it was another one of his exaggerations."

"He was prone to exaggerations?" Rocco asked.

"No, it's just that, he grew up in communist Bulgaria, with the oppression, secret police assassinations, ricin-coated umbrella tips, the works. I'd heard all the stories many times. Not that the stories were exaggerated. Most of what he'd told me had been verified by KGB files released after the fall of the Soviet Union. By exaggeration, I mean, he was paranoid, always seeing the potential for that sort of evil everywhere, lurking under the surface, waiting for an opportunity. Understandably, he was gun-shy of the slightest notion of thought control. So he would get emotional about political issues, and I learned to just roll with it. But this time, turns out his was right."

"What did your uncle fear Hoffman was going to do?"

"I don't know. Control elections? Something big I think, but, because the two were friends, my uncle convinced himself that Hoffman was just looking to make some money with marketing schemes, to 'sell more shampoo,' as he put it. But you don't kill someone just to sell more shampoo."

"Right," Rocco replied slowly, looking around at the other agents, none of whom offered any ideas of where to go next with the questioning. Turning toward the two police officers he asked, "Why don't you two run over what happened at Hoffman's home?"

"Well, I came up on him first," O'Malley began. "He was walking down the hall toward the back of the house and I called out his name, asking him to come with us, that we wanted to ask some questions, and he said, 'No.' So I drew my weapon, but before I could say anything, it was like I was pushed down to the floor."

"Why did you draw your weapon?" Rocco asked.

"What do you mean?" O'Malley replied.

"I mean, did he threaten you? What did he say? Why draw your weapon?"

"I felt threatened," O'Malley answered in a defensive tone.

"Relax," Rocco said, "I'm just trying to understand how you knew he was a threat."

"It just seemed like he was about to do something," O'Malley answered.

"Okay," Rocco continued, "so you felt pushed down to the floor. Could you get up?"

"No, it was like I had weights on me, like when they put that lead apron on you at the dentist, only it was all over me. I couldn't even raise my head."

"What about you, Officer Hardin?" Clare asked. "The report said you couldn't move O'Malley either."

"That's right," Hardin replied. "It's like he weighed a thousand pounds or something."

"You sure he wasn't just dead weight, hard to lift up with

one hand while holding a gun in the other?" Rocco asked.

"I mean I couldn't budge him," Hardin stressed. "I couldn't even lift his wrist to check his pulse."

"Then what happened?" Rocco asked.

"I went to the end of the hallway and saw the suspect. He looked over his shoulder at the back door, then he looked at me, then he was gone."

"He went out the door?" Jake asked.

"No, I was looking straight at him, then he was gone. The door was closed, there were no side doors, no corners to hide behind. I can't explain it. He just disappeared."

"So he tricked you somehow. Got you to look away for a second?" Jake suggested.

"I was staring right at him the whole time," Hardin repeated vehemently.

"What did you see, O'Malley?" Rocco asked.

"I couldn't see into that entryway. All I could see was Rick, Officer Hardin. I saw him starting to look around, saying, 'Where'd he go?' and I thought I heard a door close. I went over to look down the hall with him. We looked all through the house and even in the back yard. There was no sign of him anywhere."

Rocco looked at his fellow agents, and of the three, he noted that Clare seemed somewhat shaken. It may have been a consequence of going through all those emails. *She must have been drawn into the deception*, he thought.

"He's a master of illusion," Rocco said, looking directly at Clare. "That's all."

"He's a killer," Jonathan protested. "You're going to stop him, right?" Jonathan pressed. "You need to stop him."

"We'll stop him," Clare assured him. "We know this is more than a magic trick," she added, glaring at Rocco.

"Does anyone have any other questions?" Rocco asked. As there were none, he thanked Jonathan and the officers for coming, and he and the team left to set up their surveillance at the cafe in Manhattan.

SURVEILLANCE

03

*A*s the team drove into Greenwich Village, the fog was lifting, giving way to low-hanging clouds that moved between the surrounding buildings. The cafe, a small lunch and dinner restaurant with indoor and outdoor seating, had not yet opened. Clare pressed her badge up against the locked glass door as she knocked, catching the manager's attention. After a brief protest, the manager acquiesced, allowing the team to place microphones and cameras throughout the seating areas. Clare climbed down from a chair, having just placed a small wireless camera on the top of an exit sign.

"We still have blind spots," Clare muttered, shaking her head, "behind that rack, around the stairwell. We don't have enough cameras."

"Do the best you can," Rocco advised. Watching Clare's hair flow across her shoulder as she turned her head, he tried to remember why, exactly, he had broken off their relationship. "You want inside or out?" he asked her.

"Outside," Clare replied. "Over by that wall."

Rocco took a seat by the door to the kitchen. Looking out the window, Rocco could see Vince and Jake setting up monitoring equipment in a van on the street as Clare moved to take a seat against a low brick wall that separated the restaurant's seating area from an adjacent side street. Loading docks lined the side street, one leading into the restaurant's kitchen.

This was the part Rocco loved most–setting the trap. He thought through the different potential scenarios like projecting an opponent's moves in a chess game. Hypnosis or no, they had the upper hand. Mind tricks were just that–tricks. They had stationed themselves with triangulated points of observation, and if necessary, crossfire. They couldn't lose. This was how he liked his interactions with suspects. The deck was stacked in their favor. They would likely record damning evidence from Hoffman's conversation. At the very least, they would get enough to bring him in.

Rocco kept his eyes fixed on Clare and noticed that she glanced over her shoulder several times. It seemed to him that she was nervous. He had always known her to be very calm in the field, it was one of the traits he admired most in her. She did not appear to be herself today. It must have been something she had read in those emails. That was the power of suggestion, he thought, a hypnotist's primary weapon. Rocco was anxious for Hoffman to arrive so they could begin to undo him.

Clare tested her earpiece connection with Rocco and the agents in the van just as a truck drove down the adjacent street. The sound startled her, and she reflexly turned her head toward the wall behind her.

"You okay, Clare?" Vince asked through the radio. Clare continued to glance over her shoulders repeatedly. "Clare, Clare, are you reading me?" Vince repeated over the radio.

"Yes, yes, sorry."

"Are you all right?"

"Fine," she answered. "I'm reading you fine."

As the truck sounds receded, the sound of water hosing off the restaurant's loading dock rose. Smells of the wet loading platform, the fresh produce, the cloud of truck exhaust, the damp sea breeze, all poured in through the kitchen behind Rocco. *Power of suggestion*, he thought.

By the time Hoffman appeared, most of the indoor seats had been filled and about half of the outdoor. Vince was the first to recognize him as he approached the restaurant, speaking to a man near the front door who also had just arrived. This man remained standing by the door while Hoffman took a seat at one of the open tables in the center of Clare's field of view. Clare ordered coffee from her waitress and held a newspaper in front of her face, Hoffman visible only in her peripheral vision. "He's just a man," Rocco said to her through her earpiece.

"I know that," she answered indignantly.

Rocco looked at Clare's location against the wall, chosen for its clear vantage point, and it suddenly struck him that it also closed off any retreat for her.

"Are you all right, Clare?" Rocco asked, aghast at how awkward his question had sounded.

"Fine," Clare snapped.

"We've got him on three cameras, Clare," Jake assured her through the radio. "If he makes any kind of move in your direction, we'll be all over him."

"I'm fine," Clare stressed. "Stay put and keep recording."

Stubbornness was another trait Rocco had always recognized in Clare. Though often frustrating to deal with, it was also somewhat attractive as a sign of strength. Her displaying it now relieved some of his anxiety, and he returned to watching Hoffman speak to his waiter.

"Just coffee for now," Hoffman said. "I'm waiting for someone."

It was dark inside the restaurant and, although overcast outdoors, it was bright enough that the restaurant's glass front was more mirror than window, allowing Rocco to watch Hoffman with impunity. If he was anxious in any way, Rocco could not see it. Rather, he seemed to be the epitome of a man in control: calm and steadfast. Not waiting for someone in the usual manner where one might look over one's shoulder or down the street for their arrival. He sat more like an ancient lord awaiting the petition of a subject who would come before him with fear and trembling.

A tall thin man came up beside Hoffman's table and spoke, "Are you waiting for a machinist?"

"What on earth would I need a machinist for?" Hoffman replied, without looking over his shoulder.

"May I join you?" the man asked. Hoffman nodded, and the man took a seat opposite him. "That senator you're working with," the man began. Hoffman's eyes darted from the table to the man. "Oh yes, we know about him, he's not terribly discreet. We work very closely with the Homeland Security & Government Affairs Committee, and since he's on that committee, well, we know all about your offer to guarantee him votes."

"So?"

"So the senator only needs you every six years at reelection time. We could use you year-round."

"I'm sure you could."

"I need to know your price," the man continued speaking to Hoffman. "I need to see the app's programming. I need to have access to the database, and see how many people have the app. I need to know how it works."

"You're a needy man," Hoffman quipped.

"Well, if you want to work with us…"

"You contacted me," Hoffman rebuffed. "You need me. I do not need you."

"If you expect us to pay for this application..."

"I am the application."

"What does that mean?"

"It's a technique. I can use anything as a means of introduction. Initially, I used smart phones, but they are already obsolete. They've served their purpose, opening doors to thousands of minds that I can connect to, and millions more through them." Hoffman looked intently at the man for a few moments, then, as if bored by what he'd seen, spun his head to the side. As he turned, his gaze fell upon Clare's before she could look away. She had been watching him as he stared at the tall man as though waiting for something to happen. Caught off guard when he suddenly glanced her way, she shifted her gaze down at her newspaper.

"Well, that's all well and good, but we need to see some proof," the tall man continued. "Dr. Hoffman, are you paying attention?" he asked Hoffman, who was now quite fixated on Clare.

"I'm always paying attention," Hoffman replied. "Are you?"

"Of course."

"Really? You're not very good at it."

"What do you mean?"

"Did you know we're being watched?"

"We're being watched?" the man asked, glancing around the seating area. "Where? What did you see?"

"I see what they see," Hoffman said as he turned back to face the tall man, "and they see us."

"John, are you hearing this?" Clare asked Rocco through her wireless.

"Every word," Rocco answered.

"How do you know?" the tall man fired back at Hoffman, as he continued to glance around the seating area. "Who are they?"

"I don't know," Hoffman said slowly, scanning the surrounding tables, "not yet."

"Is that possible?" Clare asked the others over her wireless as she glanced at Hoffman's reflection in the restaurant's front window. "He sees what we see?"

"Whatever he sees, or thinks he sees, don't look at him," Rocco said. "Let the cameras do that."

"Dr. Hoffman," the tall man began.

Hoffman held up his hand, silencing him, then wrote on a slip of paper that he slid over to the man. "We'll meet there and I'll show you something then," Hoffman assured him.

"Keep your eyes off him, Clare," Rocco warned over his radio.

"I'll only look at his reflection," Clare replied.

"You're looking at his reflection in the window?" Rocco asked, as he realized with a chill that Hoffman was now staring at the window. "Clare, I think he's made you," Rocco whispered through her earpiece. "I think he's staring back at your reflection!"

"What?" she said, looking away from the window. Her hands were shaking as she turned another page of her newspaper. "What do I do?" she asked, her pulse quickening, sweat beading on her forehead.

"Get out," Rocco told her through her earpiece, "get up and leave now. Take the car, I'll catch up with you later." He could see Hoffman writing something on a piece of paper, then get up and give the paper to the man standing by the doorway. This man read the note and, nodding to Hoffman, made a call on his cell phone. The tall man, meanwhile, had slipped out of the seating area and scuttled across the street.

Clare scrambled to get her things together and threw some money on the table for her check. She stood up, kept her eyes on the ground, and shoved in her chair, tripping over it as she made her way through the tightly packed tables to the sidewalk.

"Take it easy, Clare. I've got eyes on Hoffman," Rocco assured her through her earpiece. "Listen, Hoffman spoke to a man by the restaurant door. Make sure you're not followed."

Clare walked around the corner to her car and headed uptown. At a yellow light, she turned, checking her rearview mirror for any trailing vehicle. Circling the block, she headed north again. A yellow cab fell in behind her and when stopped at a light, Clare noticed that the cab driver was speaking into his cell phone and appeared to be looking at her reflection in the rear view mirror. She turned off the boulevard and when the cab turned along with her, she moved a hand onto her sidearm, unsnapping the leather strap. As she entered the ramp for the tunnel to Queens, the traffic slowed to a crawl and she drew her weapon from its holster, holding it at her side. She kept her eyes fixed on the cab, but it continued past her onto an adjacent street, and a small car occupied by two women pulled up behind her. She holstered her gun and continued on into the tunnel.

As Clare emerged from the tunnel in Queens, a man on a motorcycle was watching the cars come out of the tunnel. Talking on his Bluetooth earpiece, he merged onto the road with Clare. When Clare pulled up to their meeting place, the motorcycle continued past her, the man muttering into his Bluetooth.

Rocco was still watching Hoffman at the cafe. Though the tall man was long gone, Hoffman remained standing on the sidewalk near the street methodically looking at all the buildings up and down the block, the cars on the street, including Vince and Jake's van, and everyone walking by on the sidewalk. Having finished his assessment, he turned his back on the scene and walked away. Rocco announced to Jake and Vince that he would follow Hoffman on foot.

"You want us to follow along behind you?" Jake asked.

"I think he'd see the van," Rocco said. "Better stay put."

"What if we follow on foot?" Vince asked.

"No, too conspicuous. I'll let you know everything I see as I go."

"Don't underestimate this guy, Rocco," Vince warned.

"I'll hang back, don't worry." Rocco said as he stepped out into the sea of pedestrians crowding the downtown streets. From where he was, Rocco could see Hoffman going into a hotel lobby.

"I'm following him into The Regis," Rocco reported to Vince and Jake. Meanwhile, Hoffman breezed up the lobby stairs and into a mezzanine lunch area. Picking up a newspaper, he sat at a table where someone had just finished eating and peered around the side of the paper toward the lobby. Rocco slid in through the revolving doors and quickly glanced around the lobby. He ran up the stairs, scanned the lunch area, then went back downstairs into a side hall. Hoffman slid up and followed him through the lobby, stopping just short of the entrance to the hall. Rocco, finding no one in the side hall, returned to the lobby, and just as he was about to turn the corner, Hoffman stepped out in front of him.

"Looking for someone?" Hoffman asked, as Rocco recoiled in surprise.

"Excuse me, no," Rocco blurted out, as he tried to move around Hoffman, avoiding eye contact with him.

"You look familiar to me," Hoffman said, sidestepping to remain in Rocco's path. "Do I look familiar to you?"

"No, no," Rocco answered, not looking up at him.

"Look at me," Hoffman ordered.

"Please, I'm meeting someone. I'm late," Rocco stammered as he pushed his way past Hoffman keeping his eyes fixed on the floor. Leaving the hotel lobby, Rocco hailed a cab and jumped in, mumbling to himself under his breath.

"How could I be so stupid? He was waiting for me."

"Didn't catch that," the cabbie replied, "where do you want to go?"

"Brooklyn."

"Anywhere particular in Brooklyn?" the cabbie asked with a smirk.

"I'll tell you where to turn as we go," Rocco answered, keeping a watchful eye out the back window.

Within an hour, Rocco and the rest of the team had reassembled at the Brooklyn warehouse. The four sat around the table where they had been that morning, the unspoken question hanging in the air between them, "How did he know?" Their eyes darted to and fro, catching each other's glances then quickly looking away. Rocco broke the silence.

"All right, so he made us," Rocco said with a sigh.

"How?" Vince asked. "What was that stuff about seeing what we see?"

"Something tipped him off," Rocco said, his hand

waving away any notion of supernatural clairvoyance. "But not before he gave us something. Did you catch that stuff about the senate committee? We need to find out who's on that committee and..."

"Already on it," Jake replied. "Sixteen members, none up for reelection this year. Two are up for reelection in two years, a Henry Miller and another, Justin Smith."

"Get a judge's order for phone and computer surveillance and let's get people tailing them 24/7."

Clare, who was silent at the table, though still visibly shaken by the experience asked, "Why did he say the smart phones were obsolete?"

"Maybe he works through laptops now?" Rocco asked. "Jake, you had the app pulled?"

"Yeah, but you know, it already had over a million downloads."

"Hey," Vince showed his phone to Jake. "It looks like it's still live."

Vince tapped his phone a few times.

"What are you doing?" Clare exclaimed. "Don't look at it!"

"It's okay. We're not registering," Vince explained, "just continuing as a guest."

"I'm sure it does the same thing! Didn't you see what just happened?" she stammered. "He recognized me. Get it off your phone now!"

"Vince," Rocco said, waving his hand toward him in an attempt to diffuse the tension, "leave it. Maybe it takes time to come off the servers. We should all get some rest tonight. Tomorrow we'll start over. I've asked a few advisors to meet with us here."

"What sort of advisors?" Vince asked, tapping his phone again, then turning to Clare. "App's gone now. No worries."

"Experts in hypnosis, science, and the military," Rocco replied.

"Any ideas where Hoffman's going next?" Jake asked. Rocco shrugged and looked across at Clare.

"Why ask me? Ask your *experts* tomorrow," Clare sniffed, turning away from Rocco and staring down at the floor.

STRING THEORY

04

*T*he following morning, invisible rays of ultraviolet light pierced the warehouse windows while infrared waves of heat rose from the individuals in the room. Electromagnetic waves splayed out in spheres with weak forces around each person, colliding, and reflecting. All were unseen, unfelt, and unnoticed, interacting and influencing each other beyond sight and sound. At the same time, within the normal range of sense perception, the agents sat with each other at the table, joined now by the advisors promised by Rocco.

The first advisor was Marcus Jones, a military consultant to the bureau. After twelve years as a Navy SEAL, he had gone into consultant work, both for government agencies and private firms. Spending several years preparing nonmilitary personnel for missions, he then worked as a bodyguard for corporate executives traveling overseas. He had been a regular consultant to the FBI for the past two years. Because

Hoffman had a history of providing the military with programs for mental manipulation and propaganda, Rocco had tapped Marcus for help on this case.

Although dressed in jeans and a casual shirt, Marcus Jones conveyed an unmistakable aura of a soldier. Everything, from his erect posture, his calm, circumspect demeanor, his shaven head and sinewy physique relayed his underlying expertise.

Next to Marcus was Dr. Paul Lejour, a retired vascular surgeon who had a special interest in mystical phenomena and mind research, having published several papers evaluating supernatural occurrences such as levitation, bilocation, and apparitions. He was born in France, but had spent most of his life in the United States, having now only a slight remnant of a French accent. He wore a suit, and was tall and lean with short white hair, smooth skin, and high cheek bones. He had been a consultant for the Bureau the previous year on the case of a Long Island con artist posing as a meditation instructor. The con man solicited wealthy clients purportedly to teach them advanced techniques of meditation for stress relief. His clients uniformly felt a sense of peace and tranquility following their sessions until they discovered their bank accounts had been emptied online shortly thereafter. He was found to be using hypnosis to get pin numbers and online passwords from his clients, which he then used to siphon off funds. Dr. Lejour was instrumental in preparing agents to go undercover in a sting operation against the con man, training them to resist his hypnotic effects. Given the apparent mind manipulation in this case, Dr. Lejour was brought in to help mentally prepare the agents.

The third advisor was Dr. Friedrich Schroeder, a physicist who had significant experience with string theory. He had been used by the Bureau to help with the "Einstein killer," a serial killer in the D.C. area who had left messages with obscure references to astrophysics. Dr. Schroeder had identified patterns and clues in the notes which eventually led to the arrest of the killer.

Dr. Schroeder was a retired university professor, who, in addition to consultant work for the FBI, also wrote a column, "Physical Wonders," that was carried in various Sunday newspapers across the country. He wore round, wire-rimmed glasses, and had a remarkably pleasant affect, beginning almost every statement with a smile. He was clean shaven, with his white hair combed neatly backwards, consistent with his appreciation for order. He was a native of Germany, though now a U.S. citizen, and unlike Dr. Lejour, spoke with a heavy accent. Despite his highly specialized and erudite field of expertise, he thoroughly enjoyed conversation on any topic and was quick to engage others with his warm, disarming smile.

The advisors were introduced to each other and their backgrounds and credentials shared. Dr. Lejour, noticing the swirly lined picture hanging on the wall, got up and stood in front of it.

"I love these things," he said, moments later exclaiming, "I see it!" Rocco shifted in his seat and sighed. As the doctor returned to the table, he shared some excitement regarding the case. "I found the information you shared about the police officer being too heavy to move very interesting," Dr. Lejour began. "This is something well known in cases of apparitions and demonic possessions." Hearing this, Dr. Schroeder chuckled. "You're skeptical of such things, Friedrich?" Dr. Lejour asked.

"I'm not a religious person," answered Dr. Schroeder with a smile.

"You don't need religion to appreciate the extraordinary," Dr. Lejour replied. The two men sat on opposite sides of the table as if poised for a debate on the relative merits of faith versus skepticism.

"Dr. Schroeder," Rocco interrupted, not wanting to waste any more time on apparently irrelevant questions, "our suspect claims to be able to connect with minds through another dimension. What does string theory have to say about that?"

"String theory physics," Dr. Schroeder explained, "is basically a mathematical representation of reality, and for that mathematical equation to work, it requires more than four dimensions, ten, or some would say eleven in all. But ideas of traveling through these dimensions, parallel universes, connecting minds–this is more science fiction than science." Rocco nodded an exaggerated nod in appreciation of this rationale disclaimer.

"What about non-local connections?" Dr. Lejour asked, seeming to draw Dr. Schroeder back into the debate.

Dr. Schroeder shrugged. "Albert Einstein called it, 'spooky action at a distance.' It is when two particles, separate from each other, spin in unison as if they were connected."

"An invisible connection!" Dr. Lejour pronounced with his hands raised in triumph, offering this unseen connection as an example of the many such invisible interactions around them.

"So can brains connect like that?" Marcus asked.

"I don't see how," Dr. Schroeder said, smiling. "Subatomic particles influencing each other enough that they spin together is one thing, but brains connecting?"

"Not brains, minds," Dr. Lejour corrected. "Those subatomic particles aren't physically connected; their *essences* are, in another dimension. Likewise, brains can't physically connect, but their essences can, and the mind is the essence of the brain. Look at animal behavior–the delegation of duties among ants or bees, the precise migration of birds–such instincts reveal a *natural order*, a transcendent connection of minds. While humans have little instinct, I believe we still have this ability to connect. Think of couples married for many years finishing each other's sentences; groups of women living together coming to have synchronized hormonal cycles; twins on opposite sides of the country becoming aware when their sibling is sick; mothers with their 'mother's intuition.' These are resonating minds, signs of connections that transcend physical space and time."

Rocco began to wonder if it had not been a mistake to bring in these doctors as advisors, leastways Dr. Lejour. In contrast to Dr. Schroeder's clear, pragmatic approach to the issues, which he found thoroughly reasonable and appropriate, Dr. Lejour's giddy excitement regarding all things paranormal was getting on his nerves.

Clare, on the other hand, seemed to be drawn to Dr. Lejour, hanging on his every word.

"How can we prevent such a connection?" Clare quietly asked Dr. Lejour. "That's what we're interested in, right?" she added glancing at Rocco.

"Well, unlike animals, our minds don't automatically connect through instinct. How we direct our will determines which minds we connect with."

"When we saw Hoffman yesterday, he seemed to know we were watching him. He said, 'I see what they see.' Is that possible?" Clare asked.

Rocco turned toward the window and took in a slow, deep breath, hoping the doctor would not encourage Clare who seemed to be more and more inclined to accept a supernatural explanation for everything.

"Interesting," the doctor said slowly. "Did you sense anything about him?"

"Like what?" Clare asked.

"A presence, maybe?"

"No," Clare answered quickly.

"Well, sight is in the brain," Dr. Lejour explained, "so technically, no, he could not see what you see. But, the mind provides understanding to what the brain sees, so in that sense, yes, he could."

"What's the difference?" Vince asked.

"It's a matter of details," Dr. Lejour said. "Suppose you are on the street and see armed men looking at you from a street corner in front of you, from a window above on your side, and from the sidewalk behind you. Your brain takes in numerous concrete details, the name on the street sign at the corner, the appearance of the men and the buildings, the floor that the window is on. But your mind distills abstract understanding from that plethora of details, realizing one thing: it's a trap. If someone were to connect with your mind, they would not see those concrete details, but would share the abstract understanding that you were trapped."

"So Hoffman understood that he was being watched?" Clare asked.

"Most likely," Dr. Lejour replied.

"But not the details," Vince added with a look of sudden enlightenment. "That's why he kept looking around."

"That would make sense," Dr. Lejour said.

"What if it was just a shot in the dark?" Rocco asked, turning back to the group from the window. "Maybe he figured there was a good chance he was being watched, and he just said that, put it out there as a test to get a response from us."

"He is purported to be an expert in mental influences, propaganda, and deception," Dr. Schroeder remarked. "Maybe he fooled you."

"He fooled us all right," Jake said barely beneath his breath.

"In any event," Clare interrupted sharply, "in the off chance that it is more than just cleverness, do you have any suggestions for how we can defend ourselves?"

"Certainly," Dr. Lejour answered with a smile. "You must focus your wills such that your minds interact with each other's and not his. Mental exercises at a dream center is something I used with the agents on the hypnotist case. It was very helpful then and I think it would help you now too."

"Fair enough," Rocco acquiesced. "We'll give it a try. When can we get in there?"

"We can start tonight," Dr. Lejour said, beaming with enthusiasm.

POWER

05

*O*n the other side of Brooklyn, outside a small apartment building, not far from where the police officers had confronted Hoffman, the stock broker, Kyle Williams, paced back and forth on the landing. He had pressed the call bell of an apartment several times, and, receiving no response, was typing Hoffman's number into his cell phone. The two had met almost a year earlier as a result of solicitation calls Williams had made to the faculty at Hoffman's university. As a ploy to expand his client base, it had failed miserably. None of the faculty would speak to him or return his calls, with one exception–Hoffman. They met several times over lunches, during which Williams ran down a list of investment opportunities for Hoffman, while Hoffman appeared more interested in the salesman than the sale, studying Williams's face as he spoke. Before long, the meetings became more a series of interviews conducted by Hoffman, rather than sales pitches from Williams. "What motivates you?" Hoffman would ask Williams, who invariably ended up expressing his longings in terms of financial success. Every fantasy teased out of Williams always ended with his being completely liquid, able to buy anything he wanted. "I may not know science," he told Hoffman once, "but I know money, and I can help you with yours." Hoffman showed little interest in this offer and referred instead to an opportunity for Williams to become wealthy through him. This was the hook that had held Williams fast to him ever since.

"Oh, there you are," Williams said, as Hoffman appeared from the corner of the building.

"Let's go," Hoffman answered. He led Williams through the electric door to a first floor apartment. Once inside, Williams glanced around the front room which had a solitary piece of furniture, an upholstered sofa with no light or table beside it. In the next room, there was a narrow bed with racks of equipment on either side, and beyond that was a small kitchenette.

"You live here?" Williams asked.

"You could say that," Hoffman answered, walking back around Williams to the door. He locked the door's dead bolt with a key which he returned to his pocket, then he placed a call on his cell phone. "Spinosa, is everything in place for the morning?" he asked quietly, speaking into his phone.

Williams was listening but his eyes remained fixed on the floor, cowering like a submissive dog. "Good. Keep it quiet," Hoffman continued. "I don't want any more interruptions. I'll be there at ten o'clock." Hoffman returned his phone to his pocket and moved closer to Williams. "Are you ready?"

"For what?"

"To meet the users of the app."

"Meet them?" Williams asked incredulously. "There are over a million." He paused, considering the notion of actually meeting one million people, then continued. "About the app, have you seen the user list and the stats?"

"Of course."

"The numbers are fantastic! Not only the million users, but also connections to all their contacts and friends. The app has an opt-in agreement set as default, so you can use any of that information. You've got one hell of a database there. What are you thinking? Track their search patterns? Retargeting ads? Sell the database?"

"Calm down," Hoffman interrupted, "The app has been useful, but it's like the clinking of a glass at a reception. Once you have everyone's attention, you don't keep clinking the glass."

"Well, surely you're going to use the data."

"I told you. I'm going to meet them right now."

"But the connections, they're too many of them. You need extensive programming to filter out specific characteristics, locations, search habits. There's no way to understand all that information at once."

"Let me worry about the understanding." Hoffman sat down on the edge of the bed and rolled up his shirt sleeve. "It's time to stop clinking the glass." Tying a rubber tourniquet around his left upper arm, he motioned to Williams to take a seat next to the bed. He made a number of adjustments to small metal devices that were clamped to poles alongside him. Each had a syringe within it and was attached to a branching network of tubing. He switched on a machine at the head of the bed which was about the size of a portable clothes washer. It made some beeping sounds and lit up digital readout screens. He tore open an alcohol wipe and began to prep the skin of his left forearm.

"Do you know what it takes to be great?" Hoffman asked. "To be a great man?" Williams looked back at him with a blank stare. "Will. An abundant will, a will to do anything, especially that which you naturally recoil from. No fear, no repugnance, no resistance whatsoever, just pure will." As Hoffman opened an intravenous catheter and prepared to place it through the skin of his arm into his now bulging forearm vein, Williams began to shift about in his chair, looking away from the scene. "You have a problem with needles?" Hoffman asked him.

"Yeah, little bit."

"Your weakness is disturbing. Look at me." Williams

gladly turned his attention away from the needle to look at Hoffman, when suddenly his expression went blank, his eyes widened and his mouth opened. "Take this needle and put it into my vein," Hoffman said to Williams, who complied without a word, grasping the object of his fear. Hoffman's hand guided Williams' as he placed the needle through his skin and slid the catheter up into his vein. Hoffman then brushed his assistant's hand away and connected the catheter to a small cap which he flushed with a syringe of fluid.

Williams sat back in his chair, and looking up from the blood on his fingers, he continued to watch the professor. Hoffman was laying out his materials on the side of the bed. He took a tongue depressor and placing it on his own tongue opened his mouth widely, tilting his head upwards. Taking a spray can with a small tube attached to the nozzle, he began to spray the inside of his mouth and the back of his throat. This seemed to leave Hoffman with some difficulty swallowing, but he continued his preparations with the same calm, determined manner. He connected a set of hoses to the machine at the head of the bed, and typed in some numbers on its keypad, after which the machine began expressing air intermittently through the tubing. He stuck an electrode to each of his temples and attached a set of tongs to them. He then connected himself to the branched tubing on the poles via the intravenous catheter in his arm. Looking again at Williams, he picked up a short, wide tube, with an oval balloon structure on its end.

"Don't touch anything, and don't leave," Hoffman ordered, as he tilted his head back and placed the tube into his mouth and down his throat. The scene was reminiscent of a sword swallowing circus act, and would have seemed humorous to Williams, if he had not been so frightened. Once the tube was in place, Hoffman spoke only with his eyes which continued to stare at Williams while he taped the tubing to his upper lip and cheek. His breathing in and out of the tube sounded like a snorkeler gliding on the surface of a lagoon. He made some final entries into the syringe-holding devices on the poles, then lay back on the bed, connecting the tube in his throat to the air pumping machine at the head of the bed.

One of the syringes was automatically injected into his IV tubing and within a few moments, Hoffman's eyes, still fixed on Williams, closed. Another syringe was emptied and the surfaces of his hands began to quiver, along with his upper eyelids and portions of his face, as if small creatures were scurrying beneath his skin. Then, there was no more motion, no sounds, except for the machine pumping air every few seconds. Lights blinked on the machine attached to the electrodes on his head and the final syringe was emptied into the professor's bloodstream.

Williams looked at Hoffman's body, motionless save for the rising and lowering of his chest in time with the rhythmic sounds of the air-pumping ventilator. Williams began to move several times, then stopped, glancing back at Hoffman's closed eyes, scrutinizing them from different angles. Then, keeping his gaze fixed on Hoffman's face, he crept to the top of the bed. He ran his hand over the surface of the ventilator machine's control panel, fingering the "off" button lightly, the button that, if pushed, would stop the flow of air into Hoffman's lungs. The corner of his mouth raised slightly as he turned to look at Hoffman again.

He moved away from the bedside and leafed through an old, worn notebook on a shelf below the blinking equipment. Checking Hoffman's face again, he pulled out his cell phone and began taking photographs of the notebook's pages. He carefully replaced the notebook on its shelf and went into the kitchenette. Opening the cupboards he found in place of plates and glasses, bottles of medication and other medical supplies. He took photographs of these as well.

An alarm sounded as Hoffman began to breathe on his own against the machine. Williams jerked his head around, then rushed to close the cabinets in the kitchenette. He started back toward Hoffman, then halted. With a look of panic, he rushed to the door, and, grabbing the knob, pulled repeatedly against the dead bolt. Looking back over his shoulder, his gaze rested on Hoffman's pocket where the key was securely hidden. He released his hold on the door knob, and stole quietly to a window facing the side of the building. He pushed up against the window frame which did not budge, despite his flipping the lock back and forth. The sides of the window frames were held shut with screws and brackets. Hoffman's arms and legs began to move.

Williams hurried back to his previous place at the bed-side. Hoffman's eyes opened, but were jerking to one side over and over. This slowed and he was again focusing on Williams. He pulled the tube from his throat, and as he took his first breath without the tube, he reached across and grabbed Williams by the front of his shirt, dragging him down to his face.

"I thought I told you not to leave," he said to Williams with a raspy voice. Williams said nothing, pulling back against Hoffman's grasp. Hoffman released Williams who stumbled back from the bed.

Removing the electrodes from his head and the IV from his arm, Hoffman turned to Williams and asked, "What were you thinking about?"

"Nothing," Williams answered, taking another small step backwards.

"Tell me."

"Nothing, really. I was a little worried about you is all."

"You thought about killing me, didn't you?"

"No! Of course not!"

"Yes, you did. How couldn't you? I was in your power." Hoffman stood up from the bed and moved closer to

Williams whose hands trembled as he slid them into his pockets. "I have hope for you yet."

"You can read my mind?"

"Of course," Hoffman replied, taping a gauze pad to his forearm. "You're afraid of me. That's good." Hoffman turned from Williams and began detaching the tubing from the machines.

"Could you see them, the users?" Williams asked sheepishly.

"Like drops of water in an immense ocean."

"How can that help you? So much information, how can you distinguish anything?"

"I recognized them," Hoffman said, looking across the room, then back at Williams, "every one of them."

"What was it like?" Williams asked.

Hoffman looked at Williams for a moment, then past him to the wall. "You can't imagine the power," Hoffman said, as though speaking to the empty space behind Williams. "You can't imagine."

RESONANCE

06

*T*hat evening, Dr. Lejour sat on the front steps of The Dream Center waiting for the agents to arrive. The center was housed in an old meat packing building in Manhattan. Some twenty years earlier, a large hook on rollers would slide out on a rail over the loading dock where quarters of beef would be transferred from refrigerator trucks into the cooler inside. In place of the loading dock, a small brick porch and stairway now stood, outlined with a wrought iron railing. From the outside, it was an unimpressive sight, indistinguishable from the row of similar brick buildings lining the street, but inside, extraordinary things were happening. Where once the meat of animals was systematically butchered and packaged for sale, now, the mysteries of the mind were dissected, entered into spreadsheets, and cross-referenced. The nature of sleep was examined, particularly its curious necessity. What was it about consciousness that required this regular hiatus, not imposed upon other vital organs of the body? The heart, liver, kidneys functioned day and night. Even the brain continued working at night, but without conscious thought. Why must consciousness cease every sixteen to twenty hours or we suffer extreme stress and even death? For Dr. Lejour, the answer was clear. Unlike heart, kidney, or liver function, consciousness involved the interaction with another dimension: the brain with the mind. This trans-dimensional activity must be particularly draining, requiring regular breaks. And what of the mind detached from the brain during sleep? What does it do? Can you understand your mind apart from your brain? These were the types of questions addressed at The Dream Center.

Dr. Lejour sat quietly on the front steps watching dog walkers and joggers pass by. Clare and Rocco startled him as they came up from behind the brick porch.

"Oh!" the doctor cried, jumping up from his place on the steps, "Agent Rocco. Agent Clare..."

"Sorry to scare you Doctor," Clare said, smiling.

"I was just thinking," Dr. Lejour said as he moved over to make room for them on the step. They sat quietly in the cool evening air for several minutes until Rocco broke the silence.

"So, Doctor," Rocco began, "you read the police reports. Do you think Hoffman disappeared into thin air as the officer said?" Clare cast a frown at him, to which he mouthed, "What?" in return.

"Well, there is precedence. The resurrected Christ could pass through walls," Dr. Lejour offered.

This is perfect, Rocco thought. *Even she has to see how ludicrous his ideas are now.* His comment did give Clare pause.

"Who do you think Hoffman is?" she asked with a raised eyebrow.

"Just a man," Dr. Lejour replied. "but a man who understands the supernatural."

"So he can perform miracles?" Rocco asked.

"Life is a miracle," Dr. Lejour retorted with a grin. "No scientist has ever created life. Yet, by understanding the miracle of life, scientists have been able to modify life forms through selective breeding, in-vitro fertilization, and gene splicing. No, I don't believe Hoffman is capable of miracles, but by understanding the mechanics of miracles, the connection between the brain and the mind, matter and essence, he may nonetheless be capable of supernatural acts."

"The mechanics of miracles?" Clare asked.

"Miracles generally occur through physical means. The more we understand those means, the more some aspects of the miraculous might be available to us. Are you familiar with the Shroud of Turin?"

"That cloth?" Clare asked. "The one that's said to be the burial shroud of Christ?"

"That's how many people think of it," replied Dr. Lejour, who went on to describe some of the characteristics of the shroud. While there had been opposing views on the shroud's authenticity, and conflicting carbon dating results with suspicions of medieval forgery, the shroud has several mysterious characteristics acknowledged by most investigators. The image on the shroud is of a man who had been scourged and crucified and then wrapped in a linen cloth after death. That the man may have been Jesus Christ was of historical and religious interest, but there were also scientific questions raised by the image. It seemed to have been caused by a type of radiation which created a photographic negative of the body without the distortion one would expect from a cloth wrapped around a body. Instead, it has correct proportions as seen in a photograph. One theory suggests that the body rapidly dematerialized, causing the emission of radiation which then left the photographic negative on the cloth as it fell through the dematerializing body. "Was the shroud's image caused by the body moving into another dimension?" Dr. Lejour asked. "That's a possibility, the move creating a burst of radiation. Was it a one-of-a-kind event, or could it happen again? Could Hoffman have done something like this, only to a lesser degree, just enough to move around the corner, out of sight? It's possible, though we also can't rule out simple illusion, given Hoffman's expertise."

"Can't rule out simple illusion? I'd say it's simple illusion until proven otherwise," Rocco declared. "No offense, Doc, but all this supernatural talk does nothing but make us miss something obvious, something right in front of our noses."

"I'd have to agree," Clare said, glancing at Rocco and holding his look for a moment longer than he had expected. As they both turned away, he found himself thinking again how pretty she was. The slight swell of emotion rising up in the pit of his stomach was pleasing yet disconcerting at the same time. He was relieved to see Jake and Vince arrive with Marcus and Dr. Schroeder.

"Oh, keep your detective instincts," Dr. Lejour said. "Just don't narrow your horizons," he added as he opened the door for the team.

Inside The Dream Center, there was a small waiting area, behind which an open space extended to the back of the building. In the center of the room was a large aquarium which cast a shimmering light across the whole area. Beds lined each wall with shelves of machinery on either side of them. An array of computers stood against the back wall, with a small cluster of chairs next to it. Dr. Lejour motioned to the group to take seats there.

"As I said earlier," the doctor began, "your will determines which minds you can connect with, and which minds can influence you. You'll need to focus that will very carefully, and Isaac here can help." Isaac was a graduate student in behavioral neuroscience who spent several nights a week working at the center. He spun around in his chair at the control panel and nodded his headful of long curly hair at everyone. A short white lab coat conferred a sense of validity to his position, despite his wearing jeans, a tee shirt and running shoes. The team settled into their seats around Isaac.

"It may seem odd to think of your mind apart from your brain, but we know the mind and brain can act independently," Dr. Lejour continued. "During sleep, the brain functions on its own. If you've ever spoken with a sleep walker, you will have noticed they are very concrete; they hear you and can respond, but without any higher understanding. They're like zombies, brains without minds. Since the mind is freed from the brain during sleep, it is more receptive to resonance with other minds. We'll be fostering that resonance now between your minds while you sleep."

Dr. Lejour stressed that discipline was the key to directing their wills. "Contemplatives use physical and mental discipline to suspend the senses and imagination, turning from concrete thoughts in the brain, directing their minds toward nonphysical realities: the natural order." Dr. Lejour moved the chairs into a circle which he then stepped outside of.

"Discipline your will. Try not to think of past events or worry about future ones. Focus on the abstract concept of yourselves as a team," Dr. Lejour said, "on your working together, thinking together."

Rocco stared at the aquarium just beyond their circle.

Its inhabitant, a small octopus, had begun to move about, creeping out of a corner hiding spot to spread out over a rock on the aquarium floor. Almost as soon as it settled into place, it camouflaged itself, matching the surrounding pattern of colors so closely, that had Rocco not watched it move onto the rock, he would not have noticed it there. He watched with envy as the creature rested in complete obscurity. Group encounters did not come naturally to Rocco. He looked around the circle from face to face, and judging by the scowling look he received when he arrived at Clare's, a lack of enthusiasm must have been evident on his. He would give it a try, he thought. What harm could it do?

The thought did bring a case to mind Rocco had worked on a number of years earlier. It had involved implanted memories which were being presented as "unlocked memories." While on that case, he read a scientific study in which psychologists interviewed volunteers, and using subtle suggestions, they implanted very specific memories which they said were being "unlocked." Most of the study participants believed that these totally manufactured memories were their own, and that they had truly been unlocked. A third of them even persisted in this belief after they were told that the memories were fake.

"What about the power of suggestion?" Rocco asked, breaking the silence. "How do we know we're not just going to develop a shared delusion?"

"Good question," Dr. Schroeder said with a smile.

"That is a good question," Dr. Lejour agreed, "and we'll get to the issue of discernment in a bit."

"Is this what you did for the hypnotist case?" Clare asked.

"Essentially."

"And it worked?" Jake asked.

"Oh yes, it was very successful," Dr. Lejour answered.

"It's just, I mean," Jake said, looking at Rocco. "We should be out there." Rocco nodded in agreement. "We should be doing something," Jake added.

"Discipline is never a waste of time," Dr. Lejour said. "Even if you think Hoffman is just using the power of suggestion and playing the odds, it will still help you resist him."

The group settled back into silence, looking at each other, the floor, the wall of computers, or the aquarium. They remained like this, with Dr. Lejour walking around the circle, for over an hour, and except for a few additional words of encouragement from Dr. Lejour, they sat in complete silence. Afterwards, they prepared to sleep in their cots and were wired to the monitors.

Isaac would be waking them after the monitors revealed a cycle of R.E.M. sleep. He waited until everyone had cycled through dream sleep at least once before waking any of them. Dr. Lejour was the first, almost two hours after they had begun. He rose and walked between the remaining sleeping subjects like a gardener walking though his greenhouse at night, checking the soil for signs of life. Isaac woke the sleepers one by one until they were all alert and sitting again in a circle.

The group was quietly talking amongst themselves, reviewing their dreams with each other. A consensus was quickly reached that nothing extraordinary had occurred. Despite their lengthy preparation, not one of the participants dreamt of the team. In fact, none of their dreams seemed at all relevant to each other or to the case they were working on.

"Don't be discouraged," Dr. Lejour said, "I'm sure you've made some connections."

"What good are they if we're not aware of them?" Rocco asked, standing up from his chair. "I think we gave this a good shot, Doc, but look: we got nothing—no insights, no awareness."

"He's got a point," Jake agreed.

"Thing is," Rocco said, "we're sitting here in a circle meditating while Hoffman is who knows where, working on his next plan."

"I have to agree," Clare concurred. "I really wanted this to work, Doctor. I think we all did."

"We just don't make good monks, Paul," Dr. Schroeder added with a smile.

"I know it can be challenging," Dr. Lejour said,

nodding his head. "Such realities are, by nature, mysterious. Connections between minds are above thoughts, so we should not expect to see them per se. But in time, you will recognize patterns and will start to make inferences. It just takes patience and persistence."

"And time," Rocco added, "which is something we don't have much of."

"Please sit, Agent Rocco, for just a few more minutes," Dr. Lejour pleaded as he handed out notecards and pens to the group. "Try not to think about the case, or anything else you should be doing. For the time being, try to be a bit more like an animal. Animals don't plan out next week's agenda; they act instinctively moment to moment. Become more like them, docile to the natural order. I'm going to ask you all a question and I'd like you to write your answers down quickly, 'A,' 'B,' or 'C.' Don't think about it or reason it out. Simply pick the first answer that comes to mind."

Looking to see that he had everyone's attention, Dr. Lejour presented his question. "Complete this surgical axiom: Never let the sun rise or set on, A: a gall bladder attack, B: appendicitis, or C: a bowel obstruction."

Dr. Lejour began to pick up the cards almost immediately, rushing the group, and the team hurriedly wrote down their answers. After collecting all the cards, Dr. Lejour looked them over and smiled broadly. They had all written the same answer. "Six of you, all answering the same way, isn't that remarkable?" Dr. Lejour exclaimed.

"It was multiple choice," Dr. Schroeder offered.

"Yes," Dr. Lejour replied, "the better to identify hunches. Why did everyone answer, 'C,' a bowel obstruction?"

"You told us to answer quickly," Vince said, "and that's just what came into my head."

"Jake, why a bowel obstruction instead of appendicitis? Isn't appendicitis more familiar to you?" Dr. Lejour asked.

"I don't know," Jake answered, "the bowel obstruction just sounded right."

"It sounded right," Dr. Lejour said, leaning into the circle with enthusiasm. "Don't you see? You knew it intuitively. Where did that intuition come from? It came from my mind." The group leaned back in collective disbelief.

"Seems like a stretch, Doc," Jake said.

"We read your mind?" Clare asked.

"Our minds resonated within the natural order," Dr. Lejour said. "That axiom is ingrained in my understanding from years of training as a surgical resident, like a favorite nursery rhyme might be for any of you. Through an alignment of our wills, you were able to share in that understanding. That's resonance, a connection between minds above the level of thoughts, and here you've achieved it, after just one session. Isn't that remarkable?"

KINDRED SOULS

07

*A*fter going home to sleep the rest of the night, the team returned to the Brooklyn warehouse the following morning. A flock of seabirds could be seen rising from the East River in front of the warehouse, turning in unison like a white banner waving before the upper floor windows. Inside, assistants were bringing out coffee and water from the kitchenette and setting them on the table.

By the window, the agents were talking over the last night's experiences as they waited for Dr. Lejour to arrive.

"That was something," Vince said, "the way we all answered that surgery question the same. What's the idea, we do that exercise every night?"

"I think the doctor expects us to," Rocco said. Jake looked at Rocco and sighed. "I've got my doubts too," Rocco said. "We're just covering all the bases."

"As long as we're not missing something in the

meantime," Jake replied.

"Like what?" Clare asked.

"Like the fact that we're dealing with a man, just a man, who's trying to sell his propaganda services with a gimmick app. I say we track him down and stop him."

"Just like that?" Clare asked. "And what do we do differently from the other day, or do we just give him another shot at us?"

Clare spun away and marched to the table.

"He's not an easy man to confront, Jake," Rocco said, watching Clare cross the room. "Besides, we don't have anything substantial to charge him with and he knows it."

As Clare approached the table, she saw Dr. Lejour entering the room and hurried over to greet him.

"Good morning, Dr. Lejour," Clare beamed. "It's good to see you."

"Good morning, Agent Clare, it's good to see you too. I hope I'm not too late."

"No, we all just arrived," Clare answered, then added in a hushed tone, "Can I ask you something?"

"Of course," the doctor replied. "What is it?"

Clare glanced back at the others and led the doctor a few steps further away from them. Quietly, she continued. "If our minds are in another dimension. Then, what happens when we die?"

"Ah," Dr. Lejour sighed with a grin, "that's a good

question. What is a person? Is it this matter that makes up our bodies, our skin and bones? But our bodies grow, change, deteriorate, and the cells in our bodies turn over every seven years, yet we remain the same person. The essence of a person must transcend this physical stuff, wouldn't you say?"

"I suppose so."

"So, when the physical breaks down and dies, the essence remains."

"In some invisible dimension," Clare scoffed.

"Invisible to the senses, yes, but not to the mind."

Clare smiled at the doctor as he nodded and sat down at the table. Rocco came up beside her.

"You really like him, don't you?" Rocco asked quietly.

"He reminds me of my father," Clare answered, still watching the doctor. "Something about his jacket. It's funny, it's like I remember the smell of it."

"You smelled the doc's coat?" Rocco asked, laughing.

"No," Clare snapped, looking back at Rocco and rolling her eyes. "Just the look of it, but it reminded me of a smell. When my father would come home, I'd run to him, and he'd pick me up and spin me around, and I'd hold on to his jacket. All my troubles would just disappear and I'd feel safe and happy. What I remember most is the smell of his jacket. It was a nice, wool smell."

Rocco watched Clare watch Dr. Lejour. He admired her sensitivity, and the fact that she would remember such a detail like the smell of her father's wool jacket. What would she remember about him, if anything? He had started to walk away when Clare continued.

"Every morning, as he drove off to work, I would wave from the end of our driveway. I could see my waving hand in his side view mirror, getting smaller and smaller as he drove down the road, with his hand out the window waving back until his car was completely out of sight."

As Clare reminisced, looking over at the doctor, Rocco imagined her, pressed against the fine wool and silk of her father's coat, spinning around, and her waving with such enthusiasm each morning.

"You must have been adorable," Rocco mused.

"Past tense, I like that."

"I didn't mean," Rocco started, but halted. "Shall we?" he asked, motioning to the table.

Clare nodded, and the two joined the others at the table. Clare took a seat opposite Dr. Lejour, beside Dr. Schroeder.

"Good morning, Dr. Schroeder," Clare said as she pulled her long blonde hair into a ponytail.

"Good morning," Dr. Schroeder replied, and with a twinkle added, "So, is there a Mr. Clare?"

"No," Clare answered, laughing. "No Mr. Clare."

"It must be hard, being an FBI agent. Such a lovely girl. You'll find the right man, if it's meant to be," Dr. Schroeder said.

"If it's meant to be?" Clare asked. "You believe in Providence, Dr. Schroeder?"

"Providence, fate, luck, whatever you want to call it. I don't believe in useless worrying in any case," Dr. Schroeder answered with his typical smile.

"Do you have children?" Clare asked him.

"Two daughters, grown and married, with six grandchildren," Dr. Schroeder said as he pulled out his wallet photographs. The two shared family histories and memories with quiet laughter.

Rocco sat beside Marcus and asked him if he had experienced any of this mental connectedness in the special forces.

"I never underestimate the mental component of a mission," Marcus explained. "As far as last night goes, it was a good exercise and not a bad start. I agree with the doctor here, discipline is critical."

Dr. Lejour, within earshot of their conversation, nodded in appreciation.

"It all about will power," Marcus continued. "Doc, you mentioned directing our wills along the same lines, that's SEAL training in a nutshell. We focus our wills on the team, and that intense discipline allows us to overcome everything: fatigue, cold, hunger, pain. The physical ability is necessary, but secondary to the mental. It's not easy and there are no shortcuts, but it's definitely worth doing. I think the doc's on the right track."

"So, all we have to do is think like a SEAL," Vince chuckled. "That's all, Boss." Rocco looked out the window and sighed.

"You will," Dr. Lejour said, quickly filling the gap in the conversation. "You may not realize it, but you've already taken a step in that direction."

Rocco stood up and moved to the window. Clare slipped away from the group to join him.

"What's on your mind, John?" Clare asked as she came up beside Rocco at the window.

"It's déjà vu," Rocco answered. "Back to square one."

"That reminds me," Clare chimed in with a twinkling smile, "on the way in here, I had the wildest déjà vu."

"Oh yeah?"

"I was stopped at a light and could see this small backyard with chickens in it."

"Here in Brooklyn?" Rocco asked.

"Yeah."

"And that was your déjà vu?"

"No, I'd never seen backyard chickens before, but that wasn't it. It was when this kid calmly walked over to one of the chickens and it sort of hunched down and let him pick it up. It was all very smooth and calm. That was the déjà vu, that smoothness, the way the kid picked up the bird. It was like I knew that trick, like I had picked up lots of birds before."

"Have you?" Rocco asked, looking intently at Clare.

"Of course not!" Clare shot back, indignant that he should ask such a question. "I've never touched a bird. But it was so vivid, such intense nostalgia, like I'd done it countless times before."

"I have," Rocco admitted, "and it was just like that. You would expect them to kick and scratch, but they're very calm, like they belong there in your hands. My brother and I perfected the technique picking up pigeons on the roof of our building."

"Well that's it then. You must have told me about it and that's why I remembered it."

"No," Rocco answered, "I wouldn't have told you. Never told a soul. My brother made me promise. My Mom thought pigeons were like rats, carried the plague or some such thing, told us never to go near them." Then, with a hush, he added, "Not a word of this to anyone."

"I'll take it to the grave," Clare promised, laughing and holding her hand up as a pledge, "your deep, dark secret."

Rocco turned to Clare with a hint of childlike excitement in his eyes. "You think that's what déjà vu is?" he asked. "Something seems really familiar, but you don't remember having experienced it before, because you haven't; it's someone else's memory."

"You think I remembered your memory?" Clare asked, cocking her head.

"I don't know," Rocco snapped, offended by her skepticism. For once, he had lowered his guard and was willing to entertain an unorthodox idea, scores of which she had been entertaining from Dr. Lejour without hesitation, and now she was a skeptic? Why now, when he was ready to believe? His glance caught her eyes, their crystal blue color and graceful curves, accented with her playful smile. How he wanted to believe! How he longed for a connection of minds, a bonding of kindred souls, *their* kindred souls. She would know him as he knew himself with more than friendship, more than relationship, with a union of minds that would vanquish the inner isolation he had so long endured.

Wishful thinking.

The thought forced the image out of his mind. *If you want something badly enough, you'll believe anything*, he reminded himself. The tightness rose in his chest and spread to his arms and the nape of his neck—his equal and opposite reaction to the darkness rising in his soul. The two opposing forces, like the beveled edges of a knife blade, honed his will, and he regained his bearings.

"You're right, that's nuts," he said. "I'm sure it was just a coincidence."

"Though," Clare mused, looking at Rocco with a whimsical glance, "it could be a sign."

"A sign?" Rocco spat. "I've told you about my brother, haven't I?"

"Yeah," Clare said, pausing, "some."

"The day before he died, I was at his bedside. He'd been unconscious on a ventilator for days. The doctors and nurses had done all they could, but he was dying; everyone knew it. Most of my relatives considered him gone already, but not me. You see, when I was little, my brother told me we would always be together, no matter what. So I knew, somehow, he wasn't going to die. I sat by his bedside around the clock, waiting for a sign. One night, as I sat there looking at him, tubes taped to his face, his eyes all puffy, I thought I heard the words, 'Pray for him.' I looked over my shoulder, thinking someone else was in the room, but there wasn't anyone there. It couldn't have been my brother since he had a tube in his throat. The words just came into my head. I took it as a sign. I could stop his dying if I believed. So I sat there, and I prayed, nonstop. Every hour or so I'd whisper to my brother, 'It's me, John. Can you hear me?' actually expecting him to open his eyes and look at me. I kept praying, waiting for the miracle, right up until the time they took the tubes out of him and pulled the sheet over his face. So much for my sign."

Rocco turned and looked out the window again, surprised that he had shared that story with her. It was not something he had ever shared with anyone before. "I'm sorry," he said, still gazing out the window. "I didn't mean to dump all that on you."

"Don't be." Clare looked up at Rocco's chiseled features reflected in the glass. "Signs can be hard to interpret."

"If my hearing those words was a sign, it was either a lie or a cruel joke," Rocco replied as he turned to face Clare again. "I needed a sign that he would still be there for me, so I imagined one."

"He is still there, John," Clare said quietly. "Don't you believe that?"

Rocco shook his head and looked down at the floor. "Wishful thinking." Glancing at Clare again, he added, "That's what this is all about. Hoffman's just playing people like a palm reader, telling them what they expect to hear, using our own imaginations against us."

"You really think that's all this is?"

"Yeah, that's all it ever is: people saying what you expect to hear."

"You're just being stubborn again," Clare growled indignantly.

"What do you mean?"

"You set your mind against something and that's that," Clare said, becoming more irritated. "You never leave an option on the table, do you?"

"What are you talking about?"

"Nothing," Clare snapped as she spun around to return to the others at the table. "Nothing you would understand."

CONFRONTATION

*B*ack at the table, Dr. Lejour had been leading another discussion.

"What are your ideas about the officer being too heavy to move?" Dr. Lejour asked the remaining agents at the table.

"We figure it was some sort of hypnotic effect," Jake answered.

"On both the officer and his partner? His partner had not even seen Hoffman yet."

Jake and the others shrugged.

"I'll tell you what I think," Dr. Lejour continued. "I think Hoffman altered the gravitational field around the officer." Rocco had just returned to the table as Dr. Lejour made this last remark. With a groan he took a seat next to Jake. "You see, like our minds, the essence of gravity is also in another dimension. Einstein," the doctor continued, "said gravity was due to distortions of 'spacetime,' a sort of grid in space. But there is no physical grid in space. Where is it? The essence of gravity, like the mind, is in another dimension where extraordinary activities of the mind can affect it."

"Or maybe the officer just thought his partner was too heavy to move," Dr. Schroeder suggested. "It was a stressful encounter."

"It's not unprecedented," Dr. Lejour continued, unabated. "You remember I mentioned Hindu and Christian mystics? During prayer and meditation, their minds are so focused on the transcendent they alter the order of gravity around them and they levitate. With demonic possessions we see an opposite alteration. Hostile influxes into the mind, similar to what the police officer experienced, can increase gravity. Victims of possession have been found to be so heavy they could not be raised from the floor."

The example of levitation caught Vince's attention.

"You know," Vince said, "I saw something like that once. There were these two Hindu guys meditating. The one guy was sitting cross-legged on the sidewalk and was holding this wooden pole at arm's length in front of him, and on top of the pole there was another cross-legged guy balanced there. Had to be at least partial levitation."

"Sounds like a typical circus act to me," Rocco remarked.

"No," Vince protested, "it wasn't just the balancing. I know, they were little guys, but still, they had to weigh one hundred pounds each, at least. How could that guy support the other guy holding a pole at arm's length? I couldn't hold a hundred pounds at arm's length, at least not for very long. And, if I did, my arm would be shaking and twitching, at least after a minute or two, but I tell you, I stood there for ten minutes and that guy's arm didn't budge more than if he was holding a cup of coffee in his hand."

"Must have been a trick," Rocco insisted. "Wires or something."

"No, I watched until he put the other guy down. People were walking all around them. And the guy on top, sitting cross-legged on that pole–it was a pole only this big around," Vince demonstrated a width the size of his fist. "The guy was only on one…" Vince paused, turning to Clare, "excuse the expression, butt cheek. And he was still totally level in the air. It was the craziest thing I've ever seen."

"So, if he was levitating, why the need for the pole?" Rocco asked.

"Like I said, I think it was partial levitating," Vince explained. "The guy was just very light."

"Like a cup of coffee," Rocco suggested with a smirk.

"Yeah, exactly," Vince agreed.

Rocco found the image of a cross-legged mystic weighing as much as a cup of coffee vaguely amusing.

"There's something else you should know," Dr. Lejour added. "In the dimension of the mind, time is different. One moment there can encompass hours, even days or weeks here, so insights from the mind can include premonitions of the future."

"Premonitions?" Jake asked, with a sideways glance.

The scene was one familiar to the doctor. For the past twenty-five years he had been encountering it: the empty stares, the raised eyebrows, the atmosphere of disbelief, the looks that seemed to say, "Oh, you're that doctor." It began in his fifties, when, as a very prominent vascular surgeon on staff at a prestigious university hospital, he witnessed an extraordinary occurrence. A patient of his who had arrested on the operating room table and was revived, afterwards described a near-death experience. In it he became aware of conversations of his family members in other areas of the hospital where he could not have heard them. The inexplicable nature of the event led to the start of Dr. Lejour's passionate hobby of researching supernatural occurrences. As he shared his findings with others, he was always given at least a brief audience, due to his prestige as a skilled vascular surgeon. After he retired, however, he became more marginalized and was considered simply strange by his colleagues and associates. Were it not for his recent success with the Bureau's hypnotist case, both he and his ideas would have faded into relative obscurity.

"Premonitions?" Dr. Schroeder echoed, smiling broadly at Dr. Lejour.

"Friedrich, we know time is relative," Dr. Lejour pointed out, noting Dr. Schroeder's amused look. "Einstein demonstrated that in his theory of Special Relativity. It varies, depending on the observer's point of view. Certainly the point of view from another dimension allows for a great deal of variability. From there, your minds will gain understanding of an entire segment of our time: not only the present moment, but also the events that led up to it and the consequences that will follow it."

"So we can see the future?" Clare asked.

"A short segment of it, yes. This is a great advantage you have over Hoffman. By directing your wills toward the natural order–toward unity and passive perception–you can see things that Hoffman cannot. He sees the future as he wishes it to be, not as it naturally will be."

"Well don't keep us in suspense Doc," Rocco interrupted with a grin, "tell us where Hoffman is going next."

Over the chuckling, Dr. Lejour protested, "Insights in the mind will be abstract, not concrete, like I told you at The Dream Center."

"But Doctor, how can these premonitions help us without concrete information?" Clare asked.

"Exactly," Rocco agreed, sending an affectionate look of affirmation toward Clare, who did not reciprocate.

"Don't worry," Dr. Lejour replied. "when you are calm, your wills disciplined, the abstract insights of premonition will become intuition guiding your concrete thoughts."

Rocco walked away from the table, tossing a wadded up piece of paper onto the floor. *This is a waste of time!* He thought. The tightness quickly made its way from his chest to the back of his neck, and he was filled with the familiar rush of anger. He paced back and forth in the center of the room, his thoughts racing. *He's playing us for fools and we're just going along with it! He played me for a fool. He was right in front of me! Why didn't I bring him in? What was I thinking? Why am I buying all of this nonsense? If I have to listen to one more of these lectures, I swear...* Rocco stopped pacing, and looking up, was startled by a face staring at him through a window in the door, the face of a tall figure standing against the hallway wall.

Hoffman! He thought. He reached for his weapon and began to call out to the others, but no sound came from his throat. It was as though the momentum of breath and voice initiated by his will and dispatched from his mind had been aborted, stifled at its source. Instead of sounding the alarm, he was being crushed, pulled from every point along his body down to the floor. His anger grew feverishly. Like a wild animal pinned to the floor he channeled the fullness of his rage toward his oppressor. The anger within him flared in opposition to this overpowering foe. He hated Hoffman with every fiber of his being. Objects around him became a blur of motion and color. His chest felt so heavy he could barely breathe. He tried to look back at the others but could not move his head.

Hearing the dull thud of Rocco's body striking the floor, Clare jumped to her feet and started toward him, but Marcus pulled her back down, pointing to figures outside the door.

From the other end of the table, Dr. Schroeder, beyond Marcus's reach, sprang up and rushed toward Rocco.

"Mr. Rocco!" Dr. Schroeder called out. "Are you all right?"

"Doctor! Get back!" Marcus yelled.

"There's something wrong. He's fallen down," Dr. Schroeder explained, turning to face the agents. Marcus slipped behind Clare, and had nearly reached Dr. Schroeder when shots were fired from the other side of the door, shattering the glass and hitting Dr. Schroeder in the chest. He fell to the floor next to Rocco. Marcus hurried back to Clare and Dr. Lejour, turning the table on its side to protect them, while Jake and Vince positioned themselves behind pillars along the side wall.

"Help me push this up to them," Marcus said to Clare as he pulled his duffle bag behind the table. "You too, Doc. Keep your head down behind the table top."

The heavy wooden table grated along the concrete floor as three armed men rushed in to the room, taking positions behind two pillars by the door.

"Stand down, we're federal agents," Vince called out just before exchanging gunfire with the men, while Jake called in for backup. The booming percussions of gunfire came at them from all sides, echoing off the walls.

Marcus pushed the table with his back and pulled his assault rifle from his duffle, slapping in a magazine. Once the table was alongside Dr. Schroeder, Marcus spun around the table's end laying heavy fire across the two pillars and the door. Fragments from the pillars flew in all directions with concrete dust billowing through the air. The intensity with which Marcus had returned fire stunned the attackers long enough for him to drag Dr. Schroeder behind the table. He swapped magazines and repeated the maneuver to bring in Rocco, but was unable to move him, scrambling back behind the table without him.

"Where's John?" Clare cried.

"I couldn't move him," Marcus answered. "Help me push the table closer."

"Where was he hit?"

"I didn't see any wounds."

"What do you mean?"

"I don't think he was shot. Come on, push." They inched the table up toward Rocco. "Can you bring him closer to the table?" he asked Clare, motioning to Dr. Schroeder.

Clare, coughing on the cloud of dust that had now rolled over them, slid her hands under Dr. Schroeder's arms and strained to drag him a few inches closer to the table, the concrete grit scraping her wrists. The thick smell of blood rose from Dr. Schroeder's saturated clothing, as his gasps became louder and more forced.

Dr. Lejour scrambled alongside Clare and tore open Dr. Schroeder's shirt. "Friedrich! Friedrich!" He did not respond. "Do you have first aid supplies in your duffle?" he asked Marcus.

"Yes, take them."

Dr. Lejour searched through Marcus' bag as Clare and Marcus continued inching the table forward toward Rocco. A bullet hit the floor just beside Dr. Lejour, spraying particles of concrete into his eyes.

"I can't see!" Dr. Lejour called out. Before another round was fired in his direction, Marcus pulled him up to the back of the table and, pouring water from a canteen, cleared his vision. The table was now just in front of Rocco, so Clare grabbed his wrist to pull him closer, but couldn't move even his hand. His eyes were partly open and he did not blink nor move any part of his body.

"He's breathing," Marcus said, running his hands over the sides of Rocco's head, chest, and abdomen. "Haven't found any injuries, but I can't roll him to check his back."

Together, Clare and Marcus pulled on Rocco's shoulder without success. Looking at Rocco's motionless face, Clare holstered her sidearm and reached into Marcus' duffle alongside Dr. Lejour.

"Give me something," she barked out to Marcus, who directed her to his other automatic weapon. "We need to drive them out of here!"

"You take left, I'll take right," Marcus said. "Find everything you need, doctor?" he asked Dr. Lejour.

"Yes, thank you," Dr. Lejour replied, pulling out an IV to place into Dr. Schroeder's arm.

"Jake! Vince!" Clare yelled, catching their eyes, "On three!" She signed the countdown with her hand, then she and Marcus moved forward from either side of the table, spraying rounds across the columns and door. Jake and Vince came at the men from the side, firing behind the pillars. Flanked and outgunned, the three men retreated to the hallway. Marcus and the agents returned to the table, their guns trained on the doorway, ready to fire at the first sign of their return.

Clare looked through the broken glass of the door and spotted Hoffman against the hallway wall. She leveled her weapon at him, steadying it on the table's edge. Just as she rested her finger on the trigger, he turned and looked at her, and her hand froze.

Hoffman's brow gathered over his eyes into a fierce frown as his teeth clenched together. He stood as still as one of the concrete pillars, an immobile fixture around which Spinosa's hired guns now scrambled like mice.

Clare struggled to slide down the backside of the table. Slumping onto the floor, she called out, "Hoffman's out there!" Marcus moved to her vantage point but when he looked at the doorway, Hoffman was gone. As he continued to search the area outside the door through his gunsights, he was suddenly joined by Rocco, kneeling alongside him.

Rocco's ears were ringing, the taste of concrete dust and gunpowder in his mouth. He looked over the table with Marcus, then back at the others, trying to piece together fragments in his memory. When had all this happened? Clearly, they had been in a gunfight. Why couldn't he remember it?

"John!" Clare stammered. "You're all right!" She ran her hand down his back, still looking for injuries.

"I'm okay. Listen, Hoffman's out there."

"We know. What happened to you? Were you hit?"

"No, I... I just couldn't move."

Rocco took Clare's hands which were trembling.

"Are you okay?" he asked.

She nodded. "What did you feel?"

"It felt like he was holding me down. Then, all of a sudden, I could move." Clare smiled at this, which Rocco found very odd.

"I think that's because I drew his attention away from you," Clare explained with a satisfied look.

"You sure you're okay?" Rocco asked, even more concerned than before.

"I'm fine," Clare answered as she returned to her knees
behind the table. "Dr. Lejour, how is Dr. Schroeder?"

"Not good."

THE PROTOCOL

09

Dr. Lejour and Marcus were bent over Dr. Schroeder, who was panting with short, shallow breaths, and no longer moving.

"He has a tension pneumothorax," Dr. Lejour explained. "We can't wait for the EMTs. We need to let the pressure out of his chest." Without a word, Marcus pulled out gloves and a sterile kit from his duffle and placing them before Dr. Lejour, he poured a cleansing prep solution over Dr. Schroeder's chest. Dr. Lejour opened the sterile kit and found among the surgical instruments a metal trocar. After donning sterile gloves, he raised the small silver spear and, to Rocco's astonishment, drove it into Dr. Schroeder's chest. A gush of air came through the site and Marcus helped Dr. Lejour attach a one-way valve to keep the pressure from building up again.

"They look like they've done this before," Rocco muttered

to Clare. The two watched as Dr. Lejour's hands moved like a musician's along a cello's neck, sliding, twisting, first slowly, then suddenly, always purposeful, rhythmic, and smooth.

Marcus checked Dr. Schroeder's pulse and lifted his legs to help raise his blood pressure. He was breathing normally now and beginning to move. Clare rolled up her jacket and placed it under Dr. Schroeder's head. "Do you think he'll be all right?" she asked anxiously.

"He's stable now, as long as he doesn't bleed out into his chest," Dr. Lejour answered as he adjusted the fluid dripping in his IV. "We need to get him to a hospital quickly."

"The EMTs should be here soon," Jake said, "along with our backup."

Rocco surveyed the scene of their unprovoked attack. "What's with this guy?" he thought out loud. "He finds out we were watching him so he attacks us? Who escalates a conflict like that?"

"A guy who's got something to prove?" Clare suggested.

"You think he's got issues?" Vince asked.

"Oh, he's got issues all right," Jake said. "You heard him at the cafe. He's a megalomaniac."

"Yeah, but not reckless," Rocco added. "He did this for a reason."

"Making a statement?" Clare asked. "Telling us to back off?"

"Or sizing up the opposition," Marcus suggested.

"We'd better clear the rest of the building," Rocco said.

"Got it," Marcus replied, picking up his automatic rifle. Tapping Jake and Vince on the shoulder, he led them out the door into the hallway. Clare slid over by Rocco, who was now kneeling beside Dr. Lejour.

"What happened to you, John?" Clare asked.

"I don't know."

"What did you feel?" Dr. Lejour asked.

"I felt nailed to the floor."

"For how long, would you say?"

"Oh, I don't know, a few seconds."

"Seconds? More like a few minutes," Clare corrected. "We moved the table up to you, brought Dr. Schroeder back, then Marcus tried to pull you back a few times. Did you black out or something?"

Rocco cast a confused glance at Clare, trying to recall the events she was describing.

"You're probably both right," Dr. Lejour suggested. "Remember space, time, and gravity are interrelated. As gravity is increased, time is slowed, so when Rocco became very heavy, he actually did experience only seconds of time, while the rest of us experienced minutes."

"You really think Hoffman is capable of doing something like that?" Clare asked.

"The interrelation of orders, space, time, and gravity is something that exists, not something Hoffman does. He's just found a way to take advantage of it," Dr. Lejour corrected.

"What about a hypnotic suggestion?" Rocco offered, "Something he put into my head when I bumped into him at the hotel the other day? Maybe it just took effect now?"

"No," Clare said, shaking her head, "that wouldn't explain it. We couldn't move you. Marcus dragged Dr. Schroeder behind the table in a second but he couldn't budge you. Neither could I."

Rocco looked at Clare and raised his hands in resignation. "Okay," he sighed.

"So, what chance do we have against that?" Clare asked.

"As I said last evening, the key is mental discipline," Dr. Lejour replied. "With the exercises you've begun, you can deny him access to your minds."

Dr. Schroeder came to and looked around him.

"What happened?" he asked.

"Friedrich!" Dr. Lejour cried out. "Don't worry, you're going to be fine."

"You've been shot," Rocco added. "We're getting you to the hospital right away. I hear the sirens now."

"Oh dear," Dr. Schroeder murmured as he closed his eyes.

The sound of glass fragments scraping beneath the door filled the room as Jake and Vince entered.

"EMTs are outside now, and local cops," Jake reported. "Marcus is bringing them up. How's the doc?"

"Better," Rocco answered.

As Jake passed the pillars, he stopped and knelt on the floor. "Looks like we hit one of them. We've got some blood."

"Get the word out to the ERs: any gunshot wound comes through their doors, I want to know about it," Rocco ordered. The EMTs entered with Marcus and strapped Dr. Schroeder onto a stretcher. Rocco had Vince, Jake, and Dr. Lejour go with them, and called in a forensics team to examine the room. Speaking with one of the Brooklyn police officers, he discovered that a traffic unit had just followed a black sedan speeding away from the warehouse to a nearby apartment complex, dropping off a tall man who entered the building. The unit had continued in pursuit of the black sedan.

"A tall man?" Clare asked, overhearing the conversation. "Sounds like Hoffman."

"He may still be there," Rocco said hurriedly. "If we move, we might have the upper hand."

However, when the three arrived they found that a second police unit had already searched the building. The landlord was familiar with a tall man matching Hoffman's description, whom he knew as Paul Smith. He had let the police into his apartment and they had found no one.

"Mind if we take a look around?" Rocco asked the police officers, flashing his ID.

"Not at all," a man in a suit answered from behind them.

"I'm detective Dobbs, Aidan Dobbs," he said, holding out his hand.

"Agent Rocco, FBI, this is Agent Clare Bristol, and Mr. Marcus Jones."

"You're on the Hoffman case?" Dobbs asked.

"Hoffman? I heard this man was Paul Smith," Rocco answered, looking curiously at the detective.

"Look," Dobbs continued, lowering his voice, "I've been involved with this investigation from the beginning, with that weird report from those officers at Hoffman's house. Our department was embarrassed about the whole thing and was just about to close the case. Then, I hear there were gunshots where the FBI team was meeting. I assume that was you. A man was down? Is he all right?"

"We think he will be," Rocco answered. "The rest of my team is with him now."

"The department's position is that you got caught in a turf battle between two crime families. I think they just want the whole thing to go away. The son of that physicist in Manhattan has been coming by the station every day, getting hot with us for not doing anything. Says Hoffman killed his father. Anyway, I think there's more going on here, so if I can help you, you let me know." Detective Dobbs handed Rocco his card and led them into Hoffman's apartment.

Rocco, Clare, and Marcus entered the apartment, examining the entranceway, living room, and bedroom, and stopped at an array of equipment arranged around a small bed. It was the apparatus Hoffman had used in front of Williams the day before.

"What's all this?" Clare asked.

"There are drugs and supplies for general anesthesia here," Marcus said as he checked through the kitchenette cabinets. He moved from the cabinets to the ventilator machine at the head of the bed, then to the equipment on the poles alongside it. Hoffman's notebook was no longer on the rack. Tongs rested on the pillow of the bed, connected with wires to a small machine. "Looks like the professor's been running some experiments."

"On animals?" Clare asked.

"No cages," Marcus pointed out, shaking his head and pointing around the room. "No cages, no animals."

"On what then, people?" Clare groaned. Marcus picked up the set of tongs and held them up to his temples. "What are those?" Rocco asked.

"Electrical leads, I'd say," Marcus suggested.

"Like for shocking?"

Marcus shrugged and placed them back on the bed.

"Maybe it's his protocol of drugs and electrical stimulation," Clare suggested.

"Take pictures of it, the equipment, the drugs, everything, and we'll show them to Dr. Lejour," Rocco said quickly. "Then let's get out of here." He felt an uneasiness there, a vague sense of nausea coming upon him that became more acute the longer he stood by the bed. He moved back against the wall and as his eyes scanned the apartment, his vision became blurred and he felt a rush of heat coming over him.

"John, are you all right?" Clare asked. Her voice sounded like it was coming from inside a drum.

"I'm fine," he lied, beads of perspiration appearing on his forehead. He'd felt this way once before, during his investigation of the child murderer. Not while going through the grisly evidence at the scene of the crime, but afterwards, when he was examining the perpetrator's apartment, seeing where he had lived and slept, his things, being among them. It was as though he could feel him, his presence creeping over him, suffocating him, the way he was now feeling Hoffman's presence. He left the apartment and waited for the others on the landing outside.

After the apparatus had been thoroughly photographed, the three drove to meet up with the others at the hospital. Jake and Vince were sitting outside the operating room, while Dr. Lejour, using his privilege as a vascular surgeon, had gained access behind the electric doors to speak with one of the surgical residents. It had been necessary, he discovered, to remove a section of Dr. Schroeder's lung, but they had controlled the bleeding and he was in stable condition.

"He had a rough go of it initially," the resident explained.

"We had to bring him back a couple times."

"You coded him?" Dr. Lejour asked.

"Yeah, for about twenty minutes or so. Then we got him back in sinus rhythm and he's been stable ever since."

Dr. Lejour thanked the resident and returned to the waiting area. As Rocco, Clare, and Marcus entered the room, Dr. Lejour greeted them with a smile that let them know all was well.

"He's okay?" Clare asked anxiously.

"He'll be fine," Dr. Lejour replied. "He's in recovery now. They'll let us see him once he's in his room."

Clare shared the photographs of Hoffman's equipment and drugs with Dr. Lejour, who agreed with Marcus that he was probably performing a general anesthetic. He also thought that the tongs looked like those used for electro-convulsive or shock therapy. Such therapy was normally used for recalcitrant depression, the type that had failed medical treatment.

"But why would he be performing such procedures?" Dr. Lejour asked. "He's not a psychiatrist."

"Marcus thinks there were timed, automated pumps on the IV poles," Clare added.

"Automated?" Dr. Lejour exclaimed. "You don't think he was performing electroconvulsive therapy on himself? That would be mad!"

NEAR DEATH

10

*I*t was noon when a nurse in green scrubs came through the electric doors and told the agents where Dr. Schroeder had been taken. The six of them rode the elevator to the twelfth floor, Rocco standing beside Dr. Lejour.

"This shock therapy, Doctor," Rocco muttered quietly, "what does it do?"

"It resets the brain, like restarting a computer."

"Why would Hoffman want to do that?"

"I can't imagine," Dr. Lejour replied as the door opened and the agents made their way to Dr. Schroeder's room. He was awake and greeted the team with a broad smile as they entered.

"How are you feeling, Dr. Schroeder?" Clare asked.

"I've been better, but I guess I could also be worse," Dr. Schroeder answered with a raspy voice.

"I'm sorry, doc," Rocco said. "I never expected Hoffman

to come at us like that. We'll be sure to keep you out of harm's way in the future. You too, Dr. Lejour."

"We are in over our heads, aren't we Friedrich?" Dr. Lejour suggested.

"Yes, we are," Dr. Schroeder agreed. "You know, I dreamt about you all. It seemed so real."

"What did you dream?" Dr. Lejour asked.

"I dreamt I was home, in Germany," Dr. Schroeder replied. "Although, it was different from my actual home, I still felt like I was home. Then I saw you all; you were all with me."

"Well, we were with you," Vince assured him, "in the ambulance, and outside the operating room. We were with you the whole time, Doc."

"Thank you," Dr. Schroeder said warmly, then asked, "Where are your headphones Marcus?"

"Sir?" Marcus replied.

"I'm sorry," Dr. Schroeder said, shaking his head. "I must be thinking of my dream. I'm still a bit groggy."

"Headphones?" Clare asked. "What do you mean Dr. Schroeder?"

"In my dream he was putting headphones over his head."

"The tongs," Clare said to Marcus. "Remember? You held them up to your head."

"The shock therapy tongs?" Dr. Lejour asked Marcus. "Did you hold them up to your head?"

"I was just showing Rocco and Clare what I thought they were," Marcus replied.

"They would look like headphones!" Dr. Lejour declared, spinning around the group and smiling.

"So what?" Rocco asked, unimpressed.

"So, what?" Dr. Lejour exclaimed. "I think Friedrich has had more than a dream. When you arrived here, Friedrich, you needed CPR. They said they coded you for twenty minutes. Friedrich, I think you've had a near-death experience!" Dr. Lejour proclaimed.

"Paul, you are incorrigible," Dr. Schroeder scoffed, shaking his head. "I just had a dream. I didn't see a light or a tunnel. My soul was not floating through the air."

"Of course not," Dr. Lejour quipped. "Souls aren't objects that move through space. I've studied such events for years, Friedrich. Not everyone sees light or a tunnel. Some see darkness, some light, some believe they have been to heaven, others do not ascribe any religious significance at all to the event. In all cases though, there is one thing in common: a supernatural level of perception. Everyone sees, hears, or knows something that they could not have physically perceived."

"What else did you dream?" Clare asked.

"Nothing really," Dr. Schroeder mumbled, turning an eye toward Dr. Lejour as though fearful of encouraging him further. "Nothing."

"That's what Hoffman's been doing!" Dr. Lejour exclaimed with a twinkle in his eye. "He's been creating his own near-death experience!"

"What?" Rocco asked, shaking his head in disbelief.

"Like I said, Agent Rocco, shock therapy reboots the brain, like shutting off a computer. During a near-death experience, too, the brain is shut off momentarily, allowing the mind to interact more readily with other minds. That's why people are able to perceive things they have no physical access to, like conversations between relatives in the waiting room, or like Dr. Schroeder seeing Marcus holding the tongs. If Hoffman is artificially bringing on this amplified state, that could be how he's seeing other minds. Only, he's not just observing, he's implanting thoughts, imposing his will!"

A nurse, noticing the excitement in the room, marched in and ushered the group out to give her patient time to rest.

The team obliged, leaving the floor after posting additional agents outside Dr. Schroeder's room and at either end of the hallway. Dr. Lejour continued to broadcast his thoughts out loud while the group approached the elevators.

"See you tomorrow," one nurse called out to another as they left for the day. Clare stopped and stood still as if listening intently for something. The rest of the group continued on with Dr. Lejour, until Rocco noticed that Clare was no longer walking with them.

"Hold up guys. Clare?" Rocco called back to her. She appeared startled by his voice and looked over her shoulder several times.

"You okay, Clare?" Rocco asked as he trotted back to her.

"Yeah, I just thought I heard something," Clare said, looking back again.

Rocco scanned the area behind them and the rest of the hallway. As they went down the elevator, he put his hand on her shoulder saying, "Stay close." Turning to Dr. Lejour, he said, "Doc, thank you for all your help with this case, but from now on, for safety's sake, we better just touch base over the phone."

"What about the sleep exercises?" Dr. Lejour asked.

"Oh," Rocco answered, feeling a bit relieved to be done with The Dream Center. "We'll take care of that. If we have any questions, we'll call." The group went out the front door of the hospital and at the end of the block, Rocco headed toward his car, parked away from the others'. "I'll see you tomorrow," Rocco said to Clare and Marcus. At his words, Clare stopped walking and looked in front of her as if she was trying to remember something. "Clare?" Rocco asked, noticing her odd look.

"Yes," Clare responded, "tomorrow, right." Rocco turned slowly then continued toward his car. Clare remained where she was, staring across the sidewalk and along the brick wall of the hospital building. Straining to see something, she tilted her head side to side as crowds of people walked around her. There seemed to be faces between the bodies rushing along the pavement. A handbag swung forward, revealing a pair of eyes which quickly vanished behind the crowd.

"Guys, I think I heard something down here," Clare said without taking her eyes off the sidewalk, but Rocco and the others were too far away to hear. Between the moving lines of pedestrians, Clare saw a dog trotting toward her, its eyes fixed on hers. It was a Rottweiler. "Guys?" Clare called out, keeping her eyes on the dog. She soon noticed two more on either side of the first, one against the hospital building and the other along the curb. She drew her weapon and walked backwards around the corner. The three dogs suddenly charged her, being joined by two more that sprang from the crowd. Clare turned and bolted toward the hospital entrance. Rocco noticed that Clare was no longer with the others, then saw her running down the sidewalk with her weapon drawn.

"Clare!" he shouted, running across the street. Clare scrambled up the handicap ramp to the front door, turned and saw the lead dog leaping for her right arm. She tried to steady her hand to take a shot, but the dog was so quick and landed such a firm bite of her forearm that her gun tumbled from her hand onto the concrete. As she struggled to free herself from the grasp of the first dog, a second leapt up clasping its jaws on the back of her neck, and with the momentum of its massive body, spun Clare around, pulling her down onto her back.

"John!" Clare cried out as she went down onto the ramp, looking up at a mass of fur, saliva, and snapping jaws. She fell flat on her back, thrashing with her free arm against their attack, but they were too much for her. Her arm, slashed and torn, was overpowered, and they were upon her.

THE RITE

11

*R*occo pushed his way through pedestrians and ran to Clare, who was alone on the concrete ramp, the dogs a hallucination in her mind. "Clare!" he cried as he looked at her writhing on the concrete, her right arm immobile at her side, her left arm flailing in the air at her invisible assailants.

"Let's get her in to the emergency room!" Marcus called out, reaching Clare only seconds behind Rocco. He slid his arms underneath her to hoist her up. Jake and Vince ran up onto the ramp, breathless, staring at Clare.

"Come on, give me a hand," Marcus barked.

"Is she having a seizure or something?" Vince asked.

"Just get her legs."

"Look at her face. Is she even breathing?" Jake asked, as he struggled to grab one of her legs that was kicking wildly. Clare's head was turned up and to the side, as if held there, her mouth slightly open, but not moving. Vince grabbed her other leg while Rocco kept her left arm from striking out at them.

"Lift her up now," Marcus said, and the four of them carried her writhing body into the hospital entrance.

"Where's your emergency room?" Marcus asked the security guard who directed them down the appropriate hallway. A gasping sort of sound came from Clare's throat as her head turned violently to the other side facing Rocco.

"What's happening?" Vince asked, seeing the distorted appearance of Clare's face for the first time.

Dr. Lejour's voice could be heard behind them. "I'm with them, I'm a doctor," he called out to security as he ran down the hall to catch up with them. "What's wrong?"

"We don't know, maybe a seizure?" Rocco asked.

"She's not seizing, she's struggling," Dr. Lejour corrected, as he watched the men scrambling to maintain a hold on her. "What happened?"

"No idea," Marcus answered. "She was running away from something, then fell down, and has been thrashing around since."

"It's Hoffman," Dr. Lejour said.

"What?" Jake asked.

"He got to her."

"Hoffman? How?" Rocco asked.

"She looked at him remember?" Dr. Lejour replied.

They passed through the electric doors into one of the

emergency room bays. A nurse and two orderlies ran over to them and slid Clare onto a stretcher, immobilizing her with leather restraints. Dr. Lejour grabbed Rocco's arm, pulling him to the side.

"He must have implanted a trigger," Dr. Lejour whispered to Rocco.

"A trigger?"

"A word or phrase that triggers a hypnotic suggestion. What did you say to her before this began?"

"Nothing," Rocco replied, "just, see you tomorrow." With these words, Clare's thrashing increased.

"That must have been it," Dr. Lejour remarked. "Don't say it again. Listen, they won't know what to do with this. They'll think she's psychotic," he added. "Look, let them work her up, but don't let them give her Thorazine, that will make her mind even more susceptible to Hoffman. I'll call someone who can help."

A doctor was getting a history from Jake and Vince: when did this all start, had she ever done this before, was she on any medication? The two shook their heads and answered to the best of their ability. The doctor felt that Clare was hallucinating, but they would need to do some tests to see if it was an intrinsic problem, or chemically induced.

"Could she have been drugged?" Vince asked.

"It's possible," the doctor answered. "Did she have any history of drug use?"

"We're FBI," Jake answered indignantly. The doctor shrugged his shoulders and turned toward the nurse.

"Get me twenty-five of Thorazine," the physician called out to the nurse as Clare began struggling with renewed intensity.

"No Thorazine!" Rocco yelled back from across the stretcher.

"Who are you?"

"I'm an agent, her partner," Rocco answered.

"Are you all FBI?" the doctor asked, looking up at the group clustered around him.

"Yes," Rocco answered, "and are these necessary?" He pointed to the leather restraints on Clare's wrists and ankles.

"We needed them to draw her blood and start an IV. Why no Thorazine?"

"She's allergic," Rocco lied, after a brief pause.

"Allergic? So she's had it before? This isn't her first psychotic episode?"

"No, it is," Rocco stammered. "She's not allergic to Thorazine. I just, we're on a case, following a man who can cause these sorts of effects in people, and the doctor working with us felt Thorazine would make it worse."

"Caused how? With drugs?"

"We don't know."

"Run a full toxicology screen and prep for a charcoal lavage," the doctor called out to the nurse.

Rocco had seen charcoal lavages before in cases of drug overdoses. Remembering how a tube was forced down the person's nose and throat and what seemed like gallons of black liquid were shot into the stomach and suctioned out again, he asked, "Can I talk to her first?" The doctor agreed.

"Just stay out of the way," one of the nurses snapped.

Rocco pulled up a chair beside the stretcher. Clare's head jerked around again toward him, her eyes looking past him with a fixed gaze, her arms and legs pulling constantly against the leather restraints. Did she even see him? He reached through the bars of the stretcher's side rails to clasp Clare's hand and wrapped his fingers around hers. He winced as she twisted and dug her fingernails into his palm. Still, he kept his hand in hers and moved closer. Her brow was tightly furrowed and her neck muscles so taut they looked like bars beneath her skin.

"It's me, John," he whispered. "Can you hear me?"

The demons in his mind rose to the surface, on every side, in every corner. He was at his brother's bedside again. He had even spoken the same words, the exact same words! Once more, he was weak and helpless in the face of suffering; he could do nothing but sit there. The demons moved in closer now, their hot breath on the nape of his neck. *I hate this!* He thought, as anguish and despair swirled around him like a whirlpool about to pull him under. Then, anger rose to his defense, stiffening the muscles of his neck, arching his back, and closing his free hand into a tight fist. Anger saved him. It made him a rock, firm, resolute, impenetrable.

Vince, Jake, and Marcus had moved to the side of the room to stay clear of the nurses that were checking Clare's monitors and vital signs. Marcus scanned the room, moving from one nurse to the other, scrutinizing every doctor that came into view, every orderly, every conscious patient, every potential threat.

Noticing this, Jake asked, "You think Hoffman's people would come in here?"

"Don't know," Marcus answered without looking at Jake.

"He'd be nuts... Of course, he probably is," Jake admitted, then moved away to sit by Vince on a small bench.

"I hope she comes out of this soon," Vince said, watching Clare's wrists and ankles pulling against the leather restraints, rattling the metal side rails.

Rocco did not move from Clare's side for nearly half an hour. Her hand still struggled against his, but with slightly less force. She showed no sign of recognizing him or the others, but she did seem a bit calmer. He had been able to persuade the doctor to hold off on the charcoal lavage until her blood work came back.

"Have you seen Dr. Lejour?" Rocco asked Marcus.

"He's outside the door," Marcus answered. Dr. Lejour entered, followed by a man in brown robes who appeared to be in his seventies, medium build with shortly trimmed hair, and a salt and pepper beard.

A priest? Rocco thought. *You've got to be kidding me.*

"Father Joseph," Dr. Lejour said, as they moved over to Rocco. "This is Clare, the agent I told you about, and Agent Rocco with her, and this is Marcus, another advisor, oh, and Agents Jake and Vince." The priest nodded to them, then looked intently at Clare.

"Clare," he said, coming up on the side of the stretcher opposite Rocco.

"She doesn't seem to hear us," Rocco explained.

The priest leaned over Clare and whispered to her. Clare remained fixed in her position facing Rocco, staring at the space over his shoulder.

"Keep talking to her Agent Rocco," Dr. Lejour suggested. "Let her hear your voice."

Vince led Jake a bit farther away, into the corner of the room.

"It's the evil eye," Vince whispered to Jake. "My grandmother used to talk about this. Hoffman put a hex on her somehow."

Marcus noticed one of the nurses speaking with the doctor across the room. The doctor nodded his head, and the two started toward Clare when Marcus intercepted them.

"It's Okay Doc," Marcus said as he stepped in front of the doctor.

"Who is that?" the doctor asked, pointing at Father Joseph.

"He's calming her down. It's okay. How's everything looking?"

"So far," the doctor said, reluctantly standing down, "her blood work looks fine, but some of the drug tests won't come back right away. We'll have to admit her."

"Whatever we need to do," Marcus replied. "Just give them a little time now, if you would."

The doctor agreed, and the nurse pulled the curtain around their bay. Father Joseph finished reading from a small book at Clare's side, then stood over her and pulled a small plastic bottle from his pocket. Opening the top, he splashed Clare's face with liquid from the bottle.

"Holy water? Really?" Rocco asked, looking up at the priest. "Father, she's not possessed. It's some type of mind control. Doc, come on!" he said, glaring at Dr. Lejour.

"Holy water, that's good," Vince whispered to Jake. "That's what my grandmother always used."

Father Joseph stared intently at Clare's face, then closed his eyes, mouthing some words silently. "Talk to her," he said to Rocco, without opening his eyes.

"Me?" Rocco asked. Getting no response from the priest, he put his free hand on her face and whispered to her again, "Clare, it's me, John. Can you hear me?"

Clare's eyes broke their stare and moved from the space

behind Rocco, looking rapidly all around her. They came to rest on Rocco's gaze. Her breaths gradually slowed and her face became animated again, confused, but engaging.

Rocco slid his hand out from Clare's relaxed grasp, blood dripping from the nail gouges in his palm. Marcus grabbed a roll of gauze off the counter and wrapped Rocco's hand, while Rocco kept his eyes fixed on Clare, who lay quietly on the stretcher without moving. The furrow in her brow had softened, her neck muscles were relaxed, her arms and legs resting on the stretcher. She blinked her eyes and turned to look at the rest of the group around her. They all stood in silence, a silence that had spread throughout the emergency room. Even for a big city emergency department, Clare's dramatic entrance had drawn a great deal of attention. Every doctor, nurse, orderly, and patient were staring intently at the drawn curtains around Clare's stretcher. She breathed long, full breaths, as though inhaling fresh air for the first time after being freed from some underground hole. She turned her head slowly toward Rocco with a placid look of recognition and relief.

"John," she whispered.

GOOD AND EVIL

1
2

*W*hen the Emergency Room staff returned to review the blood work with the agents, they found Clare calm and speaking appropriately. Impressed with the dramatic change in her behavior, they removed her restraints, and after ruling out a brain tumor with a CAT scan, they allowed her to leave.

Clare walked slowly between Rocco and Jake who each kept a hand on the back of her arms.

"I'm all right, really," Clare said. She gently pulled her arms away from the two, pausing to stand as straight as she could and collecting herself for a moment before moving on. "There were no dogs here?" she asked as they continued walking out toward the lobby.

"No," Vince answered. "Just us. We carried you into the emergency room."

"It was a nightmare," Clare said, "huge dogs lunging at

me, biting, tearing at my arms, so many of them! I would see one of you and barely hear your voice. Then I would see another one."

"Another dog?" Jake asked.

"They kept coming." Clare nodded. "Any time I began to feel safe, I'd see them, right behind one of you, snarling, moving closer and closer. Doctor, do you think Hoffman did this to me?"

"Yes," Dr. Lejour answered.

"How? It was so real."

"Of course it was real," Dr. Lejour explained. "You see, he would not have projected any actual images into your mind, just the abstract understanding of terror from an attack, then your own imagination filled in the blanks. For you, it was a pack of dogs, for another, it might have been a horde of insects. But the images in your brain would seem as real as what you're seeing right now. Do you remember seeing Father Joseph?"

"Yes," Clare said, reaching out to touch the priest's arm. "But, I couldn't tell what was real and what wasn't, until," she paused, "until I saw you, John." Rocco helped her onto a bench in the corner of the hospital lobby. After rubbing the back of her neck and shoulders for a few moments, Rocco moved over to Father Joseph.

"Can we talk?" Rocco asked the priest, who nodded. "Something you did back there seemed to snap her out of it, enough so that she could hear me. It would be a great help to us if we could understand what that was."

"It was the Holy Water, wasn't it?" Vince suggested, stepping into the conversation.

"Holy water is good," the priest said, nodding, "but..."

"But what?" Vince asked.

"This man, Hoffman? You need to keep the door shut to him, even the tiniest crack."

"Yes, yes, exactly," Rocco agreed. "How?"

"You have a window in the attic. How do you know if it's open?"

"You go up to the attic?" Vince asked.

"There you go," the priest replied, smiling at Vince. "To close the window in your soul, you must go into your soul."

"Yeah, okay, Father," Rocco replied. "The good doctor here led us through something like that, and this still happened. So, clearly, we need more; we need the power to repel him, the power you just demonstrated."

"It's not about power," the priest protested, raising his voice. "He only has the power you choose to give him." He stared at Rocco, whose face tightened at the priest's words.

Talk about blaming the victim! Rocco thought. How could self-deprecation be of any help to them, he wondered? It was clear to Rocco that you defeat the power of evil with the power of good; you match strength with strength. There was no other way.

"I think Father's got a point," Marcus said, breaking the strained silence between the two men. "We let him into our heads, he gets control, so, like he says, we have to keep him out."

"And how do we do that?" Rocco reiterated.

"Focus," Marcus answered, "like the doc's been telling us. We don't look at him, or think about him. We focus on each other."

"We tried that, remember?" Jake said, standing up and beginning to pace along the lobby wall.

"So, we try harder," Marcus answered calmly, but with a commanding tone.

"Agent Rocco," Dr. Lejour interjected, "I think what Father is saying, is that the only useful power against Hoffman is the power of faith."

"We're screwed," Jake mumbled to Rocco.

"What do you agents think faith is?" Dr. Lejour countered. "Faith is simply a willingness to follow the truth wherever it leads you. Right now, it's leading you to another dimension, where Hoffman is trying to break into your minds. Like Father said, to shut the window in the attic, you first have to go into the attic."

"Go into the attic," Rocco echoed while rolling his eyes.

"Father, maybe the agents could come by the friary tomorrow to consider this further?" The priest nodded. Dr. Lejour also suggested that the team now go directly to The

Dream Center. Rocco had had enough of that place, but as their confrontations with Hoffman were proving to be one failure after another, he felt inclined to agree.

"What do we do, chief?" Jake asked Rocco, who was staring across the hospital lobby.

"None of us should be alone tonight," Rocco said. "Let's do it. Father, thank you for your help today. Can we give you a ride somewhere?" The priest shook his head and held up his hand. "Then, I guess we'll see you tomorrow–" Rocco said the words without thinking, then quickly broke off, remembering how those very words had activated the hypnotic illusion in Clare. He jerked his head around to Clare, and to his surprise, she was walking calmly and quietly alongside him.

"The trigger is gone," Dr. Lejour explained. "The suggestion, the connection, all of it–gone."

"I'm telling you, we need to know what he did," Rocco said, watching Father Joseph head out the door toward the subway station.

"Tomorrow, I think you'll understand," Dr. Lejour suggested.

The sun had already set by the time the group was in their cars and headed for The Dream Center. Rocco took Clare in his car, leading the way across midtown. A panorama of familiar scenes rolled by their windshield: the audiences filing out from theaters talking and laughing, pedestrians moving through crosswalks, shoppers looking in storefront windows, tourists craning their necks to see the tops of buildings, locals hurrying home from work.

Life goes on, Rocco thought, looking at the crowd of faces. *If they only knew...* But, would they believe it? Would anyone believe what they had experienced that day?

"Life goes on," Clare said, as she looked out the window. Rocco glanced at her, barely noticing the coincidence of her remark. Of course no one else would believe it; he didn't believe it. Even if people bothered to look past the bright lights or listen beyond the noise of the street, the real threat would not be perceived by their senses. The agents' conflicts had taken place as much in another dimension as in the bullet-ridden warehouse. Besides the priest, would anyone understand or believe them? Would anyone in the Bureau? Hoffman's picture had been distributed throughout the NYPD. The eyes of every police officer in the city were looking for him, scrutinizing surveillance cameras and faces in the crowds, but to them, he was just a person of interest. Would any of them believe what he was capable of before it was too late? Other than two rookies in Brooklyn, who by now had convinced themselves that their bizarre dealings with Hoffman were some sort of trick or illusion, there was no one else who knew, no one else who would believe. Among millions, it seemed, the six of them were basically on their own.

Part II

Part 2

THE STOCK EXCHANGE

13

*T*he following morning, Clare was the first one up, drinking her coffee and looking over the others wired to the monitors. She seemed calmer than the day before, but still jumped at each sound the technician, Isaac, made moving his chair or opening a drawer. She looked across the room at Rocco, who was becoming fitful, turning violently and breathing in short deep breaths. She didn't need to look at the monitors to know he was dreaming.

In his dream, Rocco saw a young boy sitting in the front seat of a car, his short blonde hair combed neatly across his forehead. His blue eyes were round and full, anxiously darting from side to side. The boy was trembling and obviously frightened. He seemed to know something was not right. He didn't want to be there, but was afraid to run, and the car was beginning to move. His eyes glanced fitfully across the sea of passersby, broadcasting his silent cry for help, all in vain. *Doesn't anyone see?* Rocco asked himself. *Don't they care? Someone should stop the car, ask the boy if he is all right. Can't they see he's frightened? Stop that car! Don't let this happen! Why doesn't anyone do something? Someone should stop him! Stop!*

Rocco's eyes opened with a start and he gazed at a point on the ceiling as he oriented himself again to time and place. The tightness gripped his chest and flashed across the nape of his neck. It was a dream he had dreamt before, in which the eight-year-old boy, whose murder Rocco had solved years ago, is tricked into entering the car of the man who would later that morning take his life.

"That was a lot of activity," Isaac said as he came over to help Rocco remove his EEG leads. "Would you like pen and paper to jot down some notes about your dream?"

"No," Rocco answered quickly, "not this one."

"What was it, John?" Clare asked, coming to sit by him. "Was it the boy?"

How had she remembered? He had only mentioned it to her once, and that in passing. It was not something he ever talked about. How was she so intuitive? It was another one of her traits he admired. He turned to her and said, "We're never there in time–always after the fact."

"But when we solve the case, we stop it from happening again," she reminded him.

While Rocco and Clare waited for the rest of the team

to awaken, that morning, further south on the same island of Manhattan, Hoffman was already awake, dressed, and sitting in the cool morning air on the steps of The Federal Hall Memorial, across the street from the New York Stock Exchange. It was a clear morning with a cool breeze blowing across the labyrinth of buildings from the East River to the Hudson River. The brightness of the streets aligned with the morning sun cut through the shadowy streets perpendicular to them, still shaded from the light and warmth of the new day. The chrome trim of parked cars along these sunny streets sparkled in the light while the trim of those on intersecting streets remained subdued with an opaque gray film of frost. The sounds of cabs and buses rose through the air, drowning out the occasional chirping of chickadees that made their nests in the bricked corners and ledges some ten feet above Hoffman. The tall thin man Hoffman had met at the cafe earlier that week climbed the steps and sat down beside him.

"Are you trying to make things more difficult?" the man asked Hoffman.

"What do you mean?" Hoffman asked.

"Gun fights with the FBI? This complicates things. Why did you draw the FBI into this in the first place?"

"I had no choice," Hoffman replied. "Besides, can't you control them?"

"The CIA has no jurisdiction within the FBI, especially

at this level," the man answered, taking a drink from his cup of coffee. "Besides, this is covert even within the agency."

"Maybe I'm talking to the wrong man."

"No, I'm the man to talk to. You just need to dial it down a bit. We like to maintain a veneer of normalcy, with a cloak of apparent transparency. It works quite well. We can control appointments and committee chairs. It's just those damn elections that keep throwing a wrench into things. That's, well, that's why we're talking to you. You're supposedly the guy who can make it happen, instead you're acting like a bull in a china shop. A little subtlety, you know? Try to be a team player."

"Team?" Hoffman asked as he pointed to two birds hopping around on the sidewalk in front of them. The one bird had what appeared to be a worm in its mouth, and the other was trying to steal it. "Look at that—survival of the fittest," Hoffman pointed out. "The strong survive primarily because they are not team players." The stealing bird succeeded in its appropriation of the worm, quickly swallowing it and flying off. "Life consumes life," Hoffman mused. "It has always been that way, and always will be. A team is nothing but a group of followers. A leader does not follow. Would you have the master be directed by the slaves? The cattleman driven by the cattle?" He looked at the man sitting awkwardly on the steps, then asked, "Have you ever seen a herd of cattle being driven?"

"Can't say as I have."

"It's impressive, really, a few men on horseback can drive four hundred head of cattle, cattle that could very well trample the men and their horses if it weren't for their lack of understanding and their fear. It's their nature as herd animals. Human beings are also herd animals for the most part." He looked out across the sea of hurrying people before them with a self-satisfied grin, as though basking in the profound truth of his last statement. "So, you know how you work cattle?"

"How?"

"You scare a few of the cattle on the edges, the ones who are trying to go a different way. You turn these leaders down the path you want them to go, then keep the sides contained. The rest just follow along, the momentum of the herd being driven with fear and confrontation, mother cows bellowing for their calves, the heels of stragglers being bloodied by the snapping jaws of your well-disciplined cow dogs. It's orchestrated pandemonium," Hoffman added with a smile.

"So you're a cowboy too?"

"Never been on a horse," Hoffman answered with a smirk.

"Then, how do you know so much about cattle?"

"I saw a cattle drive once in a national park, and I never forgot it—two men with three dogs, moving hundreds of cattle. You can learn something from almost every situation," Hoffman said, leaning in toward the man beside him. "I might even learn something from you."

The man shifted a bit as he looked at Hoffman, who seemed to be studying him, looking through him, into his mind, assessing and indexing it, then logging it away.

"In any case," the man said, turning away from Hoffman's gaze, "there are laws. It's better if we work around them, not run roughshod through them."

"Laws," Hoffman repeated with disgust, turning toward the street. "Laws are the embodiment of fear. Lawmakers champion their cause to eradicate pain, all the while cowering in corners, cringing from the thought of the slightest pinprick. There is no strength that is not born through pain, no growth without suffering. It is suffering that hones the edge of the blade, so I say, let it come. Laws frustrate the natural process; they are the bellowing of driven cattle. Would you have me dismount and join the herd?"

The man shook his head.

"Nor I," Hoffman replied.

"Still, some common sense..."

"That which is common is never of much value," Hoffman quipped, looking at length into the man's eyes. "Have you strayed from the herd? A lost calf? Have you come to lecture me on the greatness of common values? To war against higher values, higher duty and nobility?" Hoffman turned from the man, who had shifted his gaze down to the sidewalk. "No matter," Hoffman said, looking across the street again. "The great will always stand alone, out of necessity, those with the burden to rule. You take your common values and run back to the herd. Your mother bellows for you."

The two sat with an uneasy hush between them, the man from the CIA eventually breaking the silence.

"I was told we needed to see something, something more than just a few tricks," the man said, finally.

"Tricks?"

"Yes, we need proof, proof that you can make things happen in a way that appears natural. Like I said, we work with a veneer of normalcy. We can't have any suggestion of coercion. You've made a big promise, guaranteeing votes, but your senate friend is still two years away from reelection. How do we know you can deliver?"

"I'll deliver. As to how, tell me where you want the herd to go and I'll move them any way I choose. There's more than one way..."

"Whatever, we need something," the man interrupted, handing a sheet of paper to Hoffman. "Now here are two insignificant local seats up for reelection this month. Both have more than a fifteen-point split in the polls. Just make the underdog in each win, and that will impress the people I work with."

Hoffman did not appear to be listening. His eyes were closed with a hand pressed to his forehead. A furrow developed between his tightly closed eyes. He drew his hand down from his forehead, his clenched jaw muscles twitching the skin of his cheeks. He remained like this for over a minute, then he leaned back. His face, bathed in the morning sunlight, became placid, the furrow gone, his cheeks still.

"I don't have all day," the man hissed as he lifted his cup of coffee to his lips.

"Pay attention!" Hoffman commanded, grabbing the man's forearm and splashing a wave of coffee onto his suit. The man glared at Hoffman, but his look quickly softened, and he turned away. "Sometimes you drive the cattle directly, other times you frighten them with your dog," Hoffman said, looking at the stock exchange building. "Watch across the street," he said, as he closed his eyes again. The man looked across at the New York Stock Exchange building with a sigh.

"I've been looking over there," the man said, turning back to Hoffman and taking advantage of the opportunity to study him while his eyes were closed. Except for his jaw muscles contracting intermittently, there was no motion in his face. The angles of his cheekbones were sharp, casting shadows beneath them, his nose straight, his chin broad. The man turned from Hoffman and looked again across the street. Glancing back at the stock exchange, something seemed oddly out of place. The street was filled with its usual frenzied activity, like a river swelled to its banks with multiple currents rising, cresting, submerging, and surfacing, but just outside the front door of the exchange, there was no motion. People were standing still, looking in through the glass. The group of immobile observers grew steadily until the door flew open and crowds of people came streaming out amidst a clamor of voices crying out in fear. The voices were soon joined by sirens that began to build as police cars rushed to the scene. The number of people running out of the building increased, with some being knocked over and nearly trampled.

"Something's going on here," the tall man said briskly. "We'd better get out of the area."

"A fifteen-point underdog winning an election suggests a rigged election," Hoffman said to the man calmly. "So much for your veneer of normalcy. But, create a crisis, when you are poised to respond and save the day, and no one will ever question your success."

"Are you saying you did this?"

"Who do you think?"

"What, did you rig the fire alarm or something?" They heard several people racing past them crying out that there was bomb. "A bomb scare?"

"A crisis," Hoffman replied, "ready-made."

"Instant disaster, find a culprit, rise in the polls," the CIA man thought out loud, "But how?"

"I'm connected to over a million minds, some twenty or

so happen to be Wall Street traders. I implanted the suggestion of a bomb into their minds to be triggered by the opening bell on the trading floor."

"Fantastic!" the man gushed, then added, "But, I still don't believe it."

"And I don't care," Hoffman said flatly as he stood up to leave.

"Wait, what about your price?"

"It will be high, and you'll pay," Hoffman said with a smirk.

"You know," the CIA man said, cocking his head as he stood up from the steps, "I could just have you thrown in prison and held as a terror suspect. Then your freedom would be the price of your services, so don't push me."

"Don't push *you*?" Hoffman asked, stopping and turning around to face the man again, staring at him intently until the man suddenly shrieked, dropped his coffee, and swept frantically at his legs.

"What the hell?" he asked, a terror-stricken look on his face. Scanning the steps around him, he saw nothing but passers-by who looked at him curiously. Turning to Hoffman he asked, "You did that?"

"Yes."

"Okay," the man said, holding up his hand in capitulation. "Okay, I believe. I believe." After a few deep breaths he asked, "How did you know I can't stand spiders?"

"I didn't, though I'm not surprised," Hoffman replied, turning to leave. "That was your last warning," he added. "Next time, I'll take your life."

Emergency vehicles were inching along the roadways clogged with throngs of terrified people struggling to get further away from the expected explosion. It was a perfect demonstration of induced chaos, an entire quadrant paralyzed with fear, traders, staffers, police, and firefighters all forcing their way through the swarm of humanity clamoring through the narrow streets.

"Let them know I will give them another demonstration," Hoffman said. "No, not your death," he clarified, seeing the anxious look on the tall man's face. "Something more useful."

"When?"

"They'll recognize it when it happens."

"Okay," the man said, shaking his head as Hoffman walked off the steps, disappearing into the crowds.

Two firehouses had responded already and detectives were questioning anyone who would stand still long enough to answer. The terrorist nature of the incident had triggered an automatic cascade of information sharing between agencies, including a notification sent to Rocco's cell phone.

Rocco reviewed the message just as the team was about to leave The Dream Center. Having spent the entire night at the center, they had been able to decompress from all that had gone on the previous day. The information Rocco shared about the stock exchange was welcome news to the agents as it seemed to be a return to their more conventional work. Investigating a bomb scare and a potential terrorist threat would be a refreshing change of pace for them.

As the team prepared to head across town, the mood was visibly lighter. Dr. Lejour gave Rocco directions to Father Joseph's friary, where they would regroup later that day. Marcus stayed with the agents, who were happy to have him along. Despite their better humor, there was an unspoken concern that Hoffman may have been behind this event. They had, after all, been conveniently sidetracked the day before. The possibility that they might come up against more of his extraordinary antics dampened their initial excitement.

Rocco drove downtown with Clare and Marcus, then stopped at the gridlock a few blocks away from Wall Street, continuing on foot to the scene. They joined up with the officers at the scene, who told them bomb squads were combing through the building now, but that it would be hours before anyone else would be allowed in. They had already interviewed a number of the people from the building and allowed Rocco and his team to speak with them as well.

"Did you see who started the panic?" Rocco asked a man who had been questioned by the police.

"There were people on the floor yelling that there was

a bomb. One of them was someone I work with," the first worker replied. "Him, over there," he said, pointing to a man who was being questioned by one of the detectives.

Rocco pulled the detective to the side, showing him his ID.

"What have you got?" Rocco asked the detective.

"There's this gentleman and at least three others in the area who started the panic. They all yelled out 'bomb' at the same time—right after the opening bell. They all say the same thing: they knew there was a bomb, but they couldn't say how. They all seemed a bit nervous, twitchy, like they were trying to hide something. So we thought it might be a hoax, maybe something to affect trading, but it doesn't add up," the detective explained. "There's no motive, no connection between the three of them. One of them was a visitor from Montana. This one's a trader. I was just about to ask him a few questions."

"Go ahead," Rocco said, getting an uneasy feeling about the source of the panic.

"You were one of the first on the floor to yell out 'bomb,'" the detective said to the man.

"That's what they've been saying," the man admitted. His voice wavered, and he seemed to be blinking a lot. "But I heard someone else saying it too."

"Did you see something that looked like a bomb?" the detective continued.

"No."

"But you heard something?"

"I guess so. I don't know."

"All right," the detective concluded politely but with a subtle sigh. "They'll need to ask you more at the station."

"Were you on your phone?" Rocco asked.

"Phone? On the floor? No way! The bell was about to be rung."

"Can I see your phone?" Rocco asked.

"Sure, here it is." The man complied, giving Rocco his phone. Rocco swiped through the man's phone screens, shaking his head slightly as he showed the screen to the man.

"When did you get this app?" Rocco asked, pointing to an icon of eTelepathy without tapping it.

"Oh, I don't know. A few weeks ago?"

"Delete it," Rocco advised, then showing the app to the detective, added, "Check any others who were yelling 'bomb' and I'll bet they all have this app on their phones."

"You think the app has something to do with this?" the detective asked.

"It's possible: subliminal messages, hypnosis, something of that nature."

"Hypnosis?" the man asked uneasily. "I'm not being arrested, am I?"

"No, they just have to check you out," the detective replied, "see if maybe you remember something that could assist us." He helped the man into the back of the police car and shut the door.

Rocco thanked the detective, then stood with Marcus and Clare, looking at the scene: people pushing their way through the crowds to distance themselves from the building they expected to explode at any second. Traffic was stopped for blocks, horns were blaring, sirens wailing. All the firefighters, police, EMTs, and FBI within a quarter mile had been called to the scene.

"You think it's Hoffman?" Marcus asked.

"The app's on his phone. The scare came out of nowhere—who else?" Rocco sighed.

"But why? Hoffman's not some prankster pulling a fire alarm," Clare pointed out.

"Could be a dry run," Marcus suggested.

"For what?" Clare asked.

"Diversion, instant panic," Marcus said. "Look: every responder tied up and neutralized without firing a shot. You couldn't get a better diversion."

"So what does he want to divert us from?" Rocco asked.

"Whatever it is," Clare replied, "we won't be ready for it, because we'll all be responding to something like this."

FAITH

14

***R*occo** and Marcus stood speechless, watching the pandemonium unfold before them, while Clare checked her watch.

"Dr. Lejour will be meeting us at the friary in half an hour," Clare's voice rang out beside them, breaking through the street noise. "We'd better get moving." They nodded and left their vantage point to go see the priest with Clare. As the three made their way back to the car, they came upon Vince and Jake, filling them in on the situation at the Exchange, explaining how people "just knew" there was a bomb.

"Like how we *just knew* the answer to that surgery question," Vince noted. "I bet that's what the doctor will say."

"I'm sure you're right," Rocco sighed.

The group returned to their cars parked just outside the gridlock. As the traffic finally cleared, the agents drove up Manhattan along the Hudson River. Crossing from Manhattan into the Bronx, Rocco led the team to the friary.

"You think he's lost?" Vince asked Jake as Rocco's car headed down a street lined with broken windows and graffiti-covered walls. They came to a stop in front of a stone wall lined with razor wire along its top edge. Getting out of their cars, they scanned the South Bronx neighborhood, then walked to the front door of the friary which was made of solid mahogany with hand-carved figures on its surface. Rocco pushed a small call button to the side of the door and a short time later, a young bearded friar let them in.

As the heavy door swung shut, the noise of the Bronx streets ceased as if it had been turned off with a switch. The air inside was cool like that of a stone cottage with the richness of an old wine cellar. The smells of leather-bound books and woodwork varnished and revarnished over the years mingled with that of candle wax rising from flickering flames. The agents were led around a corner and down a long hallway. Light streamed in from a central courtyard through long narrow windows, laying bands of light across the hallway floor, framed with repeating arches above and stone pillars on either side. Like an artist's exercise in perspective, the lines all converged at the end of the hallway where there was a life-size crucifix. Looking out into the courtyard, they could see a perimeter of slate roofs, well-groomed trees and shrubs, and several statues in the corners and along walkways. At the end of the hallway, the friar led them into a small room where Dr. Lejour was sitting, and asked that they wait there for Father Joseph.

"Good morning," Dr. Lejour called out cheerfully, sitting at the head of an old wooden table, roughly finished, with large knot holes in its surface. "Have a seat. Father Joseph should be here shortly."

The group sat around the table, looking at each other briefly, then at the walls of the room which were empty except for a small cross on one wall and a painting of a friar on another. Rocco's attention was drawn across the hall to a chapel which was much more richly furnished. There were lit candles beside a stone altar, casting off waves of heat into the air above, distorting the appearance of the wall behind them. The walls themselves were lined with bas-relief sculptures framed by the same stone they were carved from. The altar was made of simple but polished marble that reflected the light from the candles and from small lights along the side walls. On the other side of the altar, there was a golden box with ornate doors on its front, and beside it a candle glowing within a red glass cylinder. Rocco recognized this as a tabernacle, the bas relief sculptures as stations of the cross, and all the other sights as familiar trappings of a Catholic chapel. He rose and moved into the hallway, drawn by the smell of the wax candles evoking a vivid childhood memory. He would often gaze at the rack of lit candles in the back of his church. As a child, it had been his favorite place to pray. Staring at the flames through the deeply colored glass containers, his vision would blur and it was as if he was surrounded by the flickering lights, the warmth, and the smell of the wax.

"Would you like to go into the chapel, Mr. Rocco?" Dr. Lejour's voice broke into his memory, drawing him back to the present moment.

"No, that's fine," Rocco answered.

"I was just going in there, come with me. It's all right. They've let me in here before." The two walked across the hall to the chapel door, but Rocco remained outside. "Have you ever been in a Catholic church?" Dr. Lejour asked.

"I was raised Catholic," Rocco answered.

"Oh, and now?"

"I haven't been in a church for ten years," Rocco said, looking over Dr. Lejour's shoulder into the chapel. "The last time was at my parents' funeral. They died in a car accident on their way to one of those religious conferences."

"I'm sorry to hear that," Dr. Lejour said, looking at Rocco's face as he stared blankly away from the chapel.

"Aren't you going to tell me it was for the best, that everything happens for a reason?" Rocco asked, turning back to Dr. Lejour, the tightness flashing from his chest across the back of his neck. He knew the doctor meant well; he wasn't angry with him personally, or maybe he was. He's the one that brought it up. He asked for it. He aroused the darkness that he now needed to answer with anger, his equal and opposite reaction. "Admit it, Doc, sometimes things aren't for the best; sometimes they're just empty, dark, and pointless."

"You've suffered a great deal."

"Who hasn't? From what I've seen, it's just par for the course," Rocco retorted, glancing up at Dr. Lejour, then back down the hallway.

"You must see a lot of suffering in your line of work," Dr. Lejour said. "So did I, in thirty-five years of practicing medicine. But you know, I've always found that the greatest love comes through suffering."

"You don't say," Rocco replied flatly.

"Yes. It's through affliction that we receive grace."

"How about the murder of an eight-year-old boy? Where's your grace and love in that? Wait, don't say it, 'God's ways are not our ways.' There's another gem."

"How about that murder? It's your case you mean, right?"

Rocco tilted his head in a half nod, half shrug.

"I remember reading about it. Everyone had given up on finding the murderer except you. You wouldn't give up. Why?"

"Bullheadedness."

"I remember thinking how much the boy's family must have appreciated your persistence, the closure you brought them."

"It didn't bring their boy back."

"No. That's true. Such a wound never heals. Their loss is

forever, but so is your concern and dedication. Just knowing that you were there, working on your own time, that you cared, that they were not alone in their pain, their horror. That's often the worst of it you know, the aloneness. When people suffer the loss of a loved one, they see the rest of the world going on, caring about the most trivial things, while they are struggling just to take their next breath. Isolation is one of the most consistent and overwhelming emotions people feel in grief and personal suffering. Then comes someone like you, someone who seems to care as much as they do, someone who understands. What a comfort that must have been."

"I had no comfort for them," Rocco lamented quietly, forgetting his annoyance with the doctor for having brought the subject up.

"Yes you did, more than you know. Your love overcame the evil of that crime. The suffering may be permanent, but so is the love. It lives on. It's what makes life worth living."

Rocco shook his head slowly. "I'm sorry, Doc. I didn't mean to unload on you like that. This place just brought back a lot of memories." He headed back into the room with the others as Father Joseph turned the corner and joined them.

"Hello again," the priest said, looking at the group seated at the table. "So you want to protect yourselves better, yes?" He then walked around the table, looking at each of them with a hint of a smile. "You must have faith."

"Here we go," Jake whispered to Vince. Dr. Lejour

nodded while the others looked on in silence.

"Faith begins with trust," the priest said. "Trust that there is something more than all this." He motioned around the room. "There are things you cannot see, but can still know."

"We've talked about this, right, agents?" Dr. Lejour added. "Faith is the willingness to go where the truth leads you, even to another dimension."

"Choose to know what you cannot see, and your faith will grow," the priest continued. "How it grows depends on your will. The will to love is good. The will for power is evil. If your will is to love, your soul will be in communion with other souls of good will. When your will is for power, then you are speaking with evil, and you open your soul to the enemy."

"Love or power?" Clare asked. "Nothing else?"

"We are made to love," the priest answered. "That is our nature. Anything can be done out of love: hard work, service, making money, even chasing this man, and anything can be done for power: stealing, lying, even helping the poor. It is your heart, the direction of your will, that counts."

"So what are you suggesting we do?" Rocco asked.

"Control your thoughts. When you are angry, impatient, or when imagination runs wild, you open the door to your enemy. He has found you and will not let go easily. He will be back for you."

Clare shuddered. "Can you see Hoffman now?"

"Yeah," Jake added. "Can you tell us where he is?"

"See him?" the priest asked. "To see you must look–align your will with his, then he can see you too."

"So he's always got the upper hand," Jake sighed.

"The will to power is an illusion of strength," the priest corrected. "It can cause great harm to others, but in the end, it always leads to self-destruction. Keep your wills aligned with love and allow him to reach his end. You think about this. I'll be in the chapel if you need me." The priest then turned and went across the hall into the small chapel.

"That's it?" Jake muttered under his breath to Vince.

Rocco got up and turning to Clare said, "Hold up, I've got to ask him something." He followed the priest into the chapel and sat down next to him. "Father, I have to ask you something."

"Yes?"

"You said power is an illusion, but when you helped Clare at the hospital, you used power against Hoffman, didn't you?"

"If you seek power it will destroy you," Father Joseph warned. He looked at Rocco quietly, then added, "You lost someone, didn't you?"

Rocco paused, surprised by the priest's question, then retorted, "Everyone's lost someone. That's what being powerless is about. It's about losing."

The priest looked at Rocco for a time, as if considering something, then added, "Pray for him."

The sound of the priest's words reverberated through Rocco's memories. They were the words he had heard while sitting at his brother's death bed, the words he had taken as a sign of hope.

"It didn't work then; why do it now?"

"Then?" the priest asked.

Rocco, realizing his mistake in assuming the priest was referring to his brother, asked, "Who are you talking about?"

"Hoffman, of course," the priest continued. "Who did you think?" Rocco shrugged. "Be the light in the darkness; pray for him."

"Pray for Hoffman?" Rocco snorted. "Not likely. I'll let you do that."

"It's you who must believe. Pray for him."

"Why do you keep saying that? I'm not going to pray for him. And why do I have to believe? You're saying I can stop him if I believe?"

"Yes, believe," the priest said, looking down and nodding his head slightly, "but, you choose not to."

"I choose not to?" Rocco burst out, stepping across the chapel to face Father Joseph. "I choose not to? I want to believe. Give me something!"

"You want me to give you faith? Here," Fr Joseph snapped back, taking a piece of paper off of a small table, "I write it here, 'faith.' Bravo, now you have faith." The priest raised his hand in a gesture of frustration. "Faith is a gift from God, but it is a gift you must choose to accept."

"I said I want faith. Isn't that enough?"

"You want it, but you want it like a magic lamp–to give you whatever you please. You must suffer for faith. This man, Hoffman, he knows this."

"You think Hoffman has faith?" Rocco scoffed.

"Sure he has faith, but his will is evil. He has faith enough to move mountains, but since he lacks love, he is nothing."

"Hoffman is far from nothing, Father."

"No! He is nothing, or he will be," the priest insisted. "His will for power will consume him. Let him destroy himself. You want power against him? Seek to have none. Trust, believe, discipline your will. Pray. Do this and come back tomorrow." Father Joseph put his hand on Rocco's shoulder, then returned to his seat in the chapel.

As Rocco returned to join the others across the hall, he found them engaged in conversation with Dr. Lejour.

"One of the first concepts that Father helped clarify for me," Dr. Lejour said, "was that truth must be true from all perspectives, all disciplines. Truths in philosophy must dovetail with truths in biology, with truths in mathematics, with truths in physics, metaphysics, logic, and statistics, even truths in your police work. Different disciplines see truth from their own perspective. When you look at truth from just one discipline, one perspective, what appears to be true may be false, and what appears to be false may be true."

"So how can you tell?" Vince asked. "We just know our work, not all those other fields."

"It's about consistency," Dr. Lejour replied. "Take bilocation—my research into that phenomenon first led me to Father Joseph many years ago. Bilocation is the purported ability of a person to be in two places at once. Now, physics tells us that a body occupies a unique location in space and time, so it cannot be in two different places at the same time. Truth is the absence of contradiction, so when there is contradiction, the thing is either untrue, or we need to look at the question from a different perspective. As we have discussed, the mind is in a dimension without space, so a person's mind can be *seen* by another person's mind at a place far away from the person's physical body. Looking at bilocation from the perspective of another dimension, there is no contradiction, and what seems to be impossible becomes possible. Ah, agent Rocco!" he said, turning his chair to include Rocco in the conversation.

"As Father said, the will to power opens the door to evil," Dr. Lejour continued. "Thoughts of pride, envy, or anger align your will with that of your enemy, so you must keep your will aligned with the will to love, our natural order." The doctor reiterated how minds aligned with the natural order had access to each other and to premonitions while those with a will to power did not. "Remember, those with a will to power make their own order, and minds aligned with different orders have no overlap with each other. That is why, with your minds within the natural order, Hoffman cannot affect or even see you. As at The Dream Center, you must focus on the team, suspend your thoughts, your imagination, and direct your will toward love. This will increase your minds' awareness of each other and keep them inaccessible to Hoffman."

"What if we've tried all that and still don't see anything?" Vince asked.

"Don't try to *see* anything," Dr. Lejour replied. "Remember, when you use your minds apart from your brains, insights will come to you as abstract knowledge. It's like that picture in the warehouse, the one with the swirly lines you try to see the hidden picture in."

"Great," Rocco grumbled, as he sat down at the table next to Clare.

"Look," the doctor continued, "animal minds interact all the time through instinct. Their natural order promotes survival: for predators, to kill, for prey, to escape. But, our natural order is not merely to survive, but to love, and love cannot be forced–it must be chosen. So choose quickly because as Father said, you cannot afford to waffle between the will to love and the will to power. Hoffman has seen you. Every momentary lapse into the will to power gives Hoffman access to your minds which he will promptly take advantage of. The natural order is your means to defeat him, but it's up to you to choose it."

MARIONETTES

15

After leaving the friary, the team returned to the warehouse on the East River. There were few signs of the gunfight that had gone on there the day before: gouge marks in the table and the concrete pillars where bullets had been dug out for evidence, and stains of blood on the floor where Dr. Schroeder had been dragged. Otherwise, the room looked the same. The table had been righted to its previous position with glasses and pitchers of water placed on it. Assistants moved in and out of the kitchenette bringing plates of sandwiches to the table along with notepads and pens.

"You think we're okay coming back to the same place?" Clare asked, as they pulled up outside the warehouse.

"We've got the entire block covered, rooftop snipers, blockades, men on every floor of the building," Rocco answered. "It's probably the safest place in the city for us right now."

They did feel safe as they entered the warehouse, having passed agents and police officers at every doorway and stairwell. Dr. Lejour took a seat at the table while Marcus and Rocco walked slowly and methodically around the room, checking the view at each window and looking back frequently toward the entryway. Clare stood at the door, staring at the gouges in the table and the stain on the floor, while Jake sat down with Dr. Lejour.

Vince moved over to the door by Clare.

"You all right?" Vince asked her.

"Yeah," Clare answered, smiling briefly. "Yeah, I'm fine." Her eyes followed Rocco as he walked around the room with Marcus.

"Weren't you two an item?" Vince asked, noticing the focus of her attention.

"What?"

Vince motioned with his head to Rocco.

"Oh, yeah, sort of, I guess."

"I always thought you guys were pretty simpatico. What happened?"

"Well," Clare answered, looking at Vince, then over at Rocco, "one day, John said that we should be less serious, and that was that."

"Did he say why?"

"He said a lot of words, but... no, he didn't say why."

"Maybe you should ask him again?"

Clare looked at Vince with a frown. "He's as stubborn as ever."

"Yeah, he can be... but, he's a good man, you know? For what it's worth."

"For what it's worth, yeah," Clare answered. The two stood at the door watching Rocco and Marcus sweep the room. "You think he can see us?" Clare asked.

"Rocco?"

"No," Clare laughed, "Hoffman."

"Well, my grandmother used to talk like evil could always see you, but you could keep it away from you."

"How?"

"Her thing was holy water... and sometimes garlic, and some prayers too."

"Did it work?"

"I don't know. I didn't believe a word of it. But I'd never seen anything like I saw yesterday–what you went through."

"No, me neither," Clare said. "I don't ever want to again."

"Don't blame you."

"I'm scared, Vince," Clare admitted quietly, looking at him, then at the floor. "I keep thinking I'll look up and he'll be there, looking at me."

"That's not going to happen."

"How do you know?"

"We're not going to let it happen."

"Right," Clare said with a tone of sarcasm. "So, do you

have any holy water or garlic on you?"

"No, but you know," Vince whispered, "I was thinking of grabbing some holy water at the friary this morning, but then I thought, stealing from a priest–that can't be good, so I didn't."

"I'm sure they would have given it to you," Clare said, laughing again. Then she looked over her shoulder into the hallway where the police officers were standing.

"I know," Vince said, nodding, "I can't stop doing it either. It's like, is he behind me? I feel like he's everywhere."

Clare smiled, leaning to look around at the other side of Vince's face. "Who are you winking at?" she asked, looking across the room at the door.

"What?"

"There, you just did it again," Clare laughed. Then watching Vince's face, added, "You don't notice yourself doing it?"

"Doing what?" Vince replied.

"That little twitch," Clare explained. "I've never seen you do that before." Vince seemed to have a new facial tic. His signature held tilt was so familiar to everyone, that neither she, nor anyone else ever really noticed it anymore, but this was different. It was a sort of flickering, irregular squint on the left, upper side of the face. She smiled at Vince as they moved over to the table. "There it is again," she pointed out laughing. "I'm sorry, it's just, no, it's cute. I'm not used to it, that's all."

"What?" Vince laughed back. As Clare turned from Vince to join the group at the table, she noticed Jake who motioned to two chairs beside him. As Vince came alongside her and the two moved toward Jake, she suddenly let out a muffled cry, held her hand to her mouth, and pointed at both Jake and Vince.

"What is it?" Rocco asked Clare, who continued to stare at Jake, then at Vince, then back again.

"Come on," Rocco reassured her, "sit down over here."

The others, obviously concerned about Clare's outburst, followed her gaze, and one by one, they too gasped as they saw what had so frightened Clare. The faces of both Jake and Vince were twitching every half minute or so in exactly the same manner, at exactly the same time. This bizarre synchronized tic, that under other circumstances would have seemed like a choreographed skit, in the face of a mind controlling murder suspect, was terrifying.

"You two had to look at that app again!" Clare exclaimed, pacing nervously around the room.

"What are you talking about?" Jake asked, looking confused. Vince shrugged his shoulders and sat opposite Jake as though nothing were out of place, even as his face twitched in unison with Jake's.

Rocco cast a suspicious glance toward Jake and Vince. "Now what?" he asked, remembering the odd twitching of the man's face at the Stock Exchange.

"They both looked at Hoffman's app the other day," Clare explained to Dr. Lejour and Marcus, "before we met you both," she added, as though making an excuse for their reckless behavior. "But why would there be nothing until now?"

"You don't feel anything out of the ordinary?" Dr. Lejour asked Jake and Vince, who both shook their heads. "Maybe being back in this room, where Hoffman had been before?" the doctor suggested.

"I don't get it," Vince said. "What are you guys talking about?"

"If it's this room, we'll get out of here," Rocco said. "Where else could we go?"

"How about the safe house in Manhattan?" Clare suggested.

"Have you been there?"

"I was there last week."

"Fine, set it up."

"You know," Dr. Lejour began, "this may not be such a bad thing after all."

"How so?" Marcus asked.

"This visible tic is an excellent gauge of Hoffman's influence," the doctor replied. "Jake and Vince will need to free themselves, focus and direct their wills away from Hoffman's, and as they do so, this facial tic should disappear. Their progress, or lack thereof, will be evident on their faces." Both Jake and Vince continued to look on in confusion and disbelief.

Rocco informed one of the officers that they would be staying elsewhere and no longer needed the police protection. As the officer left, Detective Dobbs came up the stairwell.

"Agent Rocco, I'm glad I found you here," Dobbs said entering the room.

"Detective," Rocco replied.

"How is everyone?" Dobbs asked slowly, looking around at the agents' perturbed faces.

"All right," Rocco replied, "just going for a change of scenery."

"Well, I have some information for you," Dobbs said excitedly. Rocco nodded to the others to join them. "We've managed to track down the car Hoffman drove off in yesterday and have the owner in custody. I can get you in at the station if you'd like to ask him a few questions."

"Excellent! We'll follow you," Rocco declared, then paused, wondering what to do with Jake and Vince. The doctor noticed Rocco's concern and moved over to him.

"If you'd like," Dr. Lejour offered, "I could ride in the back with Jake and Vince and work with them while you drive with Clare in the front."

"I'd like that, yes," Rocco answered.

"What, you can't trust us?" Vince asked.

"You don't even see each other doing it, do you?" Marcus asked.

"Doing what?" Jake protested with a twitch.

"Come on with us," Rocco said, leaving Marcus to drive the other car behind them. Sitting in Rocco's car, Vince broke the awkward silence after a few minutes.

"Hey Doc," Vince whispered, "you don't have any holy water, do you?"

"No," Dr. Lejour answered with a smile, "but I can help you in other ways." He went on to coach them to focus their wills away from Hoffman's, similar to what he had done at the Dream Center. By the time they had arrived at the police station, both Jake's and Vince's facial tics had diminished substantially. Just before getting out of the car, they noticed each other's for the first time.

"I see what they're talking about!" Jake announced. "It's that little twitch on the side of your face. Sure."

"You're twitching too!" Vince exclaimed.

"You're becoming aware," Dr. Lejour explained. "Once you're aware of the influence, it can no longer affect you. You are your own masters. He can only control you through trickery. Remember, he has no power over you." Dr. Lejour put a hand on each of the ginning agent's shoulder. "They've done it!" the doctor announced. "Congratulations gentlemen, you've done it. You've out-foxed the fox!"

As the team gathered outside the police station, Clare moved by Rocco and asked, "Are you sure they should come in?"

"Hey, we're fine," Jake protested, "really."

"Jake, you come with me," Rocco said. "Vince, stick with Clare."

Dr. Lejour followed along behind with Marcus. Upon entering the precinct house, Dr. Lejour and Marcus sat on a bench in the holding area, while the others found Detective Dobbs. The suspect was already in an interrogation room, and Detective Dobbs brought the group into the observation area behind a two-way mirror.

"Jake and I will start this," Rocco said. "Then we'll go from there." Looking at Jake, he added, "You sure you're up for this?"

"I'm fine, really," Jake insisted.

The suspect was a man in his early thirties, dressed in a suit with an open collar shirt and slick black hair. He sat slouching as he waited, facing his reflection in the mirror as though looking through it, into the darkness where the team was watching him.

As Rocco and Jake entered, the man sat up in his chair and turned to look at the two agents. His foot began to beat up and down quietly as he looked from Rocco's face to Jake's face.

"So you're Hoffman's driver?" Rocco asked him.

"Who's Hoffman?"

"The guy the police saw you driving."

"I don't know anything. Someone stole my car."

"Stole your car?" Rocco asked, sitting down across from

the man. "And what? Brought it back afterwards and parked it in your driveway? Try again."

"I told you, I don't know anything."

"You're an accessory. You know what that means? It means if the man that was shot dies, you go down for murder."

"I had nothing to do with that! Look, some guys paid me a few bucks to drive them to this warehouse and wait for them. Then I dropped them off, and that was that. I don't know anything about any shooting."

"What do you know about Hoffman?" Jake asked him.

"I told you, I don't know any Hoffman."

"We don't have time for this," Rocco snapped at the man. "This is a national security issue, which means we'll hold you as a terror suspect until we get the information we need, so cut the crap."

"It also means," Jake added, "that anything Hoffman does in the meantime, you'll be held responsible for."

"All right, look," the man said finally. "All I can tell you is what I heard them talking about in the car. I never ask questions."

"We're listening," Rocco said.

"They were talking about the GW."

"The George Washington? The bridge?"

"Yeah."

"What about it?"

"I don't know..."

"Look, pal..." Jake said as he pushed away from the desk and stood up. Rocco watched Jake for a moment, beginning to question his decision to bring him into the interrogation room.

"I swear, I don't know," the man answered. "All I know is the one guy kept talking about the bridge and when they were supposed to be there."

"Which was?" Rocco asked.

"Eight AM tomorrow."

"Where on the bridge?"

"By the toll booths, upper level. The guy doing all the talking was adamant about the time."

"What else did they say?"

"Nothing, just... the guy kept saying it will be like nothing they'd ever seen."

Rocco and Jake left the room and joined the others behind the two-way mirror.

"You think he's holding out on us?" Clare asked Rocco as they entered the back room.

"I'm sure he is," Rocco answered. "The thing is, can we trust anything he's telling us?"

"Could be a set-up," Vince said.

"I don't know," Jake said. "He seemed pretty shook up by the talk of accessory to murder."

"Either way," Rocco replied, "we have to act on his

information. We'll need increased security and surveillance, both levels of the bridge, inbound and outbound," Rocco said to Dobbs. "We'll put a tracer in this guy's wallet then you can let him go."

"Let him go?" Dobbs asked.

"He won't be hard to find again. It's Hoffman we want. Maybe we'll get lucky and this guy will lead us right to him."

THE SAFE HOUSE

16

"**W**ho do you want to follow this guy?" Vince asked. He was typing information into a handheld device paired to the minute tracer he had placed into the suspect's wallet.

"Dobbs's men can follow him," Rocco replied. "They'll let us know if he meets up with anyone of interest. Is the safe house ready, Clare?"

"All set. There's no one else there so we'll have the place to ourselves."

"All right, let's go," Rocco said, leading the team out to the car.

The safe house was an apartment within a Manhattan precinct building, with no entrance from within the police station proper. It had four bedrooms, a kitchenette, a conference room, and an office. It was frequently used to protect key witnesses in high profile criminal cases involving organized crime. After picking up clothing and supplies at the doctor's and the agents' apartments, Rocco drove the group to the precinct building.

"Back up into this alleyway," Clare told Rocco, "then we can unload out of sight." Clare jumped out and placed her thumb on a fingerprint scanner alongside a sliding wall at the back of the alley. The wall rolled open and Rocco backed in. The alley was not open to the sky, but had an overhanging extension from the precinct building as its roof. Clare touched a pad on the other side and the wall rolled shut.

It was dark in the alley, with only a small amount of light coming through frosted glass bricks above the sliding wall. Clare hit a switch by the keypad and lights came on. There was a wrought iron fence at the end of the alley that ran up to the ceiling. A sign in the center of this fence read, "Danger: High Voltage." Behind the fence were two transformers on platforms with a brick wall behind them.

"Okay, let's unload," Clare said.

"This is it?" Jake asked.

"Wait until you see this," Clare said with a smile. She reached through the bars of the fence and slid a brick sideways, revealing another keypad. She pressed her thumb onto the screen and a hidden gate in the fence unlocked. Clare slid the gate open and invited the others to follow her.

"Where are you going, Clare?" Vince asked.

"Come on, you'll see."

As they walked behind the fence, they could now see

that the brick wall behind the transformers was actually two angled walls that had the appearance of one wall when viewed from beyond the fence. They walked between the two diagonal walls where they could now see the doorway to the safe house apartment. Clare locked the gate and concealed the keypad with the false brick.

"Very clever," Dr. Lejour remarked. "But you know, there's no visible gate in that fence."

"That's the point," Clare said. "If you have a gate, it can be broken into."

"But, wouldn't someone wonder about that? How would a serviceman get to the transformers?"

"Hmm, guess they didn't think of that," Clare said.

"You'd better tell them to put a dummy lock on one side, Clare," Rocco said laughing. "Keep looking, Doc. If you notice something, odds are someone like Hoffman would too."

They entered the door and climbed a staircase up one floor. Inside the apartment, Clare pointed out its security features, such as reinforced walls to withstand explosive blasts, and emergency exits through submarine type hatches, one in the ceiling leading to the roof and then a fire escape, and another in the floor leading to a tunnel that crossed the street.

Clare programmed the keypads for all their fingerprints, even Dr. Lejour's. Rocco encouraged the team to take advantage of the secure location to rest.

"We need to be sharp tomorrow," he reminded them all.

"We may not get a chance like this again." Looking at Dr. Lejour he added, "Focused minds–promise." Rocco moved toward his room, then turned, saying, "Oh, I've spoken with an agent at the hospital. Dr. Schroeder is doing well and will be going home tomorrow." Looking back at Dr. Lejour he added, "We need to get you home too, Doc. If you wouldn't mind staying here tomorrow while we go to the bridge, then we can arrange to get you off the case and out of the city after that."

"I'm perfectly fine, agent. No rush."

Everyone settled in for the night, Jake and Vince taking a small room with two cots. Jake was looking at a local street map on his laptop as Vince watched over his shoulder.

"Looking for pizza?" Vince asked.

"No," Jake chuckled. "Actually, my father's synagogue is near here."

"Oh yeah?"

"When I was assigned to this case in New York, I had this weird concern that I might bump into him. Now, I kind of hope I do."

"Really? Why?"

"I feel I owe him an apology."

"What for?"

"For not respecting him, not respecting what he did. You know he's a rabbi?"

"Yeah, you told me once."

"Probably didn't tell you what I said to him. It's just, his religion—it always seemed to me that it was just good-natured advice, advice put down by men a long time ago, old men telling young men what to do, what not to do, what to eat. I never did like being told what to do. But, with everything we've seen... I don't know. There are a lot of unanswered questions out there, and while I may not agree with his answers, he's not totally off-the-wall. I think he deserves his son's respect in any case. He's a smart, reasonable man. I'd just like to tell him that."

"Then why don't you? You said he's right around the corner."

"Maybe I will," Jake replied. "So, what do you make of all this stuff: near-death experiences, minds in other dimensions?"

"Well, I've always believed we have souls that live on," Vince replied. "I was brought up with the idea but never gave it much thought."

"You go to church?"

"Yeah, when I'm upstate with my folks, I go to Mass with them."

"But not here?"

"No, not too often."

"I don't know," Jake said, looking out the small window across the Manhattan buildings. "It just seems so contrived."

"What's that?"

"Religion: man-made rules, man-made customs and traditions, all conveniently given the stamp of approval from God. Just accept it all on faith and don't think."

"You go to synagogue?" Vince asked.

"Not for a long time. A few years ago I was home for Thanksgiving and my mother was talking to some of my nieces and nephews about what heaven and hell were like, describing an eternal banquet where no one can bend their elbows. In hell, everyone is starving, but in heaven, everyone feeds their neighbor and they're full and happy. I'd heard that story before, but this time I decided to make a snappy remark. I said how people born without arms can still eat, they just eat right off the plate, or maybe use their feet. My Dad said I was missing the point as usual, and wasn't listening. I said something back, and he told me to leave and not come back until I'd learned some respect. I haven't been back since."

"This is the time to go," Vince suggested. "I mean, you're thinking of it, we're right here, just do it."

"You know, I will. Next time we have a break. Thanks."

"Make sure you wear your Kevlar though. You never know, maybe Hoffman put this into your head to trap you."

"You're always thinking," Jake said with a grin. The two heard a conversation starting in the living room. "Sounds like another lesson from the professor. Maybe we should sit in?" Jake suggested, and they joined the others sitting around Dr. Lejour.

"There will be signs of your alignment with the natural order," the doctor explained. "You'll develop a sixth sense about each other, when one of you is nearby or when you're in danger. Animals will seem to be unafraid of you."

"Animals?" Rocco asked with a chuckle. "What good is that?"

"I'm speaking of signs," Dr. Lejour clarified. "I'm not saying this will help you per se, just that you'll notice it; it will seem odd. When you do notice it, you can feel more confident that you are within the natural order."

"Where Hoffman can't reach us?" Vince asked.

"That's right."

"And where we read each other's minds?"

"Don't expect to read minds," Dr. Lejour clarified. "It's more like looking over each other's shoulder–seeing what they see."

"That's just what Hoffman said," Clare remarked.

"It's not easy, I know. You must be patient. Do you know the origin of the word, 'patience?' It comes from the Latin for suffering. That's why we doctors refer to the sick people we treat as patients. Every goal that is truly worthwhile will require patience to achieve. In other words, it will entail suffering."

Life entailed suffering, whether one was patient or not, or so it seemed to Rocco. If one were impatient, would there be less suffering? When one suffered, did that automatically make one patient? Vague feelings or insights were loose cannons as far as Rocco was concerned. They could be pointed in any random direction. A sleepless night could make a person irritable, and that irritable mood could affect their judgment. It was by suppressing those underlying feelings that a person could be rational and consistent. Indulging those feelings as though they were supernatural insights seemed to Rocco to be the epitome of recklessness. He began to feel hopeless and alone, and thought that none of this was going to help him. A sudden uneasiness flashed through him as he thought of his next confrontation with Hoffman.

"Resist fear," Dr. Lejour continued, "but be careful of pride, the tendency to make your own order. The will to love is a surrender, and you cannot be proud and surrender at the same time."

"Surrender, Doc? Pretty poor battle cry," Rocco said as Marcus chuckled in agreement.

"I don't mean surrender to Hoffman, but to the natural order. Be passive to that order. Let it assist you and move you, like the current in a river propelling you downstream. Align yourselves with the natural order and its strength will be manifested in you. Then, no matter what happens, you cannot lose."

THE GEORGE WASHINGTON

17

*T*he next morning, the gray steel of the George Washington Bridge could be glimpsed between the passing trees as Rocco drove through the wooded slopes of the New Jersey Palisades. Rocco's team arrived at the upper level entry point an hour before Hoffman was to be there. Rocco, Clare, and Marcus parked behind a line of cones on one side of the traffic approaching the tollbooths, while Jake and Vince parked on the other side.

Of the five of them, Marcus was the only one that had so far avoided all contact with Hoffman. Rocco stressed the importance of Marcus maintaining this anonymity. "Never look at him. Look at us, and get your information from us," Rocco said. "Keep us honest. We start doing anything unusual, pull us back." Then over the radio he advised Jake and Vince as well. "Marcus is our anchor. He's the only one Hoffman's never gotten to. So we all touch base with him and keep our heads straight." All agreed as they waited for Hoffman, watching the morning traffic crawl by.

"I've seen three faces already that were twitching," Clare reported. "Does everyone in New York have this app?"

Rocco glanced at Jake and Vince. "Everything okay over there?" he asked on the radio.

"A-okay," Vince responded.

"Would they know if it wasn't?" Marcus asked. The three shared dubious looks.

"They're good now," Rocco said, looking for reassurance from the other two. "Let's keep an eye on them though," he added. Rocco watched the cars inch along in the lane beside them. Out of about thirty cars, he noticed two more drivers with twitching faces. They both twitched as they looked up at a sign reading, "George Washington Bridge" and "EZ Pass." Was it a coincidence or were those words a trigger? *A trigger to what?* Rocco thought, looking at the line of cars winding around the on-ramp to the bridge.

Off to the side of them, a chipmunk scampered along one of the bridge's massive suspension cables anchored into the solid rock of the Palisades cliffs and stretching to the top of one of the towers. From that dizzying height, additional supporting cables trailed down to the traffic far below. Between them, sea birds flew. On the pinnacle of that gray tower, a Peregrine Falcon stood, gazing down at the circling birds.

The falcon's head moved very slowly, following the flight

patterns of gulls near the lower level of the bridge. Its natural order was that of predator, an extraordinary predator. With piercing eyes, it followed the circling prey below it, taking in the data. Its brain, programmed to select the weakest, most vulnerable bird, processed the information and delivered a set course of action. Its head sank between its shoulders as its upper body leaned down over the edge of the tower. In a fluid continuation of the head and shoulder movement, the bird slid silently off the tower, slicing through the air toward the gull below. Without thought or choice, the program was executed with fluid precision, adapting constantly to the ever-changing position of the prey. The muscles of its wings made minute adjustments controlling wing shape and contour, minimizing drag and air resistance as it dove. The fastest living creature on Earth, the Peregrine travelled with the speed and accuracy of a guided missile as it struck the unsuspecting gull.

A second before impact, the falcon brought its feet forward from a tucked to an anterior position, pointing its talons at the gull's neck. The only thing nearby birds would notice was a cloud of feathers drifting in the air as the falcon blurred by, banking out of its dive to flap its way back to its nest, carrying its limp victim in its claws.

Above, on the bridge, traffic continued to crawl, commuters stopping and starting, making their way to work, unaware of the timeless drama of predator and prey that had just taken place below them.

Back at the entry to the bridge, on a small ledge of rock above the tollbooths, stood another predator, Hoffman. He looked down at the line of cars with the methodical intensity of the falcon, scanning the drivers, seeking out his prey. Standing behind two small trees, he had not yet been seen.

Jake and Vince had climbed up a slope outside their vehicle, now at the same level as Hoffman, about one hundred yards away. Rocco, Marcus, and Clare had also left their car and were making their way across the traffic toward the tollbooths. Rocco's eyes darted from the booths, to the cars, to the drivers, to Jake and Vince, and back to the booths. Was it the power of suggestion, or could he feel Hoffman watching him? Whichever it was, he began to wonder if they shouldn't have stationed themselves on higher ground.

"Do you see him?" Jake asked.

"No, but he must be here somewhere," Rocco answered, as he flashed his badge to a curious tollbooth operator. Alongside a lane of passing cars, they looked into all the booths in either direction, seeing nothing but toll collectors carrying out their normal duties. Rocco moved to the other side and scrutinized the surrounding terrain.

"We need a higher vantage point," Rocco announced to the others, glancing briefly toward the tree behind which Hoffman was standing. Hoffman was motionless, his eyes fixed on Rocco, unblinking, as if at any moment, like the Peregrine, he would slip off his perch, and with fierce, silent precision, come in for the kill. "Jake, Vince, we'll position ourselves opposite you," Rocco reported through the radio, as he returned to the other side of the booths.

The three moved back through the traffic, returned to their car, and drove to a high point on the other side of the road. Jake and Vince settled into their location, sitting on a flat rock that overlooked the line of traffic. Meanwhile, Hoffman began to move. He climbed down the hill and made his way toward the nearest tollbooth below, his path obscured by a line of brush between him and the agents. Passing through the toll booth, he walked into a line of cars then stopped and looked up at Jake and Vince.

"There he is!" Jake called out, pointing to Hoffman who was calmly looking up at him.

"Don't look at him," Vince whispered over to Jake, as he drew his weapon and started down the hill. "Come on!"

Jake continued to stand on the hill, looking at Hoffman who stood quietly in front of a line of honking cars, staring steadily at Jake. Vince grabbed his arm and pulled him down the rocky slope to the level of the road. "Don't forget what this guy does," Vince urged Jake, finally getting him to turn away from Hoffman. By this time Rocco, Clare, and Marcus were dashing between cars and only four lanes away from Hoffman, about to descend on him, when he quickly moved from the lane and ran up the hill beside the road. Jake and Vince joined Rocco and the others as they pursued him to the crest of the hill, only to see him slip into a waiting car that sped away. They stood on the crest of the hill, watching the car disappear down a side street and out of sight.

"Now what?" Vince asked.

"Did you see him do anything?" Rocco asked.

"I didn't realize it was him until he stood in the middle of the road, looking up at me," Jake admitted. "I don't know where he came from or what he might have been doing."

"He wanted us to see him," Rocco concluded, "but why?"

As they looked down the slope at the morning commuters, they realized that they were no longer crawling, but standing still. The entire line of cars, from before the toll booths to as far as they could see, was immobile. They ran along the ramp and onto the bridge. Moving between the stopped cars, many of which were beginning to honk their horns, they saw the point at which the traffic had stopped. Oddly, there was no accident. The vehicles in front were stopped and their drivers were standing outside their cars.

"What's going on?" Rocco asked one of the standing commuters, who promptly pointed up to a sign over his head.

"Can't you read?"

The sign merely listed the lanes for different roadways. "What about it?" Rocco asked the man.

"The bridge is closed for the mayor. He must be passing through or something." The man's face twitched as he turned from the agents and began pacing back and forth beside his car.

"That's not what the sign says," Rocco began, then Clare tapped his shoulder.

"It's happening on the other side too," Clare pointed out.

"That's not all," Jake added, looking down at his phone. "Traffic's stopped on all the bridges around the city."

"But why?" Vince asked. "A demonstration like the stock exchange?"

"A demonstration of how he can affect elections," Rocco suggested. "Remember what Silverman's son said? His father was afraid this ability could be used to control elections." Pointing to the crowd around them, he added, "They think the mayor's responsible for this. By the end of the morning, they'll all hate him."

"But, the mayor's not up for reelection for years," Vince said.

"Like you said Vince, it's another demonstration," Rocco replied. "Reporters will hear similar stories from everyone, and even though the mayor's office will deny it, people will figure there must be some truth to it. Instant scandal with a big drop in the polls—what better demonstration of the power of your propaganda?"

"There's a million ways you could do this," Jake added, "ways that aren't so obvious. He wanted this to be obvious, to show off. Like his standing in the middle of the road back there."

One of the front cars began moving again after Marcus had spoken to the driver. He went to the next car and called out to the others, "We can get this side moving, anyway."

"Get the word out to the police and the press," Rocco told Vince and Jake. "Tell them to send out a message over the emergency broadcast system: this was a city-wide prank, someone hacked into car radios or something." Motioning to Clare to join him as he approached another driver, he added, "Now, how do we stop the next one?"

"How do you break over a million subliminal connections?" Clare asked.

"At the source," Rocco answered, looking at the New York skyline stretching down along the Hudson River. "It's time for us to have a demonstration of our own."

"A demonstration?"

"A trap," Rocco answered with a smirk.

While thousands of commuters were standing beside their cars on New York's bridges, cursing the mayor's name under their breath, Spinosa was smiling at Hoffman in a small warehouse not far from the George Washington Bridge. After speaking on his phone, Spinosa reported, "My boys just hit five targets without one police response. Every unit is occupied with the city-wide traffic jam. Talk about easy money! What else have you got up your sleeve?"

"Much more than that, my friend," Hoffman replied. "This was still just a demonstration. Do you have a laptop?"

"Yeah, here."

"Search these words, 'New York rabbi, son, and FBI,'" Hoffman said. Spinosa typed into his laptop, then turned the screen toward Hoffman.

"Here you go, local rabbi's son appointed to FBI. Abraham Steinman, his son's name is, 'Jacob.' Is that what you're looking for?"

"Is there a photo of the son?"

"Yeah, here's one."

"Perfect, that's him. Print that and give it to your men. Have them stake out that rabbi's synagogue and wait for him to come."

"When will he be there?"

"Soon. Have your men there around the clock, then take him out."

The man nodded. "Those words: son, rabbi—did you get a tip or something?"

"Something like that."

"So, we take him out. Then what?"

"One thing at a time," Hoffman said, looking out one of the warehouse windows. "That's how you rid yourself of an infestation, one rat at a time."

KNOW BEFORE WHOM YOU STAND

18

*I*t took the agents the rest of the morning to make their way back to the safe house, crawling through the traffic jam near the bridge. They met together in the living room, considering how they might catch up with Hoffman again. Vince reported that the driver they had followed the other day was still being trailed by police officers, but he had not led them to Hoffman yet. Clare shared an update from an agent working with an organized crime task force. He had found a link between that driver and the Spinosa family and was picking up known associates for questioning. Dr. Lejour was sitting off to the side of the group, quietly listening, while Jake paced back and forth in front of the kitchenette.

"What's on your mind?" Rocco asked, coming alongside Jake.

"Oh," Jake answered quietly, "just thinking."

"About?"

"Well, I was thinking, maybe this evening, if we're still in a bit of a holding pattern, my father's right around the corner from here. I just thought I might see him."

"While we're on a case?" Rocco asked.

"I know, but, it would be quick. Just to touch base. We haven't talked. It's just—I'm right here, you know? I'd be back in an hour."

"I could go with him, Chief," Vince offered, listening in on their conversation. "Then he wouldn't be alone."

"That's not necessary, Vince," Jake protested.

"No, I think it is," Rocco replied. "In fact, you said he's right around the corner?"

"Yeah, a few blocks."

"Then we'll all go."

"No, really."

"It's fine," Rocco insisted, "I'm sure everyone would like a little fresh air. We'll give you your space, but we'll stick together. We can't give Hoffman the chance to shave us off one by one."

"That's just what I was saying, right?" Vince added. "Maybe Hoffman's trying to get you alone."

"You haven't contacted your father, have you?" Rocco asked.

"Of course not," Jake answered. "I was just going to catch him at the synagogue after services tonight."

"Fine, Vince, you'll go in with Jake. Marcus, Clare, and

I will keep watch outside."

That evening, the team left Dr. Lejour back at the safe house once again, as they escorted Jake to his father's synagogue. It was dusk when they arrived at the brick structure, dwarfed by the taller office buildings on either side. An alleyway on one side led to a parking area behind the synagogue. Vince and Jake left the others outside the front doors while they entered and stood in the back of the crowd. Vince craned his neck looking throughout the interior, along the walls and ceiling.

"You ever been in a synagogue?" Jake whispered.

"Once," Vince replied. "Long time ago."

"It's been a while for me too." Jake added, scanning the interior. His eyes rested on a lamp hanging from the ceiling, a flame flickering within red glass. Beneath it, a scroll was being lifted out of an ornate wooden cabinet. "That's the tabernacle, the ark of the Torah." A procession, led by his father, moved from the cabinet carrying the scroll that would be read from that evening. All the surrounding people were singing, and Jake seemed to mouth the words as the procession went by. "I know what they're singing," Jake whispered to Vince. "When I was little, I used to think they were singing for my Dad, as he walked in the procession." He smiled, then looked at Vince. "Then I realized it was the scroll everyone was singing about, God's words. They were singing to God, not my Dad," he chuckled.

The two watched and listened as the scroll was laid down. "I was always proud to be there," Jake whispered.

"Where?"

"Here, at synagogue. I was proud to be the rabbi's son. Proud to pray." Jake stared across the rows of covered heads before them. "That was a long time ago."

Vince looked at the wooden doors and ornate curtain behind which the scrolls were kept. Above the curtain were letters carved in Hebrew.

"It says, 'Remember the law of Moses,'" Jake explained, noticing Vince's interest, "and under that, 'Know before whom you stand.' I used to ask my dad who it was we stood before and he'd say, 'God.' He'd point to that red light and say that was there to remind you of God's eternal presence. I decided it was all symbolism. But, now I'm thinking, what if religion, these rituals and prayers, aren't ends in themselves, but a means to an end."

"What end?"

Jake looked up at the hanging light for a moment then replied, "Perception."

"Perception?"

"Yeah, of that other dimension, that place Hoffman's exploiting, where we're connected to each other, and to who knows what else."

"God?"

"Maybe that's what people call, 'God,' maybe it's this

other-dimensional experience."

Vince tilted his head and raised an eyebrow. "I don't know, Jake," he said. "I think God is God to most people, not some other-dimensional thing."

"Maybe," Jake replied, quietly chuckling again, "but it's made me think." The two were silent throughout the remainder of the services. Afterwards, while people were filing out, Jake's father was in the back changing. Jake told Vince he was going to talk to his father privately, and would meet up with him outside.

"I'll be with the others out front," Vince said, after looking around the synagogue again and seeing nothing suspicious. Jake made his way to a room in the back to find his father.

"Yes, what is it?" his father asked, hearing the sound of someone approaching.

Jake turned the corner and stopped at the doorway, his hands slightly outstretched. His father looked at him in silence.

"Rabbi," Jake said. His father leaned back in astonishment. It had been many years since Jake had called him that. His father frowned slightly, then began to move toward him, stopping as he noticed the corner of Jake's gun along the edge of his jacket.

"You bring a gun here?"

"I'm sorry, Dad," Jake said as he removed his gun and

holster, placing them on a small table.

"That's all right. I know, you're FBI. You have to carry a gun, but..."

"No, I'm sorry," Jake repeated. "I'm sorry. That's what I came to say."

"Jacob," his father said quietly as he came to embrace him. They stood for a few moments together, then the rabbi motioned to the chairs by his desk. For half an hour, the two talked, smiling and laughing, the pauses between the words becoming longer and less awkward.

"Can you come to the house?" his father asked him.

"No," Jake answered, "not now. I have to get back soon. When we're done with this case we're working on, I'll call."

"You're working here in Manhattan?" Jake gave his father a subdued nod. "I know, you cannot say." They stood and embraced again. "It was good to see you, Jacob. Thank you."

"Good to see you too, Dad," Jake said, and he made his way out a back door. Closing the door behind him, he started across the parking lot behind the synagogue toward the side alley. The air smelled damp and droplets of fog collected on his cheeks as he stepped into the darkness. He breathed in the air and let out a long, low, sigh. "Thanks Vince," he muttered quietly to himself, and he continued through the dark parking area. The blaring of car horns echoed down the alley lighted with the soft glow from the street. He was making his way there when another sound rose from the void alongside him. It was the crisp sound of footsteps, very near in the darkness, echoing his own, though at a slightly faster pace. He had seen no one in the lit periphery of the parking area; there was no one passing through. These were the steps of someone walking alongside him, clearly, some-one who had been waiting for him. Jake put his hand onto his waist and paused, looking back toward his father's office where his sidearm was still on the table. There were more steps now, on the opposite side of him and behind him, the alley still a good fifty yards away. Jake began to run.

Meanwhile, outside the synagogue, the others were sit-ting on a short wall in front of an adjacent office building.

"Why didn't you stay with him?" Rocco asked Vince as he checked his watch again.

"He said he wanted to speak to his father alone," Vince replied, then added hurriedly, "It has been quite a while though. Why don't we go in and check?"

Rocco had a nagging feeling that he had forgotten something, but could not remember what it was. It grew in intensity, as if it was something of great importance, then, like a person lashing out against an incessant irritat-ing noise, he snapped, "You should have stayed with him, Vince! You and Clare go in the front. Marcus and I will go around back."

Rocco walked briskly around the side of the synagogue toward the alley, and then began to run, Marcus running in stride alongside him. At the same time, Jake's father came out of the front of the synagogue, then turned to lock the door.

"Wait," Vince said to Clare, "that's the rabbi!"

"Jake's father?"

"Yeah."

"Then where's Jake?" As the two hurried over to speak to the rabbi, Rocco and Marcus were approaching the end of the alley and the dark area beyond. "I'll take left," Marcus said as he ran to the corner of the synagogue and stopped up against the wall. He motioned toward the opposite wall, then whispered, "Rocco, take the other side." Rocco didn't answer, but instead, kept running toward the dark area behind the lit alleyway. That nagging sense Rocco had of forgetting something had now become like a raw nerve, a compulsion, driving him like the crack of whip behind his ear. Without breaking his stride, he drew his weapon and ran into the darkness.

"Rocco!" Marcus called out after him.

Rocco slowed to a walk to give his eyes time to adjust to the darkness. Out of the blackness a figure emerged, a man in a suit, running toward him, not fifty feet in front of him. The sound of running footsteps echoed throughout the space before him. He was straining to make out the face of the running man when there were explosions of light and sound from both sides and the figure fell to the ground. Rocco's ears were ringing. Marcus tapped him on the shoulder and fixed a light to his hand gun, exposing several men running away from the scene.

"You check him, I'll follow them," Marcus yelled, running after the men who were making their way toward the other side of the synagogue. By this time, Clare and Vince had run around the corner of the alley, having heard the sound of gunfire, adding more light to the scene with their flashlights.

"Jake," Rocco cried as he recognized the man lying on the pavement. "Jake, can you hear me?"

"Yeah, I'm here."

"Are you hit?"

"Not sure," Jake answered, straining to breathe.

"You wore your vest," Rocco said with relief as he ran his hand under Jake's jacket checking for injuries.

"Yeah, Vince made me."

Marcus rounded a parked car into a shower of gunfire from the men who had ambushed Jake. Taking cover, he returned fire, hitting two of the assailants, while a third ran off. Clare, Vince, Jake, and Rocco joined Marcus as he approached the two men he had hit lying on the ground. Rocco kicked the gun away from one and turned him to cuff him. Vince and Marcus discovered that the second man was already dead. The group gathered around the survivor.

"So, talk to us," Rocco demanded.

"I was just taking a walk," the man answered.

"How will it go for you when they find out you screwed up?" Rocco replied.

"Hey, I need a doctor. You gotta take me to a doctor."

"You think you'll be safe there? You don't think he can reach you in a hospital?" Rocco asked him.

"Reach me? Look who's talking."

"What do you mean by that?" Rocco asked him, wondering if perhaps this man had seen Hoffman overpower him at the warehouse. "We're not afraid of Hoffman." Rocco said looking down at the man.

"It's not Hoffman you have to worry about," the man said chuckling.

"You got something to say, spit it out!" Vince snapped.

"Get me an ambulance. And I want a deal."

"Talk first," Vince said, pressing the man's shoulder to the ground, eliciting a sustained groan.

"How did you know we'd be here?" Rocco asked. "How did you know? If you expect any kind of deal, you'd better start talking."

"Hoffman told us. He said you'd be here."

"When?"

"This morning."

"That's a lie!" Rocco shouted. "Hoffman was at the George Washington this morning."

"That's when he told us. He'd just come from the bridge. He also said we'd have nothing to worry about, that no one would be coming after us," the man added. "I'm saying, you've been sold out."

"Sold out? By who?" Rocco demanded.

"Beats me. But Hoffman has an inside man, someone in the government. I know that much, and I'm the one that told you. Remember that. I want a deal."

Rocco motioned to Vince to join him, Clare, and Jake, while Marcus guarded the man on the ground.

"You think there's something to that?" Jake whispered to Rocco. "You think Hoffman's getting inside information?"

"It would explain why he seems to be a step ahead of us all the time," Rocco answered.

"So, what do we do?" Clare asked.

"This could work to our advantage," Rocco said. "We know this guy will play it both ways and sell us out. Just follow my lead and act like you know what I'm talking about." Rocco and the others returned to the man on the ground. "One more of those near-death treatments and I'll be untouchable," Rocco said in a slightly louder tone, "then there'll be no threat, inside man or no inside man."

As Rocco finished speaking, the sound of an ambulance grew louder and soon echoed off the alley walls. As the man was strapped onto a stretcher, Rocco stood just behind him and spoke quietly, but still loud enough for the man to hear. "If Hoffman does have an inside man, it won't matter, because even the Bureau doesn't know about 91st and Park."

The paramedics loaded the man into the ambulance and drove out the alley.

"What were you thinking, coming out the back door alone?" Rocco accosted Jake once the ambulance was out of sight.

"I wasn't thinking. I always used to leave that way. My gun! My gun's in there."

"Don't worry," Clare assured him, "you're father's still here. He'll let us in. Did you call him, or anyone else to say you were coming here?"

"No. I just told you guys."

"So, how did they know?" Clare asked.

"He was looking at you," Vince said to Jake. "I told you not to look at him."

"It was only a few seconds," Jake protested.

Rocco shook his head. "He probably got background information on us from his inside man," Rocco said. "He found your father's location nearby and staked it out. But," he added, looking at Vince, "just to be safe, no one makes any more eye contact with him. Agreed?"

Everyone nodded.

"So, what's with 91st and Park?" Clare asked.

"Yeah," Jake added, "what's that about?"

"Let's get your gun, Jake," Rocco answered, "then I'll tell you about 91st and Park."

91ST AND PARK

19

*T*he following morning, the agents and Marcus picked up some equipment at a medical supply store, "props," as Rocco called them, and drove to 91st and Park Avenue. The place Rocco had referred to was a vintage four-story building that was part of a real estate sting operation the Bureau had recently worked. Rocco had arranged to get the keys for the day. The building, the second in from Park Avenue, was still owned by the bureau and as such, was unoccupied. The first level was once a retail store, with apartments and offices in the three floors above. There was a homeless man who had been coming and going through a side window. Rocco gave him some money for breakfast and told him he had to leave. The group entered the first floor space through a side door in an adjacent alley. Rocco slid a short dividing wall to the center of the space, then pushed a sofa behind it so that the end stuck out just a bit from behind the divider.

"Bring me those poles, Marcus," Rocco said, motioning to the IV poles they had gotten at the medical supply store. He hung IV bags from the poles, and connected tubing which ran onto the sofa behind the divider.

"What's all this?" Vince asked.

"Bait," Rocco answered, looking out the front window.

"You're making it look like we're doing that shock therapy?"

"Near-death experiences, yeah."

"We're just faking it though, right?" Vince clarified.

"Yes," Rocco chuckled, "It's a challenge. If he's all about power, like the priest says, just the thought that we're onto his game should tear him up."

"So," Jake asked, "you're trying to lure him here?"

"Basically, yeah."

"And what happens when he gets here, and we don't have the power he has?" Vince asked.

"We'll have the power of surprise."

Marcus was walking around the space, checking the thickness of the walls and shaking his head.

"This is no place to make a stand. These walls are just drywall, low ceiling, only one door out besides the front door, and that goes into a blind alley," Marcus said.

"We won't be in here. Come on." Rocco replied, motioning to the alley door. The group went out into the alley, then climbed a fire escape up to the roof. On the other side of the building, another fire escape led to a parallel alley. The roof was flat with a small brick wall around the edges. Rocco crouched down and moved to the front of the rooftop facing the street. Peering over the brick wall, he could see well down 91st Street. "We'll watch for him here," Rocco said, "then, when we spot him, Marcus, you'll control the rooftop and the four of us will split up and go down both alleys. By the time he gets near the front door, we'll be close enough to hit him with tasers."

"What about his armed guards?" Clare asked.

"Marcus can handle them from here, right Marcus?"

"As long as they're not directly beneath us. I can't see the storefront from here."

The group of five settled down against the brick wall. Marcus was assembling his sniper rifle with a cloth cap on his scope to avoid a telltale sun flash. He also handed out small periscopes, so every angle could be watched. The morning passed by uneventfully.

Clare watched the traffic move through the intersection and the pedestrians pour through the crosswalks at regular intervals. Her eyes were drawn to the large ad on the side of a city bus, and as it passed from view, Hoffman's tall figure appeared standing at the corner.

"I see him," she whispered, as she slid down behind the wall, looking at him now through her mirrored scope. "He's on the southwest corner."

"Got him," Marcus said, peering through the scope on his rifle. "What are our rules of engagement, Rocco?"

"Clear and present danger," he replied, looking down along the line of Marcus' rifle. "Could you make the shot?"

"I could make it. No wind, no passersby. So what exactly constitutes clear and present danger?"

"I'd say you're looking at it," Clare said.

"Hard to prove after the fact with an unarmed man," Rocco said, "especially if we have enemies inside the Bureau. Marcus, you keep eyes on him and watch for any of his hired guns. We'll go down to the alleys."

"He's checking things out," Vince reported, watching through his periscope. "He's only looked over here once. He seems more interested in the building at the corner."

"Wait," Clare said, "he's seen something, no—someone."

"It's that homeless guy we kicked out this morning," Jake noted. Hoffman walked down the sidewalk to a building directly opposite the agents. Hoffman looked at the homeless man, who was sitting with his back against the brick wall, then he looked across the street at the storefront window.

"How long have you been here?" Hoffman asked the man.

"This morning," the man replied, shielding his eyes from the sun as he tried to look up at Hoffman. "They kicked me out."

"Who?"

The man pointed across the street. "In there." Hoffman looked at the man for a few moments, then looked at the storefront window below the agents, the IV poles visible beside the sofa. He looked up at the rooftops adjoining the building.

"Bad news," Marcus said. "He hasn't made our position, but I think he suspects a trap."

"Let's get down to the alleys then," Rocco said. "He may still come across the street."

The agents split up and scrambled down the two fire escapes. Rocco and Clare moved up behind two trash cans at the entrance to their alley, and Jake and Vince stood against the wall at their entrance. Hoffman was speaking on his cell phone. Three men stepped out from different buildings along the street and joined him. Hoffman seemed to be giving them directions after which they left. Hoffman looked across the street again into the storefront. He stepped into the street, stopping between two parked cars and stared intently into the empty store. Rocco stared at Hoffman's face, visible above the hood of an adjacent car, using his periscope. He watched him stare at the decoy, the empty store, straining to see, to analyze, oblivious to Rocco's gaze. Like a matador staring at the bull staring at the cape, Rocco was motionless, awaiting his opponent's move. How different this was from the time at the warehouse, he thought. Now, it was Hoffman who was caught unaware, Rocco who had the power. Was this what the priest had been getting at? "If you want power, seek to have none." Was he telling him to use diversion? Confront without confronting? Lead him to the bait, then strike? He would have to talk to that priest again.

"Don't look at him," Clare reminded him, squeezing his arm. "Just wait for him."

"Any motion yet?" Jake asked over the radio. "We can't see him."

"Negative," Marcus replied. "He's just standing across the street."

"Can we rush him from here?" Vince asked.

"He could have more guns, there's traffic, collaterals," Marcus warned.

"Keep waiting," Rocco ordered. "He'll come to us."

Hoffman looked up and down the block, back into the storefront, then turned suddenly, walking briskly around the corner and out of sight.

"He's gone," Marcus reported.

"We almost had him," Clare said to Rocco, as the two stepped out of the alley. "Who knows when we'll have a chance like that again?" Jake and Vince joined them from the other side.

"Now what?" Vince asked.

"He'll be back," Rocco replied. "He may have suspected

a trap, but he doesn't know for sure. We're still a variable outside his control. That's what brought him here. We brought him here!" he said triumphantly, then muttered under his breath, "I brought you here."

"Still," Vince said, "it's a bit of a bluff, isn't it?"

"Yeah," Jake agreed, "as soon as he finds out we don't have any special power, will he bother with us anymore?"

"Maybe not," Rocco conceded, "but it's safe to say that we know more about his game than just about anyone else. We're probably the only threat to him." Rocco looked down at his phone. "I just got a text from the Bureau. They've gotten new intel from the CIA: they say Hoffman's leaving the country. He's going to lie low for a while in Nicaragua."

"Nicaragua?" Clare asked.

"So they're pulling us off the case?" Jake asked.

"Actually, no," Rocco replied. "The CIA is asking us to stay on. Apparently, we have special authority to work out of the country."

"Ever heard of that before?" Jake asked.

"Never," Rocco answered.

"Something's not right," Clare suggested. "Why is the CIA involved? For all we know, Hoffman's inside man could be in the CIA, not the FBI."

"So do we follow him out of the country? Outside US Jurisdiction? What's our backup?" Jake asked.

"Sounds like a setup," Marcus added.

"Possibly," Rocco answered. "But we had him here," he boasted. "We had him."

Clare leaned in to Rocco's ear and whispered, "Just be sure it's not him that had us."

EPIPHANY

2
0

*T*he team shut down the storefront on 91st street and headed to the friary in the Bronx as Rocco felt the need to speak with Father Joseph again. Dr. Lejour would be there too, and it would be a chance for the group to see him one last time before he left for his home upstate. When they arrived, they found the doctor waiting for them outside the chapel.

"Dr. Lejour," Rocco said as he sat down beside him. "Where is Father Joseph?"

"Father Joseph is in the confessional over there," Dr. Lejour replied, pointing to a small wooden cubicle. "You're all invited to lunch shortly, if you'd like. There's a meeting going on in the conference room, so why don't you all just wait in the chapel?"

Clare led the group in and they took seats along the side and back. Rocco remained outside with Dr. Lejour.

"So what's next?" the doctor asked him.

"We'll be following Hoffman to Nicaragua," Rocco answered.

"Central America?" Dr. Lejour replied. "Well, that's interesting." The doctor kept looking at Rocco, appearing deep in thought. "Agent Rocco," he continued, "you told me before that you lost your parents."

"And my brother," Rocco added quickly, immediately regretting having shared that information. He never brought the topic up to anyone; why now to the doctor, of all people?

"You lost a brother?" Dr. Lejour asked.

"It was a long time ago."

"A long time ago. That doesn't matter much, does it? The loss is with you forever. I lost a sibling too—my sister." The doctor leaned back and stared across the hall. "Their absence is always there. It's like a bad knee or a limp. You may notice it less at certain times, but it's never totally gone, is it?"

Rocco felt the hairs rising on the back of his neck. With a few deep breaths, the reaction was calmed, and he joined the doctor in staring at the wall across the hallway.

"Their absence is always with you, but so is their presence," the doctor concluded.

"You realize that makes no sense," Rocco quipped.

"You're familiar with the Catholic Mass?"

"You kidding? I was an altar boy." Rocco recalled images of himself and his brother kneeling at the altar before the tabernacle, its ornate metal doors covered with a small curtain, lit candles on the altar, the smell of incense rising from the censor beside him. He remembered gazing up at the priest as he raised the Host, lost in the wonder of it all, the priest's vestments, the gold inscriptions, the silence. His momentary wonder would be shattered by a nudge from his brother kneeling beside him, whispering to him to ring the bells. He would nervously comply, hoping his slip-up had not been too noticeable. Every Sunday morning from his childhood was like that one, different times, different experiences, yet all summed up somehow in that one memory.

"Then you know what is meant by the *Real Presence*," Dr. Lejour continued, interrupting Rocco's recollection.

"I know what people believe it to mean."

"But not you?"

"I don't believe a little wafer is God, no."

"Its *essence* is God, present beneath the physical appearance of bread. That is the mystery, the same mystery we have been speaking of regarding hidden dimensions. They are unseen, yet can be perceived, indirectly, as through a mirror. Your brother's essence is still present beneath the appearance of his physical absence, but, as Father Joseph said, you must believe if you are to see him. Your brother, my sister—their physical appearance may be gone, along with their smiles, their warmth, the comfort of their company, but their essence... that is more accessible than ever. Your brother is here with you, right now; believe that."

"A minute ago you didn't even know I had a brother. Now, you know he's here?"

"Yes. Look for him in abstract insights."

"We've been through this," Rocco replied with a sigh. "I need specifics, not vague abstractions."

"Abstract understanding is not vague," Dr. Lejour insisted, "though it is an art." He pointed to a print hanging on the wall next to the confessional. "Art reflects the essence of life. You know, some people define art as simply a statement, a concrete expression." The doctor shook his head. "A two-year-old's tantrum is a statement, but it is not art. Art must do more than relay concretes. It must relay abstracts; it must speak to the soul. Your eyes may see the art, but it is your mind that says, 'I see it!' It's your mind that understands."

"Maybe your mind, Doc, not mine."

"Everyone's mind." He pointed again to the print on the wall. "That's Rembrandt's painting of the Prodigal Son: the Bible story of the repentant son who, after squandering his share of his future inheritance on wild living, falls on hard times and returns, asking to work as a hired hand on his father's estate. His father sees him, runs out to embrace him, and has a feast to celebrate his return. See how Rembrandt used concrete colors to portray a host of abstract concepts—the bliss of homecoming, the tenderness of a father's embrace, forgiveness and contrition, the light of mercy overcoming the darkness of hunger and want. Your brain does the same thing. It uses concrete images to represent abstract concepts in your mind, images like the smell of a home-cooked meal, the view from a bedroom window, the laughter of a loved one. The images are unique for each individual since they are drawn from personal experience and memory. You need to decipher the patterns: why did that memory come to mind, why did I just think that? Learn the patterns, then see what comes to mind."

See what comes to mind? Rocco thought. That was the problem, not the solution. For ten years he had been beating back those memories, tamping them down so that they wouldn't rise up and smother him. How many times had his mood been brought down by a memory rising to the surface? Wasn't that always the case? Didn't everyone have their demons, dark emotions lurking beneath the surface, waiting for an opportunity to take hold?

He had seen so many examples of it during his career: alcoholics, post traumatic stress and abuse victims, hostage situations, returning combat warriors, all had inner demons. The only way to get past suffering was to endure it then forget it. Put it behind you. Lock it up and keep it locked up.

If he had learned anything over the past ten years, it was that control was key. Control what you feel, what you allow to surface. It was the only way to survive. Give in to feelings, to wishful thinking, and you'll be overrun by your own demons.

"You sound like that crazy meteorite girl," Rocco jabbed.

"The girl in South Dakota? Funny you should bring her up. She wasn't crazy, just misunderstood," Dr. Lejour replied, referring to a story several years prior of a sixteen-year-old high school student who believed she could communicate with aliens through a meteorite that had landed on her family's farm. The meteorite itself had drawn a great deal of attention to the small town, bringing groups of reporters, scientists, and astronomy buffs in droves. Once the story of a young girl communicating with aliens had gotten out, the area was overrun with bizarre followers of various alien conspiracy theories. The girl further claimed that a neighbor boy was cured of cancer after touching a piece of the meteorite that she carried around with her. When it was later discovered that the boy was, indeed, cancer-free, the story of an alien cure for cancer went viral. Farms were trampled by the hordes, traffic jams became commonplace, and in response, the girl and her family were shunned by the local community and nearly run out of town.

After the story died down, the incident was largely forgotten, except for a journal the girl had kept of the events. In it, she described her code for understanding the communications she believed she had received. This had been published online as *The Meteorite Girl's Deciphering Code*. Since the girl described the alien communications as coming through abstract concepts in her mind, Dr. Lejour felt her code was applicable to deciphering all abstract insights.

"Misunderstood, huh?" Rocco replied. "Well, misunderstood or not, you said the images that come to mind from abstract concepts are different for each person, so how could this girl's deciphering code help anyone but her?"

"She discovered some basic patterns among abstract concepts. For instance, just as there are three primary colors: red, yellow, and blue, she felt there were three primary abstracts: love, justice, and truth. This fact can help you start to understand your own insights. If you think about it, everything is contained in those three abstract notions."

"Love, justice, and..."

"Love, justice, and truth. Remember them."

"Pretty limited, Doc."

"Limitations depend upon your point of view," Dr. Lejour replied. "Answer this riddle: how do you use fifty feet of fence to enclose the largest area of land?"

"A riddle?" Rocco grumbled. How he despised riddles.

"My last one, I promise."

"You'd make a circle," Rocco answered with a sigh.

"Of what circumference?"

"Fifty feet."

"No, you'd make a tight circle of fence around yourself and call the land you stood on, *outside*. Then, it would be the rest of the Earth that was enclosed."

"Cute. That clears everything up," Rocco quipped,

rolling his eyes. It was the phenomenon of other dimensions, the doctor explained. That was how something could seem to be contained, yet open up into the vast expanse of another dimension.

"Look at the light area in that painting," Dr. Lejour continued. "It appears to be surrounded by darkness, smothered by it, but in fact, it's the other way around. It is the darkness that is enclosed by the light. The smaller area of light is *outside*, because it is the doorway to love, a vast expanse that the darkness has no access to. Abstract understanding in your mind may seem limited compared to the immediate concretes all around you, but it is *outside* the world, a doorway to a reality so vast it dwarfs the entire universe. It is the doorway to love, the natural order. It's there in your mind that your brother speaks to you. Like I said, you will still apply concrete images to abstract understanding—sights, sounds, smells from the past that are associated with those abstracts—the dappled sunlight sprinkled through the back yard, a moment from the past when you and your brother sat there one sunny afternoon."

"We didn't have a back yard. We sat on the roof."

"Okay then, when a roof comes to mind, that is your brain associating whatever it can with the insight your mind has just received. So, when concrete images arise in your thoughts, the real question is, what is the abstract understanding that led to those images? If it is a memory associated with a loved one, what is the overall sense of the memory? Don't be fixated on the concrete, like a patient with schizophrenia, who, when asked, 'What brought you to the hospital today?' says, 'a cab.' Consider the underlying abstracts. Remember: love, justice, truth. As with the fence riddle, what appears to be limiting is in fact the most limitless thing imaginable—a mystical communion of minds. Let your brother lead you to it, and you will never be alone, and never be overpowered by evil again."

Rocco sighed quietly. "Okay, Doc," he said finally.

"Here's Father Joseph now," Dr. Lejour pointed out. "You wanted to ask him something?"

Father Joseph came out of the confessional and started down the hall.

"Father," Rocco called out as he ran to him.

"Yes?"

"I'd like to clarify something with you." The priest stopped and turned to Rocco. "I think I understand what you were telling us the other day, about not aligning our minds with Hoffman's."

"Good," the priest answered, then turned to continue on his way.

"Wait, Father, I'd just like to be sure of something." The priest stopped again. "So, as long as we don't confront Hoffman directly, we'll be safe. Is that right? Use diversion, distraction, flank him, come at him from the side?"

"Better not to come at him at all."

"Not an option for us, Father. It's our job."

"Yes," the priest nodded with a shrug, "well a glancing blow is better than a direct blow. But maybe you should stop trying to beat him at his game."

"How should I beat him then? Tell me."

"With love." Rocco cringed at the answer. While it was consistent with all the priest had said previously, Rocco had hoped for something different. Having lured Hoffman into a trap earlier that day, he had started to feel in control. He thought the tide was turning. "Something holds you down," the priest continued. "If a cord ties a bird to the ground, it cannot fly. Thick or thin, unless the cord is broken, it cannot fly."

"What holds me down?"

The priest looked at Rocco for a few moments. "Anger," he said finally, nodding his head at Rocco. "Anger is a perversion of courage, as lust is a perversion of love. The bravest of men have no anger. Foolhardy men are often filled with anger, driven and controlled by it."

"I'm no fool, Father."

"Aren't we all fools at times?" The priest turned and opened the door to a small adjacent room. "Be the light in the darkness," he added, closing the door behind him.

The others came out of chapel, following Dr. Lejour to the dining room for lunch.

"What was that about?" Clare asked as she came up behind Rocco.

"I have no idea." Rocco said.

"Then why don't you ask him?" Clare asked, nudging him in the ribs. Shaking his head in resignation, Rocco tapped on the door the priest had gone through and opened it. Beyond the doorway, it was dark, except for the flickering light from several candles along the front wall. Rocco thought he could see the priest kneeling. Not wanting to interrupt him during prayer, he took a seat in the back of the narrow room, which appeared to be a small side chapel. He watched the candle flames as they waved back and forth, and breathed in the smell of the wax and burning wicks. He became mesmerized by the flames. Different scenarios presented themselves to him of confrontations with Hoffman, but the flames seemed to seduce him, leading him back to the silence of that moment. He glanced at the priest again, but could not see his face. He was kneeling on the floor with his head down in front of him, his hood drawn over it.

Looking past the priest again to the flames, Rocco noted an odd sensation, as if there were someone directly beside him. It was a comforting sensation, like gazing out over some beautiful scenery beside a close friend. The urgency that had driven him to talk to the priest was gone. For that moment, at least, he was content to sit there in silence, thinking of nothing as he stared at the flames.

After ten minutes, the priest was still kneeling in the center of the aisle. *He could be there for hours*, Rocco thought, trying to remember how exactly he had imagined Father Joseph helping him. As he looked back toward the priest, he saw lights he had not noticed before, lights that seemed to be moving on the floor by the priest. Due to a slight breeze in the chapel, the candle flames in the front of the room flickered and waved. Rocco noticed that the lights on the floor swayed in unison with them. They seemed to be a reflection of the candles' flames on the floor beneath Father Joseph. But that wouldn't be possible unless... he was off the floor. Was he levitating? It was dark and the flickering light distorted all the images with shadows, such that his eyes could easily be fooled. He stood up and began to move closer to the priest, then stopped suddenly, turned, and bolted out of the chapel.

MYSTICISM

2
1

*R*occo trotted down the hall to join the others in the dining room. Clare noticed his face as he walked into the room and came over beside him.

"What is it, John?"

"Can you come outside with me for a minute?" Rocco asked her. The two climbed a short staircase that led to a rooftop courtyard. They closed the door to the stairs and sat on a short wall crossing the roof.

"What's up, John?" Clare asked.

"I thought I saw something."

"In that room?"

Rocco nodded. He could tell her, he thought, but then, no. She might make too much of it. It was probably the light playing tricks on him. "It was nothing," he said, shifting his eyes about the rooftop.

"Nothing? That's why you wanted to talk?"

Rocco let his gaze rest on Clare for several moments. "Have you ever... You believe everything Lejour says, don't you?"

"Most of it. Why? Don't you?"

"No. No, I don't."

"Why not?"

"Why not? Because it's not real!" Rocco declared. He stood up and began pacing back and forth.

"What do you mean, it's not real?"

"I mean... people hallucinate all the time. People see things, things that aren't there. It doesn't prove that they exist. It just means they're hallucinating."

"What did you see?"

"I told you, nothing," Rocco repeated. Clare frowned at him. "Okay," said Rocco, "what if it's like your hallucinations the other day, something Hoffman put into my head?"

"What was it?"

Rocco stopped pacing. "It looked like the priest was... off the ground."

"Levitating?"

Rocco nodded, then began pacing again.

"Well, that's nothing like my hallucinations," Clare said. "Why would Hoffman make you see that?"

"I don't know. It's just too convenient. Why now?" Rocco continued. "Why haven't I seen anything like this before?"

Clare looked at Rocco closely for several moments. "I

worked this case once," she began, "where this kid's father had disappeared a couple years earlier. Everyone had assumed he was dead, but it turned out he was alive and working a scam with stolen identities and bogus social security claims. When the kid was brought in to corroborate the mother's ID of the father in a lineup, he wouldn't go into the room. At first I thought he was scared, maybe there'd been a history of abuse we didn't know about. So I told him not to worry, it was a two-way mirror; his father wouldn't be able to see him, but the kid just got more adamant, insisting it couldn't be his father, and he refused to go in. He never did look at his father, who ended up being convicted and sent to prison."

"Why are you telling me this?" Rocco asked.

"I realized," Clare continued, "the kid wasn't scared; he was angry. When he hears, 'Hey, your father didn't die, he just skipped out on you,' he was furious. If he ever had gone in to see him, I think he would have just yelled, 'How could you do this to me?' and run back out."

"And?"

"And so, his anger kept him from seeing the truth."

"Anger? You and that priest both–I didn't see a long-lost father, I saw a priest doing something weird." Rocco said, pacing more quickly. "And I'm not angry at him. I just don't believe it."

"It's not just weird," Clare said. "It's extraordinary. You told me how you looked for a sign when your brother was dying, but what you got was let down. Then your parents died, and you were let down again. Now you see an amazing sign and it's like, 'Where have you been?' After my Dad died, I felt the same way for a while. People would say, 'Everything happens for a reason,' and it would make me mad. I was like that kid, I'd think, 'How could you do this to me?' I was mad, mad at God."

"God?" Rocco spat. "Look, I know that's where you're at, but..."

"It was easier for me to think there was no God, rather than think He would allow this to happen." Clare looked at Rocco as he stared across the rooftop. "If these supernatural events really do happen, why not before, when you really needed them?" He turned to her with a scowl that slowly softened once he caught her eyes. "That's it, isn't it?" He looked down, rubbing his hands together.

He remembered now why he had broken off their relationship several months ago. It was her unfailing optimism, her persistent hope that blared like an air horn through his shield of rage. He had been keeping his darkness at bay, contained and controlled with the anger rising from his chest. His anger was like a fierce dog chained behind a fence, one he dare not let loose, yet still, depended upon in some way. Her blinding cheerfulness had threatened to sweep that fury away. But, what would have taken its place? Without his shield, what would he become? The uncertainty of that question was too much for him to bear, so he pushed away her cheerfulness, and her along with it. Now as he felt himself being drawn once again to her charm and beauty, he recognized his old rival, hope, waiting to assail him once more.

Could it be true, that promise made to him on a Brooklyn rooftop so long ago, that he and his brother would always be together? Were they together now? Did he dare consider the possibility? Did he dare hope, or was he poised to be crushed again?

"I don't know," he said finally, turning to look at Clare again. He gazed at her face, searching for something to explain the depth of beauty he saw whenever he looked at her, something in her expression, the empathy in her eyes, her subtle, disarming smile, the harmonious whole, the work of art that was Clare. His prolonged scrutiny made her blush, a reaction Rocco had never witnessed in her before.

"What?" Clare asked timidly, her voice barely above a whisper as she looked down with a shy smile.

A feeling rose in the pit of Rocco's stomach, grabbing at him, pulling him toward a distantly familiar emotion. A passion, resisted for years, began to surface. The feeling grew and spread through him, blurring his concentration. He felt compelled to throw his arms around her, but the impulse was immediately overcome by a tightness rising to the back of his neck and down his arms. Wishful thinking was always a setup for disappointment. "Nothing," he said, his voice too, barely above a whisper, and the feeling quietly receded.

"I was in a dark place after my father died," Clare said, looking up again at Rocco.

"What got you out of it?"

"I met you."

"No, really," Rocco asked, looking at her earnestly.

"Really, I met you, and I started to feel alive again. I started to notice things, little things, signs, I guess you'd say."

"Like what?"

"Oh, I can't remember now. Coincidences, someone saying just what I needed to hear, things like that."

Rocco looked over Clare's shoulders, past the trees that lined the friary. He could make out the peaks of apartment buildings in the distance, topped with air conditioning units. "I grew up with this kind of view," he said. "I'd go to the roof to clear my head. It used to be my sanctuary."

"Used to be?"

"Yeah. The last time," Rocco paused. Like a muffled voice from behind a closed door, the tightness stirred again along his neck. "The last time I went up to our roof," Rocco continued, "I was with my brother. He'd just been diagnosed with Leukemia, after feeling weak and losing weight for a couple months. We were going out to Seattle for a bone marrow transplant, and the day before we left, I suggested we go up to the roof to clear our heads a bit. We climbed out the window to go up the fire escape as we'd always done, and he stopped in his tracks. He just froze on the landing, looking through the metal bars to the sidewalk five stories below. 'I can't,' he said. 'I'm afraid.' He wouldn't move. I practically had to carry him back in. Two weeks later, he was dead."

"You think he knew?"

"Knew what?"

"That he was going to die."

"I don't think he knew anything," Rocco said, standing up. "Not anymore. He'd been beaten by a metal fire escape, a fire escape he had run up and down a thousand times." Rocco walked toward the edge of the rooftop and ran his hand along the tar paper edge. "The doctors said he'd probably had those cancer cells his whole life. Something just happened, triggering them to multiply, some random, haphazard thing."

"Hard to understand," Clare said, now standing just behind him.

"It was then I realized, things don't happen for a reason; they just happen."

"It can seem like that sometimes."

"Sometimes? All the time."

"Look, I know it sounds trite," Clare said, "but I do think there's a purpose behind things. I couldn't see it for a while. I was so down, I remember wondering if I'd ever be happy again. Then... you don't remember the day we met, do you?"

"Sure I do."

"What did you say?"

"What, like, word for word? I don't know. But I do remember the day."

"What do you remember?"

"I remember noticing you," Rocco said, looking at Clare's face again, the silhouette of her hair and shoulders.

"And you asked, 'What's on your mind?'"

"You remember that?"

"Yeah."

"Why?"

"You were the only one to ask me, and I didn't even know you. People I did know tiptoed around me, afraid to ask how I felt, because they all knew my father had died. They didn't want to go there. You knew too, at least that I'd had a death in the family, but it didn't stop you from asking."

"I'm not known for my tact."

"It wasn't tactless of you, it was thoughtful, and I never forgot it. I stopped feeling alone in the world. We had lunch later, and I felt happy for the first time in months. Later, I came to realize that what I was clinging to so desperately in my memories was right in front of me all the time."

"What was?"

"Everything, everyone who'd ever been important in my life. They're not locked away in our old memories. They're here now, in front of us. We just can't see them."

Rocco grinned at Clare. If anyone else had said something like that to him he'd think they were crazy.

"I never thought about how they could be here, I just knew they were. Now, I guess I'd say they're in another dimension," Clare continued, smiling back at him.

"Another dimension," Rocco echoed, fighting the urge to roll his eyes. It wasn't just his own painful experiences that led to his cynicism. All he had ever seen supported the utter and complete finality of loss. Dr. Lejour was right about one thing, an absence never went away. A loss was a loss. A deceased loved one is still present? *Try telling that to a victim's family,* he began to think, but as he looked at Clare's smile, his cynicism receded. He felt unusually comfortable with her as though he was ready to accept anything she said. His defenses were down. Maybe he could let himself be taken in by the idea. What an idea it was, that the dead weren't lost, but simply present in a different way.

He dwelt on that thought, and lost himself in the comfort of the moment. It was a beautiful moment: the sunlight shuttered by the waving tree branches, the fresh smell of the air blown in from the waterways, the blue sky over the rooftops, and Clare's blonde hair tossed lightly back and forth in the breeze. His uncertainty regarding his brother's soul, his soul, all souls, remained. How could it be otherwise? Throughout his childhood, he was certain that he and his brother would always be together. Then, the stark contradiction of his brother dying shattered all that. But here, reflected in Clare's beautiful smile, carried on the cool breeze rustling the surrounding leaves, there was, once again, certainty. Souls were united in a natural order of love. At this moment with Clare, it seemed so reasonable. For now, at least, he believed.

He leaned against the brick wall and looked up at a line of pigeons on the edge of the friary's tile roof. He and Clare stood together in silence for several minutes, then two of the pigeons flew down from the roof, landing at Clare's feet.

"Hello there," Clare said to one of the pigeons that seemed to be cocking its head to look up at her. Two more landed, then a small collection of pigeons passing overhead banked into a wide curve, with all of them landing in the area in front of Rocco and Clare. Rocco hadn't yet noticed the birds that had landed. He was still looking at the sky, the waving tree branches, and the birds' wings beating against the air and gliding on the currents.

"John," Clare said, "I'm having that déjà vu again." Rocco looked at Clare, then down at the rooftop. He squatted down amongst the collection of birds. They seemed to look at him with some curiosity, then continued to search the roof for small seeds that had blown from nearby trees.

"What is this?" Clare asked, crouching next to Rocco and looking around at the birds.

"It's like they don't see us," Rocco said, picking up a

pigeon and holding it up to his face. The pigeon turned its head from side to side, eyeing Rocco closely.

"I'm pretty sure that one sees you," Clare laughed, as another pigeon hopped up onto her knee and cocked its head toward her face. "What do you mean, 'They don't see us?'"

"I mean, not as people. Even in the park, pigeons are still afraid of people. They'll only get so close."

"Maybe it's that sign the doctor talked about. They're not afraid because we're more in line with the natural order."

"Wouldn't that be something?" Rocco asked as he placed the bird back down on the rooftop. "Pigeons, of all things. Whatever you said before," he said, looking up excitedly at Clare, "remember it. If we could keep our minds like this, consistent, focused..."

"Then what, we could face Hoffman?" Clare asked. She spoke the very words in his mind. This was what he had come here for, why he had wanted to talk to the priest. He needed a protocol, a course of action. "I wouldn't get carried away with this," Clare warned. "I think our best bet is still to try to second guess him, stay a step ahead, rather than risk a confrontation."

"Yeah, sure," Rocco said, looking back over the mass of bobbing heads on the roof. But all he kept thinking was that they had found the answer. Before that moment, he didn't even believe in a natural order. Now it seemed, they had found their way into it.

OPPOSITE POLARITIES

22

*T*he following morning, the sun rose over Manhattan. Piercing the darkness, it commenced a new day with warmth and light awakening fresh possibilities, melting the frost and drying the dew. On the opposite side of the Earth, that same sun sank sullenly below the haze, giving way to shadows and blackness: the start of another night. In the precinct building that contained the safe house, there was a flurry of activity. The morning shift had arrived to relieve the night shift. Paperwork was finished, and reports were given. Behind the walls, hidden from view, the agents sat, quiet and still.

Rocco had just been notified by Detective Dobbs that Spinosa's men were on the move in Manhattan, possibly to meet with Hoffman. This could be their last opportunity to intercept Hoffman before he left the country. He shared this tip with the rest of the team who unanimously agreed to act on the information immediately. Rocco had gotten Dr. Lejour safely out of the city and back to his Upstate home the previous evening. The group geared up and was about to start down the stairs to the alley when Rocco called them back.

"Hold up guys," he said. "Let's get together on something first." The four sat in a semicircle around Rocco in the kitchenette, staring at him. "We need to be prepared to face Hoffman." Clare frowned, shifted in her chair and began to speak.

"But..."

"You can't apprehend a man," Rocco continued over Clare, "without facing him. We can try to come at him in groups, but the bottom line is, we have to be prepared to meet him face-to-face."

"Only when absolutely necessary," Clare insisted.

"Yes," Rocco agreed, smiling at Clare long enough for Vince to notice. "Only when necessary."

"You guys figure something out?" Vince asked, looking back and forth between Rocco and Clare.

"Yes," Rocco answered slowly, noticing Clare's anxious look. "The natural order. I don't really understand what or where it is and I don't care, but I know that if we get our heads there, he can't get to us."

"So what do we do?" Vince asked.

"Just," Rocco began, staring at Clare. As he remembered

their conversation on the roof, he tried to articulate the experience. What was it that had made him so confident, so certain they had found the answer? It had seemed so clear the day before. "Stay focused on each other, no matter what happens."

"But don't challenge him," Clare warned, looking steadily at Rocco.

"That's right," Rocco agreed, "don't play his game. We play our game, by our rules."

"So where are we headed?" Jake asked.

"Chelsea," Rocco replied. "That's where Spinosa's men were last seen."

The team reached the location in Chelsea and drove slowly around sequential blocks, looking for any sign of Hoffman.

Meanwhile, only three blocks down and two stories up, Hoffman stood before the large window of a loft apartment, looking down at the traffic below. The stock broker, Kyle Williams, and the congressman, Henry Miller, stood beside him, while four of Spinosa's men leaned against a side wall. The tall man from the CIA was also there, looking suspiciously at the others.

"It's all right. You can speak freely," Hoffman reassured him. "They're with me." The man moved reluctantly closer to Hoffman, handing him a manila envelope.

"There are too many people interested in you now, in

both the Bureau and our own agency," the man said in a barely audible voice. "They're getting too close to me and the others, that's why we've arranged for you to lie low for a while in Nicaragua. Here is your packet to get out of the country. There's a new identity and passport, American and Nicaraguan currency, and an itinerary of your flight. We'll arrange for the local investigation surrounding you to come to an end."

"You think it will be that easy?" Hoffman asked.

"I don't think it will be easy as all. That's why we want you out of the country. The FBI agents will follow you and will be dealt with by our people down there." He then leaned very close to Hoffman and whispered, "Your shooters will take the fall for that mess the other day and we'll quiet the professor's son by staging your death." Stepping back and speaking in a normal tone again, he added, "You'll have your new identity and can carry on your work with us more discreetly without further interruptions. Our people in Nicaragua will contact you when you arrive."

"Very well," Hoffman remarked as the tall man left the room. Looking over at Spinosa's men he asked, "Were you followed?"

"No way," two of the men snapped, looking at each other.

"We'll see," Hoffman said quietly, turning back to face Miller and Williams. Williams was the first to speak under Hoffman's gaze.

"That business on the bridges," Williams began, "was that you?"

"What do you think?"

"Well," Williams stammered, "I don't know anyone else who could pull it off."

"And the Stock Exchange?" Miller added.

"Both trial runs," Hoffman replied. "You noticed there were no casualties?"

"Well, that's a good thing, isn't it?" Miller asked.

"Good?" Hoffman retorted. "Good? Don't be an idiot! Nothing is memorable without suffering. They were simple demonstrations, nothing more. They'll soon be forgotten. But, what is coming, that will be memorable."

"I see," Miller said quietly. "Still, there's no need for unnecessary cruelty, is there?"

"Cruelty?" Hoffman's eyes lit up at the word. "Cruelty, Congressman, is simply domination, domination is power, and power is everything. It is through cruelty that we dominate our own will, harden and strengthen it, then dominate the will of others. Cruelty is an evil only to those who have not mastered it. To those of us who have, it is our life's blood. As for what is necessary... I don't suppose either of you has read Nietzsche?"

"Who?" Miller asked.

"Of course you haven't," Hoffman hissed, "You have no

idea of the privilege given you. To elevate ignorance to such heights... no matter, it suits me presently." Hoffman turned a steady gaze upon Miller. "I trust, Congressman, that when the time comes, you will be up to the task."

"What task is that?" Miller inquired.

"Whatever is necessary."

"You'll let us know, I'm sure, and we'll take care of it," Williams blurted out in an obsequious tone.

"I will," Hoffman pronounced, then turned and looked out the window again.

Miller tapped Williams on the arm, looked toward Hoffman and made the "crazy" sign with his finger to his head.

Williams glared back at him, whispering, "He sees everything!" Williams moved timidly up to Hoffman's side. "Doctor," he breathed, "what about your equipment?"

"I no longer need it," Hoffman replied, looking down at Williams with a slight grin. After examining the street in silence for a few minutes, Hoffman turned back toward the men in the room.

"Control, gentlemen, control," he spoke as he began to walk to and fro before the window, his hands clasped behind his back. "To control events, people, governments, courts, armies, it's all the same. Control the key players and you control everything. Most of the minds out there are cattle, they follow the lead without question. Control the leads and you control the masses. The key is to not let them know they're being controlled. Always let them believe they are free thinkers, that they are in control and it is they who are using you." He looked steadily at Miller as he spoke these last words. "Let them scheme plans how they might benefit from you. Let them act out their petty maneuvers while you weave the net that will ensnare them all."

"You're talking about controlling the entire country?" Williams asked.

"I'm talking about everything. Absolute control." Hoffman turned and looked down at the street again. "Anything that gets in the way needs to be dealt with promptly." Glancing at Spinosa's men over his shoulder he added, "Twice you've failed me in that regard. These agents are becoming an annoyance to me."

"Say the word and we'll take care of them," one of Spinosa's men offered.

"Will you now?" Hoffman replied, looking down at the street again. "Perhaps you'll have a chance to make good on that promise." Another of Spinosa's men rushed into the room.

"Cops are everywhere down there! We need to get out of here," he yelled, and Spinosa's men ran swiftly out of the room, barely pausing to glance at Hoffman.

"We've got to go," Williams said nervously to Hoffman.

Miller had already run from the room on the heels of the others.

"Do what you feel you must," Hoffman replied flatly and continued to scan the street below. Williams slipped quietly out the door behind the others.

On the street, police cars were speeding down the surrounding blocks, stopping any suspicious individuals on the sidewalks. Miller and Williams easily blended into the pedestrians without being noticed. Two of Spinosa's men were stopped, while the other two had slipped away into the crowds. When questioned, they misdirected the police to the building on the opposite side of the street from Hoffman. Rocco, Clare, and Marcus stood on the sidewalk, watching the police enter the building, while Jake and Vince circled around the back.

Rocco stepped away from the others, moving into the street between two parked cars. He looked across the street at a line of loft windows, moving from curtain to curtain, to hanging plant, to books and desk lamps, to... Hoffman! There was no mistaking him, his tall figure was the same as he had seen through the warehouse door. His mind was racing, his heart pounding, pulsing up into his neck. What had he done on the friary roof the day before? What had he thought? What was it? He couldn't remember! He stopped thinking and closed his eyes. He would be on the roof in his mind, even while standing before Hoffman now. And there it was: Clare's face, the light shuttered by the moving tree branches, the cool breeze, the moment when he believed. His mind was back on the roof. His breathing slowed, his pulse quieted, and he opened his eyes and looked up at Hoffman in the window.

Hoffman's eyes were closed, his finger and thumb on his forehead, a deep furrow between his eyes, his jaw muscles clenched, the skin of his cheeks twitching, then, he lowered his hand and opened his eyes.

"You!" he growled, as he stared down at Rocco standing in the street below him.

Clare noticed Rocco standing by himself and rushed to his side, following his gaze up to the window where Hoffman stood.

"What are you doing!" she cried. "Is that him?"

"Yes," Rocco answered nonchalantly. "Get the others and let's pick him up."

Clare tried to pull Rocco away, but he kept his gaze fixed on the window above.

"Marcus!" she called out, "Get Jake and Vince. It's Hoffman! He's across the street." She pointed to Hoffman in the window, then turned to get Rocco's attention. "John! Look at me."

Hoffman had his hand to his forehead again. The deep furrow between his eyes was back and his jaws were clenched, though now his eyes were open, riveted on Rocco, as though he would pour his very being into him. Hoffman seemed oblivious to the fact that the police were gathering in the building, that they would be coming for him. His mind was elsewhere, completely focused on the imposition of his will.

The two men stood frozen, linked like opposite magnetic poles. Rocco was looking directly at Hoffman, but saw only his silhouette, as though he were looking around him. He concentrated on his memory of Clare on the roof, the pigeons, the peace he had felt. The natural order would be his shield, and he would triumph, overcoming whatever Hoffman might use against him. As his self confidence grew, Hoffman's image became clearer. Suddenly, he was no longer a blurry silhouette behind the glass, but an immediate presence before him, staring at him, perceiving him, seizing him, suffocating him.

"He's getting through," Rocco muttered.

"John, come on!" Clare shouted, pulling him back onto the sidewalk to join the others. He broke his stare with Hoffman and joined the group as they ran across the street toward the entrance to the building's lobby. Hoffman was no longer in the window. There were police officers throughout the lobby, at the stairwell, and at the elevator. Rocco asked the doorman if there was another way out of the building. There was the service entrance, by a back loading dock, the doorman told them. The police had already been stationed there as well. Jake and Vince went around the building to check out the back, while Marcus, Clare, and Rocco remained in the lobby.

As Vince walked around the outside of the building, he noticed a tall man crossing the street. "Jake, is that?" Vince began, then asked the officer standing on the loading dock, "Did a man come down that stairway?"

"No sir."

"Did anyone?" Jake asked.

"Only an old woman," the officer replied.

"When?"

"Just a minute ago."

"What about you?" Vince asked a second officer standing around the corner in the street. "Did you see a man come out this way?"

"No," he answered, as he and Vince joined the others at the dock, "just a young woman with a baby."

"Did you see a young woman?" Jake asked the first officer.

"No, just the older woman."

"And, did you see the old woman?" Vince asked the second officer.

"No."

"You must have seen her," the first officer protested. "She went right around that corner. She would have walked right past you."

"The only person that came by me was a young woman pushing a baby in a stroller," the second officer insisted.

Vince looked across the street where he had seen the tall figure walking. Looking up and down the sidewalks he saw neither a young mother nor an old woman. "You think?" he asked Jake.

"He's good," Jake said, shaking his head. "Rocco, I think we lost him back here," he called through his ear piece. The police swept through the building without finding Hoffman. Rocco and the others regrouped on the sidewalk in front of the apartment building.

"If he really did trick those officers, why make one see a young mother and the other an old woman?" Vince asked the others.

"He didn't make them see either," Clare suggested. "It's like what Dr. Lejour said after my attack. He put an understanding in their heads and their imaginations filled in the details. He made those officers think the person coming toward them was not a threat and was someone they would naturally get out of the way for, or even help. The one saw an elderly woman, the other a young mother."

"So now what?" Vince asked. "Back to the drawing board?"

Rocco hadn't heard him. He was staring out across the sea of moving people and lights. For the first time, he understood what Dr. Silverman had been so afraid of—the terrible consequences of mind control, of the loss of free thought. He could imagine now, the horrors Silverman had known living under a totalitarian regime, the secret police, the assassinations, the absolute power. If they didn't stop this, the unthinkable would happen here, not through some bloody revolution, but silently, surreptitiously infiltrating the country under the guise of freedom, until the control ran so deep, it would be impossible to get out from under it. It would be like being killed in your sleep.

Rocco looked down at a text on his phone. "The Bureau just sent me the GPS coordinates for our headquarters in Nicaragua. They say the people there are on the lookout for Hoffman and will assist us in apprehending him. They've got extradition papers for us. All we need to do is fly down there, they'll share their intel with us, and we'll go and pick him up. We've got flights booked out of Miami, and we'll be met at the airport." He held up the phone to the others. "Oh, and one more thing, we're to leave our phones and IDs in Miami, and we'll be given everything we need in Nicaragua. Sounding more like a setup every minute."

"I have contacts in Nicaragua," Marcus offered. "Ones we can trust. They can fly us into a small military base, and get us through customs without triggering calls to the CIA or FBI. Then we can check that location out beforehand, and make sure it's not a trap."

"Could your contacts meet us in Miami?" Rocco asked.

"Say the word and I'll make the calls."

"We'll fall off the grid in Miami, as planned, only we won't be on their flight," Rocco explained.

"I can get us burner phones and IDs too," Marcus added.

"Some contacts you've got there," Jake commented.

"We were on multiple deployments together," Marcus replied. "Like I said, we can trust them."

"Agents!" Detective Dobbs called out as he ran across the street. "Tough break back there losing Hoffman."

"Thanks for the tip anyway," Rocco said as he greeted Dobbs. "Say, we're going to be out of the country for a while, following Hoffman." Moving closer to him, he said quietly, "We think he may have someone on the inside, in the Bureau or the CIA. For your own sake, you'd better keep the fact that we've spoken quiet."

"Understood," Dobbs said. "Any way I can help you from here, just let me know."

"We might take you up on that," Rocco said, looking around at the others. "It helps to know there's still someone we can trust."

Part III

NICARAGUA

23

*W*ith a few calls, Marcus had everything arranged. The agents took the flights booked by the Bureau to Miami, but then met up with Marcus and a fellow SEAL named Dirk outside the airport. They left their phones, IDs, and other personal items in a storage locker, got outfitted by Marcus with new IDs and phones, and drove to a private airport about two hours away. A plane was waiting for them, fueled and ready for takeoff.

As they flew over the Gulf of Mexico, Marcus reminisced with three fellow SEALs, Dirk, Madock, and Wallace, who had been doing private contract work in Nicaragua for the past year. They assured him they could keep the team undercover while in country. Vince and Jake caught up on lost sleep, and Clare moved to the back of the plane next to Rocco.

"So tell me," she began, "what was that on the street,

you and Hoffman? Why were you staring at him? Did he make you?"

"No, I don't think so. I was trying to look at him but not focus on him, if that makes any sense. It seemed to work for a few seconds, and then..."

"It seemed to me like you were playing with fire," Clare admonished him. "Next time, let's stick to our game plan."

"Fair enough," Rocco concurred as he leaned into the window, watching the clouds race by over glimpses of the Gulf of Mexico. Looking back at Clare, who was now resting with her eyes closed, he recalled that moment on the friary roof once more. He wanted to keep that memory vivid, to prevent it from fading in intensity. Already, he was losing the details. It had seemed so clear, so transparent, yet now he was at a loss to recall what, exactly, he had felt. Would the memory soon fade completely? Even as he considered ways to immortalize the moment in his mind, it was slipping away like smoke between his fingers. With a long, slow breath, he let himself fall off to sleep.

When he awoke, he saw the Nicaraguan mountains. The landscape was lush, with trees covering the mountains nearly to their peaks. Rivers wound their way between ridges and down through the valleys.

"Beautiful country," Clare noted, seeing that Rocco was awake. "I know people who come here, for hiking, birding, things like that. They say it's a real paradise."

"To each his own, I guess," Rocco muttered, "but I don't see it." Having lived his life in New York, Dallas, D.C., and Chicago, the tree-covered scene below was, to him, simply a lot of nothing.

They passed over the city of Managua, and Rocco felt a bit more in his element, though the feeling passed quickly as they continued on to an area of undeveloped wilderness. Their landing site was cut into a wooded area at the base of a mountain range. As soon as the plane landed, it was flanked by vehicles directing it to an area off the runway. As they deplaned, armed men in camouflage uniforms escorted them to a customs area.

"Your friends do know these people, right?" Rocco confirmed with Marcus, who remained silent. As they were brought into the building, Marcus and his friend spoke in Spanish to the customs officer, who looked over their paperwork suspiciously. The officer then went behind a dividing wall and spoke to someone who appeared to be his superior. He returned shortly afterwards, told them everything was in order, and wished them a good day.

"No questions asked? How did you manage that?" Jake asked.

"See the head of customs over there?" Marcus pointed out the man their customs agent had spoken to. "We helped him out last year. His daughter was kidnapped."

"Kidnapped?" Clare asked. "What, is he rich?"

"No, but that doesn't matter. The kidnappers figure most people either have relatives in the States with money, or know someone who does, so either way they can get it. If they can't, or even when they do, they usually end up killing the kidnapped child."

"Did you get her?" Rocco asked.

"We got her back safely," Marcus answered, nodding. "The police are out-gunned and out-numbered, so yeah, four of us took care of it for him."

"Nice. So now he owes you."

"More a code of honor, than a debt. We were under no obligation, and we wouldn't accept any payment. It was just the right thing to do. He knows that, so now it's the right thing for him to do, to let us in, no questions asked."

"You have any more key officials bound by this code of honor?" Jake asked, grinning.

"A few," Marcus replied, sliding his bag over his shoulder. "Always looking to add one or two more though."

The group loaded their gear into a van and headed to where they would be staying. Rocco watched the scenery out his open window as they passed from the wooded hills into scattered neighborhoods on the outskirts of the city. Cinder block walls topped with razor wire enclosed patches of grass and tin-roofed shacks. The smell of wet ashes and smoke flooded the interior of the van as they splashed through small puddles on the road left from a recent rain.

Rocco felt like they were on stage as they drove down the road, their van arresting all activity around them. Dogs with sides displaying protruding ribs stopped in their tracks and watched them until they passed. Lightly clad children stood, framed by doorways, motionless except for their large black eyes tracking the outsiders' passage through their world. The sound of the van joined that of an occasional chicken squawking or a corrugated metal roof rising and falling noisily with gusts of wind.

They drove out of the more populated area through lines of banana trees that opened up to a sea of green plants, dotted with red coffee beans. The surrounding mountains were shrouded in low-hanging clouds.

"First thing, we'll check out the headquarters we were told to go to," Rocco announced to the others. "If you and your friends have some surveillance capabilities," he added, looking at Marcus, "we can find out pretty easily if it was a setup. We need to move quickly though. It won't take them long to realize we ditched them in Miami, then they'll be gone."

The van left the main road and drove up a series of switch-backs that led to the gated entrance to the barracks where they would be staying. After unloading and getting outfitted with surveillance gear, they set off to investigate the meeting place arranged by the Bureau. Wallace stayed behind at the barracks while Marcus, Dirk, and Madock led them along a wooded mountain slope that looked down on the site. They could see gunmen throughout the area, at the entrance, along the sides, and in a tower.

"It's well guarded, but we would expect that," Jake noted. "How do we know if it's a trap?"

"That's how," Marcus answered, handing his binoculars to Rocco, and pointing to the back of the compound.

"That's it then," Rocco sighed, passing the binoculars on to Clare. "We're definitely on our own."

"What is it?" Clare asked, grabbing the binoculars. It was Hoffman. He was standing on a platform, giving orders and pointing in various directions. There was no doubting it now; they'd been set up for an ambush.

"He's on the move," Vince reported, the last one to look through the binoculars. Hoffman had walked out a back gate with two guards. They paralleled his progress along the hillside, following him down onto a dirt road, lined with small patches of grass cut through by a muddy stream, thatch-roofed dwellings, and a cinder block struc-ture with a large Coca Cola sign on the front. A long win-dow was open, through which drinks were sold along with other food items. Several men were leaning against the front wall, glancing intermittently down a perpendicular road as though waiting for someone. People came up that road, back from the town below. There was a man sitting on a flatbed pulled by two oxen, another man on a bicycle wearing a small backpack, and two young men covered with cement dust returning from a construction site. The men in front of the store seemed to be trying to look past them when Hoffman stepped into their line of sight. He stood immediately in front of each of them, one by one. The first fell backwards against the wall, then the second cringed at Hoffman's gaze, as did the third. Hoffman turned from the store and stepped into the road, being met by a man who drew a handgun. Hoffman glanced over his shoulder at the woods lining the road, then turned to the man with the gun who suddenly looked frantically in all directions, muttering to himself.

"I think Hoffman just disappeared," Jake commented as he watched the muttering man retreat behind an adjacent wall.

"What do you mean?" Rocco asked. "He's right there."

"Yeah, but I don't think that guy could see him. It's like he made him think he disappeared."

"Like he did to those cops in Brooklyn," Vince recalled.

"All he has to do is look at them," Rocco mused.

Hoffman turned back toward the store, coming upon a woman walking back from the town. He stood in her way and she stopped and looked up at him. One of her eyes was closed, and her face was disfigured by scars running across her cheeks, nose, and forehead. Her hands and arms also appeared to be deeply scarred. She stood still, looking quietly up at Hoffman who continued to stare at her. She then stepped to the side to walk by him, and he quickly moved into her path. She looked up at him again and seemed to be speaking to him.

"Look at that," Rocco said, pointing to the woman. "He has no effect on her."

"Maybe she's blind," Vince suggested, looking at the woman more closely with the binoculars. "One of her eyes is closed, and she's got some pretty bad scars."

"I don't think so," Clare remarked, "See how she's looking right at him?" A tall blonde woman came up from behind and whispered to the woman with the scars. They both nodded at Hoffman, then walked casually past him. Hoffman turned and watched them as they continued down the road.

"Look at him," Rocco whispered, "look at him watch them. He couldn't get to them and it's annoying him. I'd like to know why he couldn't affect those two."

Hoffman leaned against the wall vacated by the men he had frightened earlier as a dark sedan came into view on the road, raising a plume of dust in its wake. The sedan pulled up to the store and the tall man from the CIA stepped out along with a man with a rifle slung over his shoulder. The two entered the store with Hoffman and his body guards.

Marcus shifted his position on the hill, pointing a directional microphone toward an open window at the back of the building, and passed earphones to the agents so they all could listen in. "Once we have the situation controlled in the states," the CIA man began, "we'll bring you back in the witness protection program. You'll have a whole new identity and untraceable past, and we can get started on our first project together."

"And you're certain all the loose ends are taken care of?" Hoffman asked.

"About that," the man from the CIA began, "it seems they failed to meet our contacts at the airport today. We believe they're here in the country, but we don't yet have their exact location." The man shifted his eyes back and forth between the table and the floor.

"Why am I not surprised?" Hoffman sneered.

"The place you're staying, it may not be safe for you any more, now that we don't have control of the agents."

"Look at me," Hoffman commanded.

"No, I'm not playing that game," the man answered quickly, keeping his eyes fixed on the ground.

"You think this is a game?" Hoffman spat as he jerked the man's shoulder, turning his face to his. The man reluctantly looked at Hoffman. "Leave the agents to me. I've found a different place I'll be going to with my own security team, so you needn't concern yourself with my safety. You should be more concerned with yours." The man broke away from Hoffman's grip and looked down at the ground. "We'll speak tomorrow," Hoffman sneered.

"We'd better follow him," Marcus said, pulling out his earphone and being joined by Dirk.

"Take Jake and Vince with you," Rocco replied. "Keep your distance and stay in contact with me. Clare, you and I, and, Madock, is it? I'd like to talk to those two women, the ones that seemed to be untouchable." Madock nodded, slung a bag over his shoulder, and led the way down the hill.

LA CHURECA

2
4

*R*occo, Clare, and Madock caught up with the woman with the scarred face who spoke very little English. Madock spoke enough Spanish to learn that her name was Maria, and that her tall friend had left for La Chureca, the city garbage dump. Clare asked, through Madock, if she would come help them find her, and the woman readily agreed. She seemed to trust Clare, perhaps because she was tall and blonde like her friend.

Madock returned to their barracks and brought a Jeep down the switch-backed road, picking up the group to take them to La Chureca. On their approach, they were passed by several empty dump trucks that were leaving, raising a cloud of dust behind them. Madock parked the Jeep and as the wind shifted, a wave of the overlying air washed over them.

Rocco coughed lightly, suppressing the urge to gag. He

knew the smell of garbage—who didn't? But this was something different. It was like the worst smells he could imagine all mixed together, amplifying each other to such an extent that there was no avoiding them. When he breathed through his mouth, the taste coated his tongue. Closing his mouth, it spread to his throat. The air stung his eyes and wrapped itself around the skin of his neck and face. Madock handed both Clare and Rocco bandanas, tying one around his own nose and mouth, and pulling it up close to his dark glasses like a bandit.

"Watch yourselves in here," Madock warned. "It can be pretty rough."

They made their way along the dirt road, flanked on either side by small groups of people who were hunched over piles of trash like harvesters in a field. Black vultures covered the sky and land, some circling overhead, and others hopping from pile to pile, eyeing the humans for any uncovered finds they might steal. Dogs moved by haltingly, their noses fixed to the ground. Cows too, searched through the rubble for a bit of wilted lettuce, or old fruit. Within a thick curtain of white smoke and ash rising from a mound of burning garbage, figures appeared methodically raising and lowering what looked like sickles. Like a line of grim reapers, they combed through the debris with tri-pronged rakes, kneeling occasionally to pick up a piece of metal or glass, the coveted recyclables. Other white plumes of smoke rose from orange flames throughout the landscape. A loaded dump truck arrived and a crowd quickly assembled behind it. As the people were scrambling to position themselves, one person remained still.

"Ashley!" the scarred woman, Maria, called out. "Aquí!" It was the blonde woman.

"Her name is Ashley?" Clare asked. Maria nodded vigorously. Ashley walked toward them along one of the trucks' tire tracks. She was wearing a baseball cap with a ponytail sticking out the back, several locks of hair having fallen out of it.

"Hola, Maria," Ashley called out as she reached the group, then, looking inquisitively around the circle added, "Can I help you?"

"Yes," Rocco answered. "We're from the States."

"I can see that," Ashley noted promptly. "Your clothes," she explained, "and your hair," looking at Clare, "and your size," looking at Madock. "Are you police? Military?"

"Something like that," Rocco replied quickly. "We're pursuing a criminal from the States." Looking around the scene, he asked, "Why are you here?"

"I'm a nurse. I do prenatal care for the pregnant women who live here."

"Who live here? Really?" Rocco blurted out. "How did you wind up here?"

"My parents are missionaries, so I grew up here in

Central America, and in Africa. When I graduated from nursing school, I came back here to work."

"And you provide nursing care here?" Clare asked.

"Yes, nutritional supplements, counseling. There are programs underway to modernize this place, make it a recycling plant, and someday, even employ some of the people who've lived here. In the meantime, they make their living recycling bits of glass or metal."

Not far from them, a small child pulled up on a string of intestines, casually pushing aside a horn and a hoof.

"What is that?" Clare groaned. The child then picked up a round, rough edged object from within the pile of slaughterhouse refuse and to Rocco's horror, bit into it. He and Clare turned away, fighting the impulse to retch.

"You get used to it," Ashley mentioned, noticing their distress.

"They're living like animals," Clare lamented.

"It can seem like that. They're doing what they need to do to survive, fighting off vultures and dogs, sometimes it's all you can see, the immensity of their need. Then," she pushed her hair back up into her cap, "you spend your time meeting their need as best you can, and you don't see it anymore, you just see people, people with families, children..." She shook her head, looking past the agents to the area where they had parked their Jeep.

"See those vans over there?" She pointed to two vans

that had pulled up behind Madock's Jeep. "I know they mean well. They hope to raise awareness, and funds, which we always need. But, it's like they're on a safari, cameras sticking out the windows, taking snapshots of people like they were wild animals. Children go to school here. People pray here. Today, I saw a young man share some shards of metal, which is like gold, with an older woman who had found nothing all morning. When did you ever see an animal do that? They're not animals; they're people, beautiful people with dignity... but you came to ask me something."

"Dignity?" the word slipped out of Rocco's mouth as he wondered what dignity there was in living off garbage. Clare looked at Rocco, waiting for him to respond to Ashley's comment, then nudged his arm to gain his attention. "Right," Rocco uttered finally. "You two saw a tall man in a suit earlier today."

"By the store, yes," Ashley replied.

"He usually has a certain effect on people, but neither of you seemed to experience it."

"What sort of effect?"

"He intimidates people," Rocco said slowly.

"He can make people see things, even make them fall to the ground," Clare explained, after seeing the perplexed look on Ashley's face. Ashley explained this to the scarred woman, who shrugged her shoulders.

"You didn't feel anything, when you looked at him?" Rocco asked.

"No," Ashley replied.

"Nor her?" he asked, nodding to Maria, who shook her head after Ashley translated the question. "Can I ask," Rocco added, "what's her story?"

"Her story?" Ashley asked incredulously.

"What he means is," Clare interrupted, casting a sideways scowl at Rocco, "we'd like to know more about her, as we know about you, to try to understand why neither of you were affected by him. Hopefully, it will help us in our dealings with him. He's not a good man. He's suspected of murder, among other things."

"Okay," Ashley agreed. "I don't know how we can help you, but her name is Maria. She lives in the village, not far from me, and works at the market. We've known each other for three years now. I first met her shortly after her attack."

"Her attack?" Clare asked.

"She saw a gangster, as she called him, stealing from the market. He came back that night because he knew she had seen him, so he tried to kill her with a machete. She lost much of the function of her hands and arms from protecting herself against the blows. She got the scars on her face and lost her right eye, but she survived."

Maria looked amiably at Clare as Ashley spoke. Rocco looked only at Maria's scars, recreating the crime, the angles of the facial wounds, the position of her forearm scars, where they were deepest. The attack had come from the right side, one blow striking the top of her eye, several others hitting her face, many striking her arms held up in defense. He looked at the sequelae of the attack, the loss of an eye with the eyelid perpetually closed, the loss of her cheek contour and the shape of her nose, the lack of motion of her facial muscles, her hands barely mobile, with clawed, stiff fingers.

"The attacker," Rocco asked gently, "was he apprehended?"

"Yes," Ashley nodded, "Maria was able to identify him. He is in prison now." Rocco breathed a quiet sigh of relief. "But that was not enough, was it Maria?" She repeated her question in Spanish to Maria, who shook her head and replied in Spanish to Ashley.

Rocco listened to the rapid string of Spanish words, then suddenly interrupted, "Perdonar?" he repeated one of Maria's words, the tightness flashing from his chest to the nape of his neck.

"It means, to forgive," Ashley explained.

"I got that," Rocco interjected, "I just can't imagine..."

"Si," Maria replied, without waiting for the translation, apparently understanding Rocco's protest from the look on his face.

"She says it was necessary to forgive him," Ashley continued, "otherwise she would have remained his prisoner."

How could anyone forgive such a thing? Rocco thought. What justice was there in that? To accept it? To just let it go? Rocco stared blankly at the two women, standing before the backdrop of smoke, fire, garbage, and the incessant rising and falling of rakes. He struggled to find a common point of reference in what they said, in what he was seeing, but everything before him was foreign. He felt like a stranger in not just an alien land, but an alien world. He nodded briefly toward the women.

Clare thanked them, asking that they not talk about their meeting that day to anyone. The two agreed and offered to help them if need be. Rocco arranged for Maria to get a ride back with Ashley and stressed again the need to keep their meeting secret to avoid putting them in danger. Walking back to the Jeep, Rocco shook his head.

"I don't know what I expected," he said, "but I thought it would be more helpful."

"What do you mean?" Clare retorted. "It was very helpful. They're exceptionally good, kind people, so good that Hoffman couldn't get to them. The pure, what was it, will to love? Everything the priest and Dr. Lejour were talking about. Now we know it really can work."

"Sure, as long as you work in the slums like Mother Teresa or have the forgiving heart of a saint. Maybe you could pull off being a saint, Clare, but it's not happening with me."

"What are you talking about? You looked right at Hoffman yesterday, remember?

"For a few seconds, three stories away."

"A few seconds is a start, and three stories away makes no difference and you know it. What's more, now we know there are at least two people here we can trust. I'd say that's a great start."

THE PLAN

25

While Rocco and Clare were at La Chureca, Jake and Vince were trailing Hoffman with Marcus and Dirk. They followed him back to the original headquarters, where Hoffman met with a number of armed men, one of whom Dirk recognized.

"That figures," Dirk said, looking through his binoculars. "That one's a local drug lord. When he said he had his own security team, he wasn't kidding."

"So, do we follow them?" Vince asked.

"Yeah, but not on the roads," Dirk explained. "They'll have a tail, a vehicle or two hanging back behind them to watch for people like us following them. They'll also have their own check points. These guys are pretty sophisticated, so much so, the government's backed off on trying to hunt them down. They retreat into their 'no-go' zones, where it's understood the police and military don't go."

"Any of those no-go zones around here?" Jake asked.

"Right on the other side of this ridge, as a matter of fact. It's a box canyon. The road's all switch-backs on this hill getting down to the valley. If we stay above like this, we can travel on foot along the ridge, keeping them in sight on the road the whole time. That is, if they're going to the place I think they're going."

"Let's head out then," Marcus suggested, "assume they're taking the route you mentioned, and keep us a step ahead."

"Roger that," Dirk replied. "You boys up for the trek?" he asked Jake and Vince. "It'll be a little rough in spots."

"Sure," Vince answered quickly, tilting his head at Jake. "We're good."

Below, Hoffman climbed into a vehicle with the drug lord and a small convoy drove down the road. Dirk led the group through the trees and along a rocky hillside, moving from boulder to boulder to minimize their visibility. They were able to make it around the ridge by the time the convoy had made it down to the valley. From their location, they could now see the road leading into the box canyon.

"We'll have to go down in elevation now," Dirk explained. "There are cliffs up ahead that will stop us from going any further." The group moved down into the wooded area of the hillside, sliding through loose dirt where the grade was especially steep. After the terrain leveled out, they continued another two hundred yards until they reached a point where they could see the road. It led to a gate at the mouth of the canyon. They set up behind a cluster of boulders, and within minutes, heard the rumbling sounds of heavy vehicles off to their left. A cloud of dust rose just beyond the visible crest of the road. The group crouched closer to the stone beneath them as the column drove into view. It continued past them to the gate which opened promptly, allowing the line of vehicles to drive into the canyon. Vince relaxed from his crouched position and began to rise when Dirk's hand pressed him back down against the boulder.

"Wait for the tail!" Dirk chided him. "I told you, there's always a tail." A minute later, two more Jeeps drove down the road and through the gate. Once the sound of their vehicles faded, and the dust raised from their passing diffused through the air, Dirk rose from his crouched position, giving the okay for the rest to do likewise. "Well," Dirk continued, "now you know where he's staying."

"Have you ever looked into breeching this canyon?" Marcus asked.

"We have. There are two plateaus, one on the right side here and the other on the back wall of the canyon. They're both accessible and are good vantage points for sniper support and infiltration. The problem is getting to them. At any time there is what amounts to a small army in there. The key would be to get in while most of them are out."

The sound of voices suddenly broke through the trees, coming from just beyond a small crest along the road. The tree cover was thin between them and the hillside, so Dirk and Marcus quickly identified hiding spots next to the boulders they were on. Like a flounder scurrying beneath the ocean floor, Dirk had himself buried beneath leaves and loose earth in seconds. Marcus helped Jake and Vince with similar camouflage, then he, too, covered himself.

The voices belonged to three armed men patrolling the valley. As they approached the boulders, one of the men seemed interested in something on the ground, pointing to it. The other two followed him as he continued to point at areas on the ground. He crouched down, picked up a handful of the fresh earth that had been disturbed, and said something to his fellows in Spanish. The three moved back and forth in the small patch of ground that lay before the four buried men, one man's boot only inches from Marcus's face. The first man pointed up toward the hillside and all three looked in that direction, at which point Dirk began to rise slowly from the earth, his knife drawn. Then, one of the three men said something that made Dirk quietly recede back into the dirt. It was a reference to wild pigs, to which the others nodded in agreement, and they returned to their rounds.

Once the armed men were well out of sight, they all came up out of the dirt and quickly brushed themselves off.

"Thanks," Vince said, nodding to Marcus.

"No problem," Marcus replied. "Let's plan our approach to that plateau and get out of here before pressing our luck." The group moved closer to the road in order to see the terrain around the plateau on the side of the canyon. As they were scanning the hillside for the best approach they might make in the dark, the clanking sound of a cowbell rose behind them. It hung from the neck of a goat that had just come over the crest of the road. It stood still for a few moments, looking at them, then bleated and trotted toward them. Stopping in front of the four men, it seemed especially interested in Marcus, who was more concerned with what might be following it over the crest. It then moved to Jake and Vince, the clanking of the bell echoing throughout the canyon.

"Get out of here," Jake whispered, swinging his arm at the goat. The goat moved on to Vince, who gave the animal a similar nonverbal rejection, though less vigorously. Vince seemed somewhat taken with the goat's eyes, which seemed to stare at him.

"Maybe he's telling us something," Vince suggested.

"He's telling you to feed him," Jake replied, "and he's going to get us killed." The goat continued to move from Vince to Jake, then back to Marcus and Dirk. "We've got to get out of here."

"This way," Dirk told them, "up to those trees." The four moved away from the goat which, thankfully, did not follow them up to a dense patch of trees near the hillside. Moments after they had gotten behind the tree branches, armed men appeared on the road, marching four men across and at least ten men deep.

"That goat saved our lives," Vince whispered.

"Come on Vin," Jake replied, "you think he was warning us? He was just being nosy."

"Maybe, but it still saved our lives."

Once the men had passed through the gate and there was no further motion below them, they made their way into the wooded hillside. As they climbed up through the trees, Jake pulled a stick out of the back of Vince's hair.

"Ever hide in the dirt like that?" he asked Vince quietly.

"Nope, another first," Vince answered. "There's been a lot of that on this case."

"That's for sure. By the way, I didn't get a chance to thank you before."

"For what?"

"For encouraging me to get back with my Dad."

"That was all you. I didn't do anything."

"No, you helped me. I can't tell you what a relief it is, especially when... you know, when you think you might die before you have a chance to. It's one of those things, once you're rid of it, you realize how much it weighed on you. So, thanks."

"Forget about it. Like I said, I didn't do anything. I'm

glad it worked out though, except for you getting shot, that is."

"Yeah," Jake agreed chuckling, "except for that."

The group continued to move quickly out of the valley with Dirk not slowing his pace until they were up on the ridge.

"Hey, check this out," Vince called out to the others after they had slowed down for a rest. He pointed down to the ground next to him where there was a line of ants carrying little squares of leaves.

"Leaf cutter ants," Dirk explained after glancing briefly at the ground by Vince. "Little farmers. A scout finds a certain type of leaf, then leads the colony to them. They take pieces of those leaves back to their nest to grow a fungus on them that their larvae eat."

"The natural order," Vince said, looking at Jake. "You should meet our doctor advisor, Dirk, he'd tell you all about it."

"Probably more than you'd want to know," Jake added.

"Okay, if you say so," Dirk replied.

"Wow," Vince mentioned, "I'm having some serious déjà vu."

"Oh yeah? About what?" Jake asked.

"About this, those ants, what Dirk just said. It's weird."

The four made their way along the ridge and back to their barracks, where Rocco, Clare, and Madock had just returned from La Chureca. Marcus filled in Rocco on what they had seen.

"It's a box canyon," Marcus explained, "steep hills and cliffs on three sides, one way in and out. It's also very well fortified."

"Are there plateaus on the sides that we could approach from?" Rocco asked.

"Yeah," Marcus answered, looking at Rocco curiously. "Why, have you seen it?"

"No."

"Well, as a matter of fact, there are two, one on the north side and one in the back. But the woods and surrounding area are all pretty heavily guarded. We were nearly compromised twice today."

"If it hadn't been for the goat..." Vince began.

"The goat?" Rocco asked.

"Vince thinks a goat warned us about approaching gunmen," Jake explained.

"There's a goat on our side?" Rocco asked, chuckling. "I guess we should be thankful for small favors." Vince responded with his signature head tilt and grin.

"I think he was just curious," Jake clarified.

"Wait, was it a little strange?" Rocco asked, suddenly becoming serious. "Like the goat was a bit off, not behaving normally?"

"You could say that, yeah," Vince answered.

"Come on," Jake interrupted, "who here knows how goats normally act? What are you getting at, Rocco?" Jake asked.

"Clare and I saw something strange too, though with birds, yesterday in New York," Rocco explained, looking at Clare. "Take it as a good sign."

"A good sign?" Clare mouthed silently to Rocco with a smile.

"Dr. Lejour did say we would see signs in animals," Vince pointed out. "I tell you, that goat was trying to push us out of there before those thugs came down the road."

"So it's heavily guarded?" Rocco asked.

"Very much so," Dirk replied.

"What if we don't make our move there, but try to get him out in the open, say when he comes to meet his inside man again tomorrow?" Rocco suggested.

"It's possible to take that store," Marcus said, looking dubiously at his friends, "but the area will be crowded with locals, all in the line of fire, and I'm sure Hoffman will have his own snipers out there covering the meeting."

"What if I drew him out?" Rocco asked, "Brought him into the street so you'd have a clear shot."

"An assassination?" Marcus asked. "If you ever want to go home, you'd better have an official green light on that one."

"If he fires at me first, that's your green light."

"You think he'd be that careless?" Marcus asked. "And

where does that leave you?"

"Yes," Clare interjected, frowning at Rocco, "what are you going to do, just stand in the street and call him out, like an Old West gun fight?"

"Well," Rocco explained, "the fact that he couldn't get to those two women this morning irked him, remember? He watched them, like he was considering going after them, but it wasn't worth it to him. But if he saw me out there and couldn't get to me…"

"He'd come after you," Marcus agreed, nodding. "With enough distance between you and him, you could lead him into a trap."

"I don't like it," Clare argued. "Like you said, Marcus, there will be snipers everywhere. One word from Hoffman and John could be taken out before he ever came near our trap."

"It's feasible," Madock said, coming from the back of the circle. "Not from out in the street, but there's a spot on the opposite hill with a clear view into that store, not far from where we were earlier. You could get his attention in there by flashing a mirror, then disappear before they train their snipers on you."

"Then what?" Vince asked.

"Then, they come racing up the hill and you're dug in with the uphill advantage."

"As long as you can look at him with impunity," Clare

added. "That's a big 'if' as far as I'm concerned."

"You're so optimistic," Rocco chided Clare. "You know though, I would like to talk to that Maria again. I didn't really ask her anything earlier."

"Yeah, why was that?" Clare asked.

"I was sort of thrown off by the whole forgive and forget thing." Looking at Jake and Vince he added, "Maria's the scarred woman we saw this morning. Turns out, some creep hacked her with a machete, and she's like, 'just let it go.'"

"Really?" Vince asked.

"It wasn't like that," Clare said, rolling her eyes and shoving Rocco's shoulder. "What she said was actually very sensible. I've worked with victim support groups. The physical healing is only half of it. The psychological is even harder, to rid yourself of the fear and the anger. You can't fully recover from an assault until you're free of that anger. Not easy to do, but she's done it."

"You think that's why Hoffman had no effect on her?" Vince asked.

"I hope not," Rocco admitted, "since I'm not that forgiving. I'm banking on there being something else."

"Well if you want," Clare suggested, "Ashley told me they go to a little church near here every evening at six o'clock. We could catch up with them there."

"Let's do it," Rocco said.

PATIENCE

26

*B*y six-thirty, the group had made their way to the local church Clare had referred to. It was a square building with off-white stucco walls dotted with small stained glass windows. The front doors were held open with wrought iron hooks set in the plaster wall. Inside, they could see Ashley and Maria sitting in a side pew. All the seats were filled, with a cluster of people standing in the back. After the Mass, Rocco and Clare stood alongside the doors as the people filed out, while Marcus stayed back behind the trees with Jake and Vince, watching for any sign of Hoffman's men. Maria and Ashley were still inside the church when the priest came to introduce himself to Rocco and Clare. He was from the United States, a Franciscan friar like Father Joseph in New York. Rocco explained to him who they were, and that they were there to speak with the two women.

"Do you know them?" Rocco asked the priest.

"Of course, very well. Remarkable women."

"Maria, the woman with the scars, she's a survivor, huh?" Rocco asked.

"She suffers well," the priest said.

"Suffers well?"

"Yes."

"You think she likes it?"

"Of course not. No one enjoys suffering," the priest explained. "What I mean is, she accepts it. She knows what suffering is."

"And what's that?"

"A necessary part of life." Seeing Rocco's sour expression, the priest continued. "Imagine a life without suffering, simply going from one happy moment to the next. What would you have? The playboy, constantly seeking a greater thrill, the spoiled child, crying because the new toy is the wrong size—these are not lives filled with joy, but with misery. Suffering resets the scale, so that one appreciates what one has. If you rebel against that suffering and become angry or bitter, as most of us do, it does nothing more, but if you suffer well, if you accept the suffering, embrace it, then it lifts you to a higher plane." The priest turned to look at Maria. "That woman suffers well. She understands life much better than most of us."

Anger began to swell in Rocco's mind. He too knew suffering, and he hated it. For as long as he could remember, it was there, lurking on the periphery of his mind, like a dark figure in the shadows just out of view, threatening him, taunting him, pulling him back from every momentary happiness, as if to say, "Don't forget about me! How can you laugh? Don't you remember?"

"It's about being patient," the priest continued. "You know, the origin of the word, *patience*, means 'to suffer.'"

"Yes," Rocco sighed, "I've been told that recently." The Latin root for *patience* meant suffering. Dr. Lejour had spoken of that. But there was another memory attempting to return to his mind. He pushed it away, thinking, *Not now!* Why did he have to think of that now? But the memory would not be kept down, and it flooded into his mind.

"Be patient with me!" his brother was pleading. He was weak, days before his bone marrow transplant, struggling to get up out of a chair. Rocco leaned over to help him, as he had lost his balance. Pulling his brother up, Rocco tipped a cup of water onto his own pant leg. With an exacerbated sigh, he hoisted his brother forcibly into a standing position, squeezing his arm to do so, the arm that was excruciatingly tender due to cancer in the bone. His brother's pitiful cry of pain and plea for patience had stabbed him like a knife through the chest. It was the first time he had ever experienced self-loathing. He hated himself at that moment. He hated his impatience. That day, and any day thereafter, when those words echoed in his memory, *Be patient with me,* his self-hatred returned, drawing him into an abyss of desolation that would have consumed him, had he not countered it with an equal and opposite reaction–anger. He raged against his brother's suffering. He hated the pain and helplessness he had witnessed nonstop for nearly a week. His anger was his resistance, his bullheaded stubborn fight against despair, and it had kept him alive all these years. *Accept suffering? Embrace it?* The priest's comments seemed ludicrous. Should he surrender and embrace the demons that had for so long tried to pull him down? His mind railed against the idea. *It would kill me*, he thought.

"Should I tell her you're here?" the priest asked Rocco.

"No, that's not necessary," Rocco answered. "We'll wait." He glanced at Marcus who nodded as he continued to scan the surrounding area. Rocco turned his attention to Maria kneeling in the church. She seemed to be smiling. It was an unnerving smile, crooked and distorted by the contracted scars along her cheeks. Rocco traced the lines of scars across her face, envisioning again the blows that caused them. A nascent desire for revenge churned within him as he considered her assailant. Imprisoned or not, the effects of his handiwork lived on; the damage was done, and the possibility of preventing it long gone. He thought of all the victims he had worked with over the years, and the one common thread uniting them all was that he was always there after the fact. He could not prevent their suffering nor the evil that caused it, just as he could not prevent his brother's death, nor keep Hoffman from breaking through to his mind the night before.

The frustration of those chronic failures raised the hair on his neck. He had always thought of his anger as his protection, but from what? Certainly not suffering. He had still seen and experienced more than his share.

He turned to Clare and marveled at the juxtaposition of their two faces. It was so disturbing to look at Maria, so easy to look at Clare. He recalled that moment again on the friary roof, her blue eyes, the graceful curves of her cheek, her hair tossed by the breeze. In the face of beauty, it had been easy to believe in other dimensions, in the connection of minds, and the natural order. It was easy to think of love, to choose to love, but now, in the face of disfigurement... *What is she smiling at?* he thought, looking back at Maria. Was it some happy memory from her past? Was she in denial, smiling with the carefree attitude of a lunatic? Was she insane? No, she wasn't insane; she was calm and rational. It must be a conscious choice, he concluded. She's choosing to smile, choosing to look past evil. She's willing to love. The tightness stirred along his neck. For his part, he'd never had the heart to look past evil. His heart had been so dominated by justice that it was a heart more of vengeance than love. But, *look at her*, he thought, *she's willing to love.*

What Father Joseph had said was true—anger did weigh him down, kept him bound to his pain. Railing at the darkness, he had been blind to even the possibility of light, blind to it in Clare's hopefulness. But now, in this disfigured woman, a spot of light had appeared in the blackness, seemingly enclosed by a sea of pitch, as the doctor had described in that painting. But as he drew near to the light, like an oncoming train, it grew, becoming brighter and brighter, until, as he entered into it, he could see nothing else. A doorway to another dimension, it was indeed outside of the darkness, above and beyond it.

What he had experienced on the rooftop with Clare in a rush of emotion, he was now beginning to understand with clarity and certainty. The answer to suffering was not to endure it with bitterness, but to suffer it with love, to embrace it, and through it, enter a higher dimension, a dimension above space and time, above pain and loss. This woman existed more in that dimension than in these. That's why she was smiling. Through her suffering, she had transcended pain.

He considered the idea of other dimensions touching the world around him with finger-like projections through the sights, sounds, smells, taste in the air, and feel of the breeze. As gentle as a whisper, the fingertip manifestations of the natural order presented themselves to him. Like an aquifer running deep below ground, with no trace of its existence on the surface, save for the green life of trees that drove their roots down deep enough to drink in the water, it was hidden, its water flowing by unseen and unheard. But now he realized, he too could drink in that living water.

He looked at Maria again and stifled the anger that rose spontaneously in him. *No. Not this time.* He made a conscious decision to let it go. Through love, a conscious decision to love, he would see, enter, and remain in the natural order of love. He would transcend pain. Having spent most of his adult life using anger to resist the evil and suffering around him, he had been like a man frantically holding sand bags up against a swelling river. The notion of not doing so terrified him, yet, *If she could choose*, Rocco thought, *so can I.*

He let go of his anger, stood back and let the wall of sand bags collapse and the water rush over him, sweeping away his heart of vengeance, so that in its place there could be love. He willed to love.

It was as though weights had been lifted off his shoulders and a surge of lightheartedness rose from his chest. It was love, love that glimmered through the ugliness of Maria's disfiguring scars, just as it was love that had radiated from Clare's beautiful face, and it was love that directed and sustained the natural order within which his mind had connected with

Clare's on the friary roof, and now with Maria's.

Jake, Vince, and Marcus came to join Rocco and Clare at the front of the church. Two black birds landed on the ground near Rocco, followed by several more. Rocco glanced at them briefly then back at Maria.

"It's a good sign," Clare said, noticing Jake and Vince's curiosity about the birds. "Just act like they're not there." A black bird landed on Vince's shoulder.

"It's looking right at me!" Vince exclaimed, pointing at the bird on his shoulder. "It's like that goat. Do you suppose?" He looked around them quickly.

"I don't think it's warning us, no," Clare reassured Vince. "John, didn't you want to talk to Maria?"

"No," he said. "I think I've seen enough."

"You don't want to talk to her?" Clare asked again.

"No. I think we can go ahead with our plan now." He began to key in a number on his cell phone. "I'm going to touch base with Dobbs back in New York and see if he's heard anything."

It turned out a lot had happened in one day. Several of Spinosa's men had been arrested for the shooting at the warehouse, and the police had heard from the FBI that Hoffman had died in a car crash in Nicaragua, so the case was closed.

"Well, we know better," Rocco assured Dobbs.

"How so?" he asked him.

"We've seen him meeting with his contacts."

"Can you arrest him?" Dobbs asked.

"We hope to, once we draw him out, away from his guards," Rocco shared.

"Well, be safe. I'll keep my eyes and ears open up here."

"I appreciate that," Rocco replied as he hung up. "Let's get ready for the morning," he said to the others, and they headed back to the barracks for the night.

THE TRAP

27

*T*he next morning, Rocco was the first one up. He made a pot of the local coffee, then stood outside the door of the barracks and watched low-hanging clouds change their shape as they filtered through trees on the hill below. He listened to the crowing of roosters echoing through the valley, thinking how other-worldly the scene was, when the screen door creaked open behind him.

"Morning, John," Clare said, coming alongside him with a mug of coffee. Her hair was in a ponytail pulled out through the back of her cap. Rocco glanced over his shoulder at her, then took a second look.

"What?" Clare asked with the shy smile she had been showing him more regularly.

"You look good," Rocco replied, surprising himself with his own answer.

"Yeah, right," she laughed. "I have jungle hair this morning."

Rocco shrugged and looked out at the wispy clouds again. "Have any unusual dreams this morning?" he asked her.

"Not that I can remember," Clare answered. "Did you?"

"Yeah, pretty weird," Rocco replied. "Maybe it's the anticipation." He continued to drink his coffee and stare across the valley.

"Well?" Clare asked.

"Well, what?"

"What was it?" Clare laughed again. "You can't say, 'I had a weird dream,' then nothing." She shook her head, smiling.

"Okay," Rocco sighed. "Look, I don't know whether to make anything of it or not. I was seeing the sky, and it was really blue with only a few clouds, then it became like a puzzle, with a piece in the middle missing. Then, I was sliding down a hill in between trees. When I got to the bottom, I saw Hoffman's men, and they were all running away, and then I saw Hoffman."

"Where?"

"I don't know, but he was dying. I remember that. It was very vivid. He was dying alone."

"A premonition?" Clare asked.

"Or just..."

"Wishful thinking?" Clare interjected with a sigh.

"I was going to say, being hopeful," he said in defense of his train of thought, though what difference there was between *wishful thinking* and *being hopeful* he didn't know.

On the other side of the screen door, Vince, who had overheard the conversation between Rocco and Clare, asked Jake, "You dream anything, Jake?" Jake seemed distracted and didn't answer. "Jake?"

"Yeah, what?" Jake replied, "Dream? You know, I don't put much stock in dreams. I never remember them anyway." Jake stared out at the trees through the screen door with a distracted look.

"I don't remember any dreams from last night either," Vince admitted, as he pushed the screen door open to join Rocco and Clare. "I have to wake up right in the middle of them, or that's it, I forget them," he explained with a head tilt to Jake, then Clare.

After a few more minutes of watching the clouds in silence, Rocco asked, "Is Marcus up?"

"He's laying out a map on the table right now," Jake answered.

"Good, let's work out our plan."

The group circled around Marcus, who went over what he had learned from Dirk, Madock, and Wallace about the landscape surrounding them. The spot Dirk had referred to, where one could see through the store window, was in a gravel-lined wash on the side of the mountain. There were trees along both sides of the wash with multiple locations suitable for sniper coverage. There was also a small access road where they could station their two vehicles.

"Once they pass this point," Marcus explained, pointing to a spot on the map, "then we can engage. If Hoffman turns back down the wash, Dirk and I will intercept him from our positions here. If he continues forward, we'll separate him from the men behind, and Madock and Wallace, stationed on either side here, will isolate him from any others that are with him. Then Rocco, you and your people neutralize them and come down to help us apprehend Hoffman. It all depends on how many people he brings with him. There are only eight of us. If he comes up with a handful of men, it will be no problem, but if he has a small brigade like we saw marching into their compound yesterday, then I'd say we fall back to the vehicles and get out of here until we have a better advantage."

"Sounds good to me," Rocco said, looking over the map.

"Remember, no eye contact with Hoffman," Clare reminded the group, "and when we go in to apprehend, we have at least three of us."

"We'll get him this time, then we'll have proof of the cover-up and betrayal within the bureau. We'll close the case and expose the mole all at the same time," Rocco said with satisfaction.

"Let's not count our chickens before they're hatched," Jake warned.

"Ditto," Marcus added.

"Fair enough," Rocco agreed. Then, moving closer to Clare, he asked her quietly, "You having any more of that déjà vu?"

"Not right now, no. Why, are you?"

"Yeah. Big time. Everything's coming together perfectly. I feel like we can't lose."

"Are you sure you can trust that feeling?"

"What's not to trust? It's a good plan. We just keep our eyes open, right?"

"Right," Clare answered slowly.

"Load up the vehicles," Rocco called out. He glanced out the screen door again for a few moments.

Clare stared at Rocco until he turned back to her.

"What?" he asked as he turned around.

"As soon as he spots you, you high tail it for the van," Clare insisted. "No stare down, face off, or whatever it was you were doing the other night. Okay?"

"Sure, as soon as he knows it's me," Rocco clarified.

"Then he'll be after you," Clare sighed. "I'll be glad when this is all over."

"It will be, soon," Rocco assured her.

Within an hour, the group had finished preparations, and was loading their gear into the vehicles. Vince was looking over the stack of duffle bags, weapons, and ammunition Dirk and the others were placing into the van.

"You guys definitely come prepared," Vince commented to Dirk.

"We don't like to leave this stuff in the barracks when we're all out," Dirk explained. "Besides, you never know."

"It'd be nice to have them with us all the time, wouldn't it?" Vince asked Jake, who smiled in agreement.

The group drove the vehicles to a site just above the wash where they could unload and set up. Dirk gave Clare the microphone equipment, then he and Marcus took their positions on opposite sides of the wash about one hundred yards below the others, while Madock and Wallace stationed themselves in tree stands midway up from them, with sniper rifles. Clare directed the microphone toward the open store window below and shared an ear phone with Rocco. The two listened and waited.

"There's someone in there speaking English," Clare noted. It was the man from the CIA, who now moved into view and began to pace back and forth in front of the store window.

"Typical," the CIA man said, glancing at his watch.

Two Jeeps rolled down the dirt road to the store, raising a cloud of dust in their wake which blew past the front of the store. A few moments later, Hoffman strode through the cloud, followed by several body guards.

"Finally," the man from the CIA said, turning toward the front door as Hoffman entered. "You're here."

"Astute observation," Hoffman quipped as he sat down at a table beside the open window.

"We have some information regarding the agents," the CIA man began.

"What is that?" Hoffman asked.

"They were seen with some paramilitary personnel. We're checking into that as we speak."

"They will declare themselves, I'm sure," Hoffman replied.

"We will need to move quickly in that regard," the man from the CIA added. "There are a lot of questions being asked in the Bureau. People are starting to dig too deeply."

"I wouldn't worry about that," Hoffman retorted. "They'll show themselves soon, and when they do, I'll take care of them." Hearing this, Rocco nodded to Clare with a grin.

"Now, if he would just look out the window," Rocco thought out loud.

"There you go," Clare pointed out, as Hoffman stood up and looked at the hillside in their direction. "Now's your chance." Rocco slipped out his earpiece and moved from behind the trees into the wash, flashing a pocket mirror toward the store window. The sunlight reflecting off the mirror simulated a flash from binoculars or a rifle scope. One of Hoffman's bodyguards saw this and called out to the others, diving out of sight. Hoffman remained at the window, motionless except for his eyes, which slowly and methodically scanned the hillside until they came to rest on Rocco.

"This is it," Clare announced to the others through their headsets. "He's spotted John."

"What's he saying?" Jake asked.

"Nothing," Clare replied. "There's some background chatter in Spanish that I can't make out. Wait, now there's something."

"Get away from the window!" the man from the CIA called out. But Hoffman only held up his hand and continued to look up at the hillside.

"Let them know," Hoffman said quietly, without taking his eyes off of Rocco, "it's the north face."

In the wash, Rocco also kept his eyes fixed on his opponent. Even at this distance, which was at least one hundred and fifty yards, he could see that Hoffman was looking directly at him. Rocco tried to concentrate on the choice he had made the evening before when he was looking at the ugliness of Maria's scars. All he had to do was hold on long enough to draw him out, he kept reminding himself. But, in fact, it seemed all too easy. He didn't feel Hoffman trying to break through to him, to control him, to reach him in any way. It was almost as if he weren't trying.

"John, it's not working," Clare warned through their earpieces. "He said something about the north face, and he's not coming out."

"The north face?" Rocco asked. Looking at the sun's position, he realized that the hillside he was on was in fact the north face of the mountain. "I hear something," Rocco whispered. "Wallace, Madock, there's motion behind you!"

"Get out of there, John!" Clare yelled, "Now!"

"He's got people up there," Marcus confirmed, "all over the hill!" In the meantime, Hoffman stood silently in the store window, staring at Rocco.

"Everyone, back to the vehicles!" Rocco ordered as he turned and disappeared into the trees. Branches were rustling on either side of the wash, the sounds coming closer to the agents as they raced up the hill. Wallace and Madock slid down from their tree stands and were joined by Dirk and Marcus running back up the gravel wash. Clare had started the van, and Jake the jeep, both waiting with open doors for the others. As the last of them were jumping in, shots were fired from the woods behind them, the bullets zipping through the leaves and into the dirt alongside the vehicles.

"Where to?" Clare asked, as the van's wheels sprayed dirt and leaves behind them.

"Take the road up to the right," Dirk called out, moving to the front of the van. Jake followed closely behind in the Jeep, with Madock and Wallace returning fire out the Jeep's windows. As Clare drove through a small clearing leading to the main dirt road, she came upon gunfire from the trees ahead of them as well. Two rounds glanced off the windshield leaving small fracture lines in the bulletproof glass. Dirk opened a window on his side and fired his automatic rife toward the source of the gunshots, then sent two smoke grenades along the tree line for cover. "Take the left fork," he yelled to Clare. They turned onto a rocky path and switchbacked repeatedly down the hillside. Once they were out of the trees, they quickly made their way onto the dirt streets of the town. Pulling up alongside a garage, they stopped and Wallace hopped out to speak to the owners. After a hurried conversation, he returned, motioning for them to pull their vehicles into the garage. They pulled in and closed the doors.

"We can't stay here," Wallace explained, "but we can leave the vehicles here."

"Don't we have a better chance in the vehicles?" Rocco asked.

"Not against these numbers," Dirk replied. "We're too easily spotted in them. We'll hide out and let them file through, then they'll head back to their canyon. They won't stay for long. The police and the military will engage them if they do."

"He was totally ready for us," Jake pointed out. "It's like he was just waiting for us on that hill."

"Or maybe on both hills," Clare suggested, "north and south. Once he saw you, he told them you were on the north face."

"How did he know?" Vince asked. "I thought he wasn't getting into our heads anymore."

"We'll figure that out later. Right now, let's stay focused," Rocco replied. "Dirk, where can we go from here?"

"There's a place down the street. The owners are no friends of the drug lords. They'll help us."

Dirk led the group down a narrow dirt road to the side door of a small cinder block house with a corrugated metal roof. An older man spoke with Dirk in Spanish, then motioned for the group to come in. They crowded into the front room, which had a table with some stools next to an open fire that burned under a chimney. A woman was preparing food over the fire with several children beside her. The older man spoke to one of the children, the eldest daughter, who led them to another room that contained a bed and a small table.

"I hear them out there," Vince whispered, as he leaned to peer out the low window in the front room. "They're making their way down the road."

"We'll be safe here," Dirk assured them. The young girl pulled a curtain across the doorway, then pushed the small table off to the side of the room. She lifted up the carpet that was beneath the table, revealing a piece of plywood covering a hole in the dirt floor. Sliding the plywood to the side, she motioned toward a wooden ladder on one side of the hole. "Ladies first," Dirk said to Clare. One by one they made their way down into the hole in the floor.

"Hurry! They're coming up to the door!" Vince gasped, as he slid onto the ladder, the last out of the room. Once his head had cleared the level of the floor, the girl pushed the plywood over the hole and dragged the rug back into place. They heard the table clunk onto the plywood just as several gunmen were entering the front door of the house. Rocco clicked on a flashlight and looked around them. They were standing in a small circular space about twice the diameter of the hole they had come down. There was a tunnel that led beyond the reach of Rocco's flashlight. Rocco strained to see the extent of the tunnel when Dirk's hand slapped over his flashlight.

"They'll see us," Dirk warned, pointing to the front edge of the plywood, where the rug was not lying smoothly over the wood, allowing for a patch of light to shine through. Just then, the men entered the back room, the shadows of their boots moving past the ripple in the rug. The commanding sounds of their interrogation were answered by brief, calm responses from the girl.

She'll crack, Rocco thought. *She's just a child.* He drew his weapon and nudged Marcus, who did likewise. The red dot from Marcus's laser sight danced across the undersurface of the plywood as the others all drew their guns in anticipation of the rug being thrown back and their hiding spot exposed. But nothing happened. There were a few more questions fired at the girl, but she continued to respond in her calm, quiet manner. The shadows of the boots filed out of the room and then out of the house. After it had been quiet for several minutes, the girl moved the table, rug, and plywood back over to the side. The agents blinked their eyes at the scene of the young girl standing alone in the room. Her father entered and spoke again with Dirk. It turned out that the tunnel they were facing led to a large house across town, a house that belonged to this man's sister. There was a time, he explained, when the government was seizing private property and arresting people who didn't agree with them. Troubled times, he explained. His sister's home was a hiding place for many such people. They had dug the tunnel to move them quickly to this inconspicuous part of town whenever the police came to search the house. The tunnel had never been discovered. No one knew of it outside his family.

"He says, when we get to the house, his sister will tell us when it is safe to leave," Dirk explained. "He also says we're not to mention this tunnel to anyone. It's been kept secret for decades."

"Tell him he has our word, and our thanks," Rocco affirmed, then thinking for a moment, he added, "Ask him if he would consider one more favor. If he could mention to some of his neighbors, ones that might be more friendly with the drug lords, that a group of gringos came through, asking the way to the nearest military base."

"The nearest base is fifty miles away," Dirk said.

"I know," Rocco replied. "If they think we've headed there, maybe most of Hoffman's support will head out in pursuit, leaving him more exposed here."

Dirk relayed Rocco's request and the old man nodded with a smile. "Vaya con Dios," he said, handing Dirk a flashlight and pulling the plywood back over the hole.

SIGNS

28

By the time they had reached the end of the tunnel, the old man's sister, who had been informed of their arrival, had opened the doorway. It was in a false wall behind a basement wine rack. After ensuring that there were no more gunmen in the town, she let them out a side door and gave them directions to the garage where they had left their vehicles. Once in their van and jeep again, they drove up the hillside to their old barracks. Upon their arrival, they saw that Hoffman's gunmen had ransacked the building.

"See why we always pack up our stuff?" Dirk asked Vince with a smirk. Vince nodded and smiled. They continued driving as far as they could, then all but Wallace and Madock, who left in the jeep to procure a helicopter, continued on foot to a point where they could see Hoffman's canyon below. They watched as lines of jeeps and armed personnel filed out of the canyon.

"The diversion seems to have worked," Rocco noted. "They're probably all heading toward the military base, hoping to intercept us."

"There's Hoffman," Clare said, looking through binoculars. "He's on foot, standing outside the gate."

"Staying behind," Jake said. "Excellent! It looks like he'll be practically alone in there."

"What was that dream of yours, Rocco?" Vince asked. "Hoffman dying alone?"

"Things are coming together," Rocco replied. "We've got him this time."

"Déjà vu," Jake said. "Isn't that what you said this morning?"

"That's so weird," Vince noted, "I was just thinking that. The words were on the tip of my tongue!"

"Everything's coming together," Rocco repeated under his breath, casting a glance at Clare. "Even our close call in the house back there, having to go out the tunnel. That led to our setting up this diversion. It's all good. We've got this!"

They slid farther down the hill, making it to the side ledge they had seen earlier. From there, they could see the entire canyon. Marcus scanned the area with infrared sensors, capable of seeing images of people behind walls or in dense brush. Hoffman drove back through the gate, and entered a building with two guards, leaving two more guards outside.

"There's only four men with him," Marcus reported. "If we can get to the edge of the woods down there with a sniper rifle, I can neutralize the outside guards."

"Dirk and I will cross over to the left," Rocco announced. "Marcus and Clare, you take the right side, getting as close as you need to in order to make those shots. Jake and Vince, you two come down from that ledge and close off the back exits. Then, once Marcus takes out the guards, we'll approach the front from both sides and fire tear gas canisters through the windows. As they come out the front or the back, we'll get them one by one."

"Madock and Wallace will have a helicopter ready to extract us in minutes," Marcus added. "Once we have the package, I'll signal them."

"Remember, we take Hoffman alive if possible," Rocco continued, "but either way, we take him. He doesn't get away this time."

Jake and Vince headed out across the wooded slope to the ledge behind the building.

Dirk stood close to Rocco and noted quietly, "There's a lot of green down there." Scanning the periphery again, he added, "We'll need to move quickly and one at a time." Rocco nodded, then looked at Clare and Marcus.

"We'll cover you two as you move down and along the tree line," he suggested. "Then you cover us when we make our move."

Marcus scanned the building again with his infrared scope.

"What's he doing?" Clare asked.

"Nothing," Marcus replied, "just sitting there. It looks like he's waiting."

"Waiting for what?" Rocco asked. "For us?"

Jake and Vince were moving quickly along the slope to the back ledge. Both were experienced rock climbers and had quickly donned gear from Dirk to repel down from the ledge to approach the building below. They readied their ropes as they walked.

"So, you ever think we'd be repelling down a cliff in Nicaragua to haul in a perp?" Vince asked.

"Never would've guessed," Jake replied.

"Me neither," Vince agreed. "Couldn't get any better, right?" Vince asked, extending his hand for a fist bump, to which Jake complied with a laugh. "Just think," Vince continued, "two days ago we were in the Bronx. Speaking of which–I got this from the priest." He reached into his pocket, pulled out a small plastic bottle, and offered it to Jake. "Holy water–filled it from that big bowl in the chapel."

"I don't think it works on me."

"Works on everyone," Vince assured him. "That's what my grandmother used to say. Can't hurt, right? Just trace out the star of David or something on your forehead."

"You're nuts, you know that?" Jake laughed as he took

the bottle from Vince. The two splashed a bit of the im-promptu repellent on themselves, while at the same time, in the Bronx, the bowl of holy water from which their bot-tle had been filled was dipped into by Father Joseph. The priest entered the friary chapel alone and knelt near the altar.

There were FBI agents at the front door of the friary, investigating the whereabouts of the missing agents.

"Have you seen or heard from agents Rocco, Bristol, Steinman, or Ambrosi?" an agent asked one of the friars at the front door.

"Not that I know of," the friar replied. "I can check the phone messages from the morning if you don't mind waiting."

"We understand that they met with someone here, a Father Joseph."

"Father Joseph is in the chapel right now. He'll be in there for a couple of hours. You might want to check back later."

"We'll wait," the agents replied, looking for a seat in the front room of the friary.

In the adjacent borough of Manhattan, additional FBI agents were speaking with representatives from the CIA and legislators, including Congressman Miller.

"Where are our agents?" they asked Miller. "We've been told Hoffman is dead. Why would our agents still be in

Nicaragua looking for him? Who arranged this?"

"I should think they would have received their orders from the Bureau," Miller replied.

"If they did, don't you think we would know where they are? We've had no contact with them. Who's responsible for this?"

"Trust me sirs, we'll get to the bottom of this," Miller assured them. "Mark my words, we'll get to the bottom of this."

At police headquarters, federal agents were meeting with the mayor and the police chiefs with more of the same questions. Detective Dobbs was within earshot of their questioning the mayor. "You," one of them called out to Dobbs when he noted him lingering nearby. "What do you know about Agents Rocco, Bristol, Steinman, and Ambrosi?"

"Who? Me? Oh, nothing," Dobbs stammered, slipping around a corner and down the hall. He pulled out his cell phone and nervously tapped in a number.

"The Feds are here asking questions," Dobbs whispered into his phone. "The guy in charge, I don't recognize him. They seem pretty determined. What do you want me to do?"

"Nothing," the voice on Dobbs's phone replied. "We have it in hand."

"Are you sure?" Dobbs persisted.

"Absolutely."

"It's not like they'll just forget about it."

"Very soon they will," the voice assured him. "Very soon." The voice was that of Karl Hoffman, who ended the call, tossing down the phone. Turning toward the armed guards beside him, he asked, "Are you ready, gentlemen?"

DARK NIGHT

29

Marcus and Clare got down to the edge of the woods, about fifty yards from the front of the building, without the guards noticing them. Marcus then climbed into a small cluster of boulders just on the periphery of the open field and radioed Dirk and Rocco that they were in position.

"You'll have to move quickly, but once out in the field, they won't see you," Marcus explained. "There's an 'L-shaped' concrete wall about twenty feet out from the building that blocks the guards' view of the center of the field. They're pacing back and forth, so I'll let you know when the right guard is walking behind the wall, then you can move quickly to the center of the field and wait until the left guard is behind the wall."

"Funny place for a wall," Rocco commented.

"I think it's a blind," Marcus replied. "There are openings to shoot through, but right now they're far enough back they can't see through them."

"Great, you let us know," Rocco said as he and Dirk slid down the side of the hill. Rocco slung his rifle onto his back and as he was sliding down the loose dirt, grabbing tree limbs along the way, it struck him that the scene was just as he remembered it in his dream that morning. *This ends with Hoffman dying and his men running away*, Rocco remembered. *Definitely coming together*, he said to himself.

Dirk knelt behind a tree on the edge of the field, looking at the building and wall through his binoculars. As Rocco came up alongside him, he notified Marcus that they were in position.

"Not yet," Marcus replied. "He's standing still, lighting a cigarette... Okay, get ready, he's moving."

Just as Rocco was poised to begin a run out onto the field, Dirk slapped an arm against his chest.

"Hold on," Dirk warned. "There's movement on the ridge." He handed his binoculars to Rocco and motioned to the wooded hillside on the opposite side of the valley. There were armed men moving through the trees, many of them. Rocco spun around and scanned frantically through the wooded slopes between them and the entrance to the canyon, seeing tree branches moving high on the hillside. There were men coming into the canyon on this side as well! They were the drug lord's men. They had doubled back and were now surrounding the canyon from both sides and moving toward the back wall where Jake and Vince were preparing to repel down the cliff.

"It's a trap," Rocco announced over his headset. "Clare, Marcus, you read me?"

"Yeah," Marcus replied. "Where is the movement?"

"Everywhere, they're all around us, on the ridges," Rocco answered. "Jake, Vince, do you read me? Jake, Vince, come in." There was no answer from either of them. "We're coming over to you, Marcus," Rocco said as he and Dirk ran through the trees, glancing back frequently at the movement of branches behind them. As they came up to the cluster of boulders where Clare and Marcus were positioned, Hoffman emerged from the building with his two inside guards and walked calmly up to the concrete blind, motioning to the two outside guards to join them. Clare kept trying to contact Jake and Vince without success until she moved out of the rocks and up the hillside about twenty feet.

"I've got them," she announced. "Jake, Vince, you need to get out of there now. There are gunmen approaching you from both sides."

"Tell them the lead men on the south side are about two hundred yards away," Dirk called up to Clare, "and on this side, it looks like they're almost to the ledge we were on."

"We'll start down as soon as we secure our ropes," Jake radioed back.

"We're in a cluster of rocks on the north side of the

open field," Clare relayed to Jake and Vince. "When you get down..." A shot rang out, hitting Clare in the leg, and she fell to the ground. More shots were fired from the concrete blind, and then others began whistling through the leaves from above them on the ridge.

"Clare!" Rocco cried out as he ran over to her, dragging her back into the cluster of boulders. She was grabbing her leg, with blood quickly spreading from the wound in her thigh. Dirk wrapped a pressure dressing around her leg, causing Clare to cry out in pain. "What are our options?" Rocco asked Dirk and Marcus.

"If you can keep them behind that wall," Dirk suggested, "and stay behind these rocks for cover from above, I can swing around, meet up with Jake and Vince, and flank them behind the wall."

"I'll lay a line of explosives up on the hill," Marcus suggested. "That'll buy us some time to make a break."

"What about the extract? The helicopter?" Rocco asked. "She's still bleeding through this dressing. We need to get her out of here."

"Wallace can't take on an entire brigade firing from both sides of the canyon in that helicopter," Dirk explained. "It would be suicide. But if we neutralize them behind the wall, we can make a break for it down the road. So, do I go?" he asked, looking at Marcus and Rocco.

"Go!" Rocco agreed, checking Clare's dressing again, then

firing at the wall to give cover for Dirk as he went around the building, and Marcus as he carried his explosives up the hillside. Firing at the small openings in the concrete wall, he thought of the fifty or so men surrounding their band of six, and the tightness stirred along his neck again. Had he been played? Was it all a sham—the insights, the premonitions, the dream? He fired a rapid series of rounds, spraying concrete fragments across the wall. *Don't be stupid*, he thought. *Conserve ammo*. He began again, firing slowly and methodically only when the ends of rifles became visible through the openings. Clare pushed herself up to him, dragging a duffle bag of ammo, and held up a new magazine ready for Rocco when he was out. As he looked at her, rising to the moment despite the pain in her leg and the anguish of their failed plan, it struck him how courageous she was. Anger was a perversion of courage, he'd been told. He wasn't going to revert to that, he decided, come what may. He laid steady cover fire at the wall and the rising anger within him subsided.

After several minutes, Marcus returned and slid onto the rock next to Rocco.

"They're starting to come down the hill now," Marcus informed Rocco.

"How long would you say we've got?" Rocco asked him.

"I'd say about ten minutes," Marcus replied. "When we blow the explosives, we should get another five or ten after that."

"We could get to one of the vehicles behind the wall," Rocco suggested. "Odds are, they've fortified the entrance-way pretty well. But, if we surprise them…"

"We could hit that gate hard and have a decent chance of breaking through," Marcus agreed, picking up on Rocco's line of thought.

"If Dirk flanks them…" Rocco began. "Are you hanging in there?" he asked Clare.

"I'm fine," Clare replied.

"You know," Marcus said, "if we take out Hoffman, most of these others will scatter. It's not their fight."

"Do you have a shot?" Rocco asked.

"I would have taken it if I did," Marcus replied. "Not while he's behind that wall. Wait, he just stepped out for a second. He was pointing to the opposite ridge. If he would do that again…"

"It looks like they've almost made it to the ledge behind the building," Clare reported, as she scanned the back wall with binoculars.

"Let's hope Jake and Vince have gotten down by now," Rocco said, looking around the side of the building for any sign of their attempt to flank Hoffman behind the wall.

Jake and Vince were, in fact, still on top of the ledge. Vince had just crossed over the crest, picking a good route for them to go down, while Jake was finishing up securing the lines. The sounds of men moving through trees were becoming louder, then voices began to call out and shots were fired. Jake tied the last knot and bolted for the crest, when a round hit him in the leg, then two more hit his vest, knocking him to the ground. Vince scrambled back up over the crest and hoisted Jake onto his shoulder. As he crossed over the edge with Jake on his back, Vince caught a round at the nape of his neck. Falling forward with Jake on his shoulder, Vince struck the wall hard, pinning Jake's wounded leg against the rocks, sending searing pain up through his hip. As Jake reeled from the pain, he could see that Vince was wounded. He quickly secured the end of his rope around Vince, and began to push off with his good leg, to repel them both down the side of the cliff.

"Dammit! I can't believe it!" Jake swore between breaths. "I dreamt this!"

"So how did your dream end?" Vince murmured as the voices of the gunmen rushing to the cliff's edge became louder.

"Vin, you're all right!" Jake cried, as he glanced briefly at the blood spreading across his partner's shoulders. "With Thanksgiving dinner at your folks' house," Jake lied.

"That's a good sign," Vince mumbled.

"Stay with me partner, you hear?"

"You still got the holy water?"

"I got the holy water."

"Another good sign."

Jake slid down toward an outcropping below them, scraping against the rocks with his back, trying to keep Vince away from the rough edges. He couldn't see the portion of the rock face below the outcropping, but only the ground, which was a good one hundred feet below them. The rope around Vince's chest was tight under his arms and Jake was trying to adjust Vince's weight somewhat, to be less restrictive on his breathing, when he heard a voice not far above his head. Looking up, he saw a hand pointing down at him and shouts calling out to the others. Seconds later, heads appeared at the rocky edge and shots were fired at them, the gunmen holding their rifles at arm's length out over the rocks.

As the bullets sprayed dirt and rock fragments beside him, Jake pushed off from the rock as much as he could with his good leg to get past the point of the outcropping, allowing the rope to slide freely through his hands. As they fell past the outcropping, he grabbed onto the rope that was flying through his palms, crying out as it burned the skin of his fingers. When he finally managed to stop the rope, he and Vince fell hard against the rocky face. They swung out again, and as they returned to the wall, Jake repositioned his good leg to regain a controlled repel. Pushing out from the rock face, he caught a glimpse of the top ledge with a larger number of heads peering down at him. As they continued on, Vince's rope suddenly went slack, then fell past them.

They were cutting the ropes!

Still more than eighty feet above the ground, they would not survive the fall should they cut Jake's rope. Jake pushed out hard again from the rocks and let the rope fly through his torn and blistered palms. About ten feet below them, there was another small overhang with a ledge beneath it that continued gradually down to the ground. If he could get to that point, they could walk down from there. As he returned to the rock wall, he missed with his good leg, hitting the wall with his wounded leg and Vince's shoulder. Struggling to return his good leg into position, he felt vibrations along the rope coming from machete blows above. With another push from his good leg, Jake repelled past the overhang and as he returned, he let go of the rope entirely and he and Vince fell onto the ledge just as the rope above went slack, falling past them.

As Jake adjusted Vince's harness again and disconnected his, four other ropes dropped in front of him and danced in the air as the men above began repelling down the wall after them.

"Vin, you with me?" Jake asked, as he disconnected the rope that bound Vince to him, but Vince did not answer. Jake pulled Vince against the back wall of their small ledge and prepared to fire upon their assailants as they appeared. His eyes were darting from line to line, when a small object bounced off the front of the ledge they were on, and moments later, exploded in the air below. They were tossing grenades onto the ledge! Jake tried to kneel in order to throw off any grenades that made it onto the ledge, but the pain in his wounded leg made him fall back onto his side. There was a gunshot and a man from one of the lines fell past the ledge. Another shot rang out and a second man dropped past Jake, then a third. Dirk, who had been watching Jake's and Vince's descent, had gotten close enough to pick off the repelling men before any more grenades could be thrown. As the fourth and final gunmen fell past him, Jake saw Dirk running up the trail to them.

When he arrived, Dirk described the situation below while Jake explained where he and Vince were wounded. "Vince got hit in the back of his neck, and I think he's passed out. He was just talking to me. I got it in the left leg, but with a little support, I think I could walk," Jake explained. Dirk strapped a splint on Jake's leg and dressed Vince's wound.

"When was he talking?" Dirk asked, as he finished placing a field dressing on the back of Vince's neck.

"As we were coming down the face," Jake replied.

"Well, let's get him out of here." Seeing that both Jake and Vince were wounded, he radioed to Marcus that he would not be able to flank the group behind the wall before bringing these two back.

Back on the boulder, Marcus explained to Rocco and

Clare, "They can't flank them. Jake and Vince are both wounded, so Dirk's bringing them down."

Rocco reached out for a fresh magazine while Marcus continued to peer through his scope.

"We're down to four," Clare warned.

"If he would just step out again," Marcus wished out loud.

"What if we went around to flank them?" Rocco suggested.

"We'd never make it now," Marcus answered. "They're down the hillside too far and all along that ridge. We'd be picked off in a second."

"You need that shot," Rocco said to Marcus. "What if…" he stopped mid-thought and stared at the field directly in front of the wall. He saw a hooded figure standing in the field just on the other side of the dirt road, his arms at his sides. Rocco looked through his binoculars, and the figure turned toward him and removed his hood. "What is he doing here?" Rocco muttered in astonishment.

"Who?" Marcus asked.

"The priest."

"From the village?"

"No, from the Bronx. Father Joseph."

"John," Clare interrupted, "he can't be here." Looking across at the empty field of grass where Rocco was staring, she repeated, "He can't be here. Think about it. Why would he be? There's no one there, John. Are you all right?"

"Bilocation," Rocco murmured to himself, "of course. Yes," he answered Clare calmly. "I'm fine. We're going to be fine. Don't worry." Turning to Marcus he said, "I'm going to a spot by the road over there that can't be seen from the openings in the wall. I'll get there, lure him out, and you'll get your shot. Are you ready?"

"If he comes out again, I'll have him," Marcus answered, keeping his eye on his scope.

"Clare, can you give me cover fire on that wall, long enough for me to get across the field?"

"Of course, but wait, John!" Clare protested, "What are you thinking?"

"Don't worry," Rocco said with a hand on the back of her shoulder and neck. "Everything's going to be fine. It's a sign. You were right about signs. As usual, you were right. Stay in these rocks with Marcus until Hoffman's down." He checked her leg wrap, then nodded to Marcus and moved to crouch behind a tree at the edge of the field.

Clare slid across the rock to a spot where she could see all the openings in the wall, signaled to Rocco, and began to fire. As she hit each opening in succession, the rifle ends disappeared momentarily. She continued until she could see that Rocco had stopped running. Glancing beside her, she gasped, "Marcus! He didn't take his rifle!"

"Left the ammo for us," Marcus said without taking his

eye off his sight. "If he gets me the shot, he won't need it. If he can't lure him out, I'll make a run across the field and try to get a shot from the other side. Listen," he added, coming off his rifle and looking directly at Clare. "If things go south, push this to set off the explosives, then this transmitter to call in Wallace. The explosion will give him enough time to drop a line to you and they'll pull you up to the chopper, along with Dirk and the others if they're back in time."

"What do you mean?" Clare cried. "What about you and John?"

"I said if things go south. For now, just sit tight and get ready to give me cover if I need to make a run over there."

THE END

30

*S*tanding at the blind spot in the field, Rocco looked at the tree line along his left, which was still a good two hundred feet away, and the trees that he had come from, which were about three hundred feet away. He had half expected to run into Father Joseph at that spot, but now realized that Clare was right when she told him there was no one in the field. Yet, it had been so clear to him, even through the binoculars. Looking back toward Marcus and Clare, he slowly stepped across the dirt road with his eyes fixed on the end of the concrete wall. He kept his arms at his sides as his view of the space behind the wall gradually expanded. The sounds of the rifles firing from behind the wall, up in the woods, and near the ridge behind the building, all seemed to fade from his mind, and he heard instead, his own footsteps, his own breathing, his own heartbeats, and then, he saw him.

Rocco stopped walking and faced Hoffman, who was staring at him with his arms also at his sides. For several moments the two men stood, silently staring at each other. This time, Rocco knew Hoffman was trying to reach him. Instead of the disinterested gaze he had given him earlier that day from the store window, he now seemed completely determined to get to his mind. But Rocco felt nothing, no anger, no fear, no encroachment of his opponent's mind breaking through. Hoffman's gaze passed through him like water through a sieve. Rocco had done it. He had become untouchable.

Hoffman moved briskly, taking two long strides forward and to the right, and raising his left arm, aimed his handgun at Rocco.

There's your shot Marcus, Rocco thought, as though watching the scene from some distant vantage point. In place of the tightness rising in his chest, he felt a peacefulness spreading through him, rising with each breath, a warmth that moved from his chest out to his fingers, a calmness so profound and complete that he barely flinched as the bullet from Hoffman's gun tore through the front of his neck and out his back just above his shoulder blade.

The sky, a brilliant blue with white patches of clouds, was slowly rotating downward in Rocco's sight as his body fell backwards toward the ground. Then the sky and clouds ceased moving and remained motionless as Rocco's arms, legs, and back were embraced by the field of grass. The blades wrapped themselves around him like an over-stuffed comforter, while the scent of dry earth mingled with gunpowder drifted across the valley. It was the image from his dream, the blue sky and the clouds, though now there was no missing piece. The puzzle was complete.

As the recoil raised his hand, Hoffman could see Rocco falling to the ground, and admiring the accuracy of his aim, he smiled. But Marcus too, had aimed accurately. A moment after Hoffman fired, while his arm was still raised in the air, Marcus' fifty caliber round struck a vulnerable triangle at Hoffman's left shoulder, just below the bone and above the protection of his Kevlar vest. The bullet exploded through Hoffman's chest and he collapsed onto the ground.

The moment Hoffman fell, his four guards panicked, looked at each other, and ran back toward the building behind them. Marcus hit each one as they moved from the cover of the wall. The gunmen on the ridge and hillside, seeing Hoffman and the others lying on the ground, ceased firing, and began to disperse. Shouts rang out between them through the trees.

"Stay here after I blow the explosives," Marcus began, but noticed that Clare had already started down onto the field toward Rocco, hobbling with a stick as a crutch. He set the explosives off behind him on the hill which proved to be a final incentive for the gunmen above to retreat.

As Clare was scrambling across the open field, Dirk came along the side of the woods to join Marcus.

"They're running for now, but could turn back at any time," Dirk warned. "We should signal Wallace for extract."

"Already done," Marcus replied.

Clare staggered up to Rocco who was lying in the grass, blood pouring out of the right side of his neck, his face ashen.

"No! Oh, please God! No!" she cried, falling onto him and pressing her hands onto his neck. The blood pulsed out in waves between her fingers as she sobbed. Rocco's face was motionless, his gaze fixed, his skin pale. He could see Clare's face, but could barely hear her voice, barely make out the words.

Can you hear me? He thought. *Is that what she said?*

Rocco's eyes were becoming opaque, his heart racing, struggling to pump a diminishing blood volume that continued to pour out between Clare's trembling fingers. The blue sky faded from view and Rocco thought he saw Hoffman, lying on the ground, dying alone, as he had seen him in his dream. He could still feel Clare's hands on his neck, but they seemed to become an arm, his brother's arm. They were children, and he had fallen, scraping his knees on the concrete. "You're gonna be fine," his brother said to him as he carried him into their Brooklyn apartment. "It's just a scrape." It seemed that he was there, in that moment.

The image changed, and he was somewhere else, a younger child in a park, shuffling through the fallen autumn leaves, again with his brother. He could smell the leaves, damp with the previous day's rain. How wet his shoes were becoming! What would his mother say? He stopped shuffling and looked up at his brother, then only eight years old. "What's wrong?" his brother asked. He shook his head. Was it nostalgia? Were they old memories firing off in his dying brain starved for oxygen? Was he already dead?

He saw the sky and clouds again, but now only in his mind. They were frozen still like a painting, beautiful and crystalline, the image gradually coalescing into a pervasive sense of light and warmth. While he no longer saw Clare with his eyes, he knew she was there, just as he knew his brother was there. He could feel him with that unspoken connection they'd so often shared, sitting on their Brooklyn rooftop gazing at the Manhattan skyline. Now he saw no metropolis, no pigeons, no sky, nor clouds, but instead entered entirely into the connection, a pure, complete, and simple union. He was with his brother. He knew it with certainty. A warm flush flowed through him with the calming peace of that certitude.

Dying isn't that bad, he thought. In fact, he looked forward to it now, more eagerly than anything else he had ever anticipated.

The pulsing of blood between Clare's fingers had

become much weaker, barely visible within the mass of congealed blood that had wrapped around her hands. Beneath them, the blood pooled onto the ground and was swallowed up by the dry earth.

"God, no!" Clare sobbed again. Suddenly, Marcus's heavy arm pushed Clare's shoulder to the side.

"Hold pressure here, and here," he said, pressing her left hand under Rocco's jaw and her right hand just above his clavicle. "He got his carotid and jugular. Don't let up on that even for a second." He then laid a field dressing between Clare's hands, deep into the wound. He pulled out some tubing from his bag, placed a large catheter in Rocco's leg vein, and within seconds had squeezed in a liter bag of saline solution. Then he attached another bag to the tubing, squeezed in half of it, and hung it on a stick that he jammed into the ground next to him. He felt Rocco's pulse in his neck and said, "Stay with him. If you see or hear anything, call out."

"Where are you going?"

"Confirming the target."

Clare's hands were shaking, fatigued from holding so firmly onto Rocco's jaw and neck. His skin was still very pale, but his eyes seemed less opaque.

"John, it's me, Clare. Can you hear me?" she sobbed.

His breaths were slower and deeper as some slight twitching motion returned to his face, his eyes now nearly closed. Clare looked up and watched Marcus walk around the end of the concrete wall.

Hoffman was lying alone on the ground, his left arm under his neck, the shoulder dislocated, his fingers still tightly gripping his gun.

"Karl Hoffman?" Marcus called out. There was no answer. Blood was steadily pouring out from his shoulder as he gasped for air. Marcus moved closer and kicked the gun from his left hand. Hoffman stared at Marcus with what was now an impotent gaze, gradually fading to a dull opacity, and with one last rattling attempt to draw breath, he was gone.

A helicopter broke over the back wall of the canyon, with Wallace and Madock firing into the tree-lined hillsides, subduing any remaining gunmen. Dirk brought Jake and Vince over to Clare and Rocco and directed Wallace to an appropriate landing site in the open field. The dry dust flew into their eyes as the grass was blown flat by the landing helicopter. A medic who had flown in with Wallace and Madock rushed over to them just as Dirk was laying Vince down onto the grass near Clare.

"Hang in there, Vin," Jake said, sitting down beside him. The medic stopped at Vince first. "How is he?" Jake asked him. The medic glanced at Dirk, then back at Jake, pausing.

"He's gone, sir," the medic replied, "I'm sorry." He then quickly checked the pulse in Jake's ankle and the wound in his thigh and moved over to check Rocco. Jake's eyes followed the medic as he knelt over Rocco. His face seemed blank, as if he had not understood the medic's words. Wallace and Madock came from the helicopter, spoke briefly with Dirk, then gently lifted Vince's body and carried it over to the helicopter.

"Wait!" Jake cried out, "Wait! He needs this." Jake limped over to the helicopter pulling out the plastic bottle of holy water Vince had given him and pressed it into one of Vince's flaccid hands as he lay on the floor of the helicopter. For the first time since he had caught him on the ledge, he looked at his partner's face. What he had failed to understand in the medic's words, he grasped in an instant in that face—the face of death, so distinct, so universal, so absolute. With his eyes fixed on his friend's face, a face that an hour ago had been so alive with color, emotion, and life, now as pale and as still as stone, he broke into tears, collapsing onto the side of the helicopter.

"Why don't you come up here too?" Wallace suggested. "You can stay with him." They pulled Jake inside and laid him beside Vince against the back wall.

Dirk and the medic were now carrying Rocco to the helicopter, while Marcus helped Clare walk alongside, keeping her hands in place on his neck.

"Her hands don't move until they're in the OR with the surgeon gowned, gloved, and ready to work," Marcus stressed to the medic. "No one takes a look. Got it?"

"Yes sir."

"His neck vessels are transected. They'll need grafts to repair them. Make sure they're aware in case I'm not in there with them." Marcus remained at the doorway of the helicopter, standing guard as the others filed in across the threshold.

As Clare was helped in alongside Rocco, she saw Jake's blank stare as he lay next to Vince, whose face was being covered with a sheet.

"Vince?" Clare whispered. "Oh, no." She looked at Rocco's face again and then the medic's. "How is he?"

"He's got a pulse. From what Marcus said, it sounds like you're keeping him alive. Are you comfortable? You'll be in that position for a while."

"I'm fine," Clare answered, looking out the window as the helicopter began to take off. Rocco's eyes opened slightly and he could see Clare leaning over him, her hair swaying with the motion of the helicopter. She continued to gaze onto the field below them, which, as they withdrew higher and higher, took on the appearance of a garden surrounded by ribbons of mist along the edges. As he looked at her face, covered with dirt and blood, he saw again the beautiful angle of her jaw, her cheekbones, and eyes. From the threshold of two worlds, one of sight and sound, the other of mind and soul, he gazed upon her, his kindred soul. They would remain together. He knew that now, just as he knew he and his brother were, and always had been, together in a hidden dimension. The clarity and intensity of his own near-death experience was fresh in his mind. Unlike Hoffman's, brought on artificially through his will for power, his had come through an act of self-sacrifice, the realization of a pure will to love.

It was a clear and simple act of the will that no person nor thing could have any power over. It had always seemed to him that love was inevitably betrayed by pain and loss. Now he had suffered both out of love, and in so doing, had found the essence of love.

The darkness and the anger that it aroused, both of which had accompanied him for so many years, were gone. He turned his eyes to look out the side window of the helicopter as they banked into a turn. He looked down at the scene Clare had been watching. It was indeed beautiful. The patterns of valleys between mountain ridges were like the carvings on some ornate wooden doorway. Everything before him, the trees, mountains, and streams all reflected the natural order of beauty, signs of the touches from another dimension. From the spiral shape of a galaxy to the spiral of a flower's petal, they all revealed the essence of life. It was as if, out of that swirly-lined picture hanging in the Brooklyn warehouse, the one he had so loathed, a hidden image had finally emerged, an image of order, purpose, beauty, and love.

Clare noticed that his eyes were open and whispered to him, "John, it's me, Clare. Can you hear me?"

Rocco struggled to form words between his shallow breaths. Clare leaned down to him, her face next to his, her hands still shaking with fatigue from pressing on his neck. His eyes remained fixed on the landscape below.

"I see it," he whispered, as he strained to turn his head toward Clare. "I see it!"

Essence *will continue.*

PRIMORDIUM

*S*eventeen-year-old Noah Bolton is having the time of his life. His job at the biotech giant, Pridapt Incorporated, has not only earned him a college scholarship and the admiration of his peers, it has also gained him the eye of Zoe Halpern, the most popular girl at school. But, behind the perks, Noah discovers a disturbing pattern of secrecy. There is a cover-up of side-effects from the company's latest miracle drug, and hidden research in the restricted East Wing laboratory, where something monstrous crawls in the dark. Will Noah simply look the other way, or will he risk his status, his future, and even his life to bring the truth to light?

Learn more at MarioLoomis.com

ABOUT THE AUTHOR

*S*urgeon, author, and homeschooling dad, Dr. Mario Loomis, has operated in third world missions, done brain and stem cell research, and cared for thousands of patients over the years. He is now writing science fiction novels to both entertain and intrigue the mind. If you enjoyed Essence, see his other work at www.MarioLoomis.com, and please review Essence on amazon!